THE LADY BORNEKOVA

THE LADY OF BOHEMIA, BOOK 1

SARA R. TURNQUIST

MOUNTAIN
SUMMIT PRESS

If you would like to stay up-to-date on this and all other series from Sara:

https://saraturnquist.com/list

First to God, who has gifted me.
To my parents, who nurtured me.
And to my husband, who encouraged me.

THE KINGDOM OF BOHEMIA DURING THE HUSSITE WARS

CHAPTER I
JOURNEYS AND FAREWELLS

K arin was cold. She was cold and wet and tired. The dampness of the concluding day seemed to close in on the coach as if to suffocate its passengers. They lurched to one side and Mary reached out to steady her lady. Karin brushed Mary's hand away. Mary's kindness was appreciated for the hundredth time, but Karin was too road weary to indulge the overzealous handmaiden. Still, she managed a small smile before adjusting her skirts. There were patches of still-damp cloth that had gotten drenched in the rain and road puddles when they'd stopped for the carriage to be pulled out of a rut.

Father's voice warmed the still space. "Karin, need we ask the coachmen to stop to stretch your legs?"

"No, father, I'm quite all right."

"We are almost there, I am quite certain. You'll fair better once you are on solid ground again."

Karin nodded. "Yes, father, I'm sure you're right."

The car fell silent again. There had been many of these short spurts of dialogue, mere pleasantries, between Karin and her father, followed by long stretches of silence. This had been much of their conversation for the journey. *And for much of the past month*, she mused. In other circumstances, she would have welcomed the opportunity to spend time with her father, but the last weeks of tension between them did not allow for that.

Catching Mary's eye, Karin considered once more that her hand-maiden, too, was being moved far from the place she called home. But she found this change of scenery exciting—a grand adventure. Yes, Karin may have been lost in self-pity the last several days, but she could still hear the servant gossip.

Karin closed her eyes against the reality of her plight. But she was powerless. Moments later, the canter of the horses slowed. Father and Mary moved to the window. Who would catch the first glimpse of their lodgings? Feigning interest, Karin did the same. The summer palace, now off in the distance, was fast approaching.

At the heart of the structure was a portico, shielding the door which would give them access. Large burgundy walls reached toward the clouds, still dark and spewing moisture. Tall windows indicated the massive structure had but two stories, while two towers alluded to more above the second level.

The foregrounds did not appear elaborate. Among the carved-out pathways, Karin saw an ornate fountain in the yard. Trees and shrubs dotted the landscape. It was a grand estate — albeit not as grand as the palaces in Prague — but as big as any summer home or hunting lodge she had known the royal family to possess.

This particular chateau was the favorite hunting lodge of her father's friend, Viscount Vlastik Dvorak. And it would be her home for the next days, weeks, perhaps months. To be sure, she hadn't been privy to that information. It was, perhaps, an appropriate place for her exile. There wasn't another living soul within easy riding distance. These places were built for seclusion. And that was what she was here for.

Their carriage slowed and tilted as it climbed a final hill, closing upon the portico. Karin leaned back, focusing her mind in silent prayer. The horses' hoofbeats created a tempo that measured the steps to their destination and to her fate.

The carriage slowed to a stop. Karin opened her eyes. And the pitter-patter of the rain above them had ceased. This was the purpose of the portico—such an occasion as this dreary, rainy day. Horse and carriage fit underneath and their exit out would be onto dry ground.

A manservant stepped out of the massive structure and opened the carriage door. Father exited, then turned, offering his hand first to Karin and then to Mary. As she set her feet onto the firm land, she sent another prayer of gratitude.

"This way, my lord," the manservant said, ushering them into the chateau.

They stepped first into a foyer. Karin drew in a breath. Indoors at last. She embraced the warmer and much drier climate. With difficulty, she resisted the urge to shake the rain from her strawberry-blonde hair. The décor of the chateau drew her eye. Deer and elk heads, along with a variety of hunting weapons, some primitive, hung on the walls. A servant took father's overcoat and Karin's cape while a maidservant stepped closer to Mary.

"Zuzana will take you to your room," the manservant said to Mary.

The two maidens separated from the group as the manservant led Karin and her father farther into the house.

They paused in a large, circular room. Was this the receiving room?

"I will let Lord Dvorak know you have arrived." The manservant bowed and took his leave.

Karin's gaze wandered around the ornate room — too much to take in. The ceilings were massive and high, dwarfing Karin in the space. One wall boasted a large fireplace, the flames within hard at work warming the room. On the adjacent wall stood a large mahogany doorframe and door, more intricately carved with artistic design and scrollwork than anything else in the room. A family crest hung on the doorframe. At each corner of the room, and at each side of the mantle above the fireplace, stood small suits of armor looking down on them.

Karin turned in a small circle. Family portraits covered the walls. These images were the faces of the men who had established the royal lineage, made the family known and carried it through the generations. One lone round table in the room held flowers. She breathed in the sweet subtle fragrance of the seasonal blooms, a bouquet of yellow daffodils.

A voice sounded, bouncing around the space. "Viscount Vlastik Dvorak."

Karin spun to meet her host. A warm, robust man entered. She arched a brow. At some point she must have met him, but his features were not familiar. His nose was round, and his eyes were bright.

Though it was quite unnecessary, they were introduced, "Earl Petr Bornekov and his daughter, the Lady Karin Bornekova."

Viscount Dvorak rushed for father, seizing father's forearm with both of his thicker ones. "Petr, my friend! So good to see you!"

"Vlastik, how is the hunt?" Father's face broke in a wide grin.

"Good, good. You will see, it is a great time for the hunt. We have been out every day, save today. Such weather for your journey! I hope it was well."

"One wheel found some bad road. Except for the rain, I think our trip was pleasant."

"Ah, some of those roads are maybe not so good, I think. But, it will be worth the trip."

"It already is, I assure you!" There was a pause in the pleasantries as father remembered Karin. "It has been a while, Vlastik, but you may remember my daughter Karin."

"Yes, yes, but this cannot be the small girl I knew!"

Karin fought the urge to drop her gaze. What must she look like? For certain her long, curled hair was wet and matted. Did her complexion belie an even greater pallor than her typical fair skin would?

"A girl no more," Father confirmed.

"No, indeed," Karin inserted. How was she to measure up this robust man? But she could always fall back on her good breeding. She curtsied. "Thank you for your hospitality, my lord."

The man's overbearing personality made Karin feel even more small and unsure of herself.

"It is my pleasure," Vlastik said. The man's eyes gleamed bright, but they sat small in his face.

He seemed an easy man to be in company with, but perhaps not easy to trust.

"I am pleased for the excuse to bring your father to this hunting lodge!"

"My absence has not been for lack of want to join you, my friend," Father said.

"It is no matter. You are here now. Come, come, let me show you the chateau." He waved his arm.

What could they do but follow him?

The conversation soon became that of banter between two old friends as the Viscount led the party from the receiving room toward the rest of the house.

Brushing past Karin, she was all but forgotten as the Viscount led them from room to room. What was his destination? Was his purpose as innocent as it seemed?

Neither the Viscount nor Petr made any attempt to speak to Karin or include her in conversation as they toured the grand estate.

Karin attempted to take in her surroundings, but it was impossible with the speed at which they would quit each room. It also seemed as if the Viscount didn't exercise even the occasional breath, as Father had a difficult time getting a word in.

At some length, Father did speak into a rare space. "Perhaps Karin would like to retire to freshen up."

"Of course," the Viscount said.

He motioned for a young girl who passed in the hall. "Would you show the Lady Karin to her rooms?"

The servant girl nodded, curtsying to her master.

Karin nodded and hid a short sigh. She was all too happy to take her leave of the two men and even happier at the prospect of being alone, if for even a few minutes.

Smiling at the young servant, she followed her deeper into the enveloping halls.

Why was this young woman at the chateau? A great secret surrounded her arrival, and no one seemed to know it. The servants always knew everything, but this was an exception. Everyone in the house was perplexed about her arrival. Only one thing appeared to be common knowledge: she was going to be staying for quite some time. Perhaps the Viscount had plans for her. It would not be the first time he entertained taking on a young girl. Either way, her presence did not make everyone happy—one person least of all, someone who didn't like surprises, who didn't like intrusions.

Did the Viscount already have designs on her, already have a claim? That would not do. No, someone would have to do something about it before anything more progressed. Prudence may beg one wait to gain more information, but it would not do to risk the situation developing any further. Again, it would not be the first time.

Earl Petr Bornekov was not a hard man. However, he had his limits. And Karin had been able to do as she pleased, her behavior gone unchecked, for far too long. Now he faced the results of this indulgence. Was pressing upon her some of the consequences of her actions truly so bad? Somehow Karin saw it that way. But there was nothing he could do about it. This was how it was to be. Of that he was determined.

The Earl and the Viscount had been close friends for many years. It was an advantageous alliance for the Bornekov family. Vlastik had become a special friend of the royal family. Something that propelled his value far above his station. And so, Petr had chosen his words with great care when proposing that Karin might enjoy an extended holiday at the hunting lodge with the Dvorak family. Petr's friend seemed all too pleased to reconnect with him, so much so that Vlastik did not concern himself with the details of the circumstances. In this way, the plan had come into being.

During their first days, Vlastik did everything in his power to distract Petr with hunting, wine, and all other manner of merrymaking. Perhaps Petr was more ready for abstraction than he realized.

Karin kept to herself, making only the obligatory appearances. Watching his once vibrant daughter become so subdued wasn't as easy as he would have thought. It concerned him.

During the day, Karin spent much of her time walking the grounds and sitting alone. She was polite and pleasant to those she interacted with, but those instances were rare. And, though she kept her distance from him, Petr could see the effects of her sleepless nights. The weariness in her eyes and the darkness underneath were telling. This doubly concerned him, as the time for his return home approached. What had he expected? What had he hoped for? Perhaps that she would be more adjusted to life at the chateau before his departure.

Vlastik tried to encourage him often. "Do not worry yourself. She will settle in to life here."

Had he not a care for why Karin's countenance was so dejected? Perhaps he did not. It would be best, in fact, if he did not.

"My son and his friends will arrive tomorrow," Vlastik continued at a noon meal.

Karin had begged off that she wasn't hungry and had excused herself early.

"She will enjoy the company of young people closer to her age. You will see. It will lighten her spirits."

Vlastik's son and his friends? Coming here? Petr and his wife had intended this to be a time of solitude. But how could he express that without opening himself up to more questions?

"So much has changed for her, Petr," the Viscountess soothed. "Give her time."

The concerns of the coming guests aside, Petr wanted to take solace in their words. But they didn't know Karin. They didn't know how stubborn she could be and how impassioned that fiery spirit of hers was. And now he was caging that spirit.

Stepan Dvorak gazed out of the window of the large library. His gaze drifted over the grounds of the Charles University. He had come to love this place. Many of his friends chided him, teasing him for wanting to come here and study. His position and future as Viscount would not depend on anything he did or did not do at the university. Whether out of sheer determination to prove them wrong, or as a product of his character, Stepan outperformed his peers. Yes, his professor's accolades would have made any father proud — except his father did not care. His father knew this truth as well.

But now he looked over the buildings with a heavy heart. This might be the end of his time at the university he had so come to appreciate. His conversation with one of his professors echoed in his thoughts.

"What a pleasant surprise, Lord Dvorak!" Professor Evzen was quick on his feet to greet his pupil with all due respect and propriety. "What brings you here?"

Professor Evzen had been a mentor to Stepan throughout his time at the Charles University. Stepan appearing at his door was a common occurrence.

"I came for one of our chats," Stepan said. Would the weighings of his mind be evident in his stance?

Professor Evzen's eyes told him they were. *"Please, come sit."* Evzen indicated a pair of chairs at one end of the room.

Stepan crossed in front of Evzen to one of the proffered seats.

"What has brought you?" Evzen probed.

Stepan was quiet for several moments. Many thoughts clouded him. He chewed at his lip. Should he speak from his heart, weighted into his stomach? Where to begin?

"Just say what is on your mind." Evzen encouraged, sitting back in his seat. From all appearances, he was not concerned in the least.

"I do not think I will be returning." There. He had voiced it.

There was no surprise in Evzen's face. Was Stepan's plight that obvious? Stepan stared at his mentor. Surely there was something to be said.

"Please, continue."

Stepan drew in a long breath. *"I fear my father does not see the reason in my studies."*

A stoic face greeted him.

Stepan stood and paced the room for some moments as the silence filled the space. Then he stopped, staring at the bookshelf on the wall opposite Professor Evzen.

"He says that my tenure here has been an indulgence. That it is time I took my proper place."

"Is he wrong?"

Stepan jerked around to meet Evzen's eyes. They were clear and neutral. Neither challenging nor urging.

Running a hand through his hair, Stepan pushed out a breath through his teeth. *"Perhaps. But maybe not. What does a Viscount need of these philosophical things?"*

"What indeed?"

Stepan winced. If he was looking for easy answers, he had come to the wrong place. He sat and leaned forward, resting his elbows on his knees, letting his attention rest on a spot on the floor as if the answer would magically appear there.

"Any leader needs to understand better how to rule."

Evzen nodded.

Stepan sat straighter. "I could understand his hesitation when that heretic was rector. Not even I wished to remain here under his leadership and teachings. It is a benefit to us all that the Council of Constance has seen an end to his preaching."

Evzen raised a brow.

"I should hope that Hus will remain shut up and put away for the remainder of his life. Surely the king will not see him freed."

No reaction from Evzen. His voice remained even. "Come now, Stepan. You know the king only cares about the papacy...that things go his way, and the university remains in his back pocket. It is his brother which burns with hatred for Hus."

The Papal Schism...Stepan remembered it all too well. What a mess that had become. Perhaps that was what led to the current situation. Two men vying for the papacy, King Wenceslas inserting himself in the politics of the university, Hus being allowed to teach his heresy...was it all connected?

A noise behind Stepan brought him to the present.

"Here you are! I have searched half of Prague for you." His best friend stepped into the library.

Stepan turned toward the open door.

"Why the long face?" Pavel's eyes betrayed his concern.

Stepan moved from the window. "It's nothing."

Pavel frowned. Then a smile tugged at the corner of his mouth. "It's time to forget all of this and think about the hunting trip."

"Yes, yes, it is. Did we convince Radek to come?"

"I spoke with him on my way here. After he finished his last lecture, his thoughts about going changed. You know how he can get so engrossed."

Stepan nodded, smiling. Radek was by far the quietest and most serious of their small group. "I am set to leave at first light."

"I haven't seen Zdenek or Luc today, but I'm certain we can find them before nightfall and ensure they are prepared."

"The hunting chateau will be the perfect getaway," Stepan said to himself more than to Pavel. "And my father will be happy to see us."

"He'll be thrilled to see you for certain," Pavel said, smiling.

Stepan nodded back, but he was not convinced.

Karin rose just before dawn after yet another sleepless night. Dressing with haste, she wrapped herself in a shawl against the cool morning air. She was restless. But as she gazed around the room, she knew it was not for lack of comfort in her accommodations. Her room at the chateau was far more than adequate.

The room was every bit as spacious as she had come to expect from the rooms in this manor with their high ceilings and large living spaces. If the chilled air circling around the room had a color, it would no doubt match the pale blue featured in the tapestries. She held the shawl tight and walked the perimeter of the room around the mahogany furniture. *Such a fine sitting area. Such a fine room.* The gold and blue themes proved rather soothing. Karin sighed. Why couldn't her mind be still in such a marvelous atmosphere?

Some nights she slept for stretches of minutes from exhaustion, but her sleep was disrupted by the lightest sound and quite impossible to recapture once interrupted. She thought about her life, her childhood, her mother. Never could she have imagined finding herself in such isolation — her parents' idea of imprisonment. And to what end she still was not sure. Leaving the warmth of the rushes, her feet bore the cold of the floor as she gazed out the window.

It was true she had disappointed them. But was her sin truly so great it required such measures? Karin expected her mother to speak for her or at least with her, to give her some further explanation, but there was none. Her mother had been more silent than ever. What was happening? What would happen? Night after night, the questions remained.

Shaking her head to clear the uneasy thoughts, she wrapped the shawl taut around herself and slipped out into the early morning. She found solace in her walks, which she took daily. On one of these walks, she had found a place within fair walking distance of the chateau yet secluded enough for her to sit, think, and pray.

Her special place was near a blue stream — a place where the water tripped over stones as it made its way through the forest. The flowers were bright and the grass green and soft. Pieces of the chateau were still visible, yet her safe place was hidden well in the tree line. It isolated her from the goings-on of the hunting palace and the people within.

Dawn broke over the horizon. Karin paused to breathe in the new day and whisper a prayer of thanks. Her body swooned a bit, but she opened her eyes and kept going. Was she so tired? She was weaker today, but so it had been the day before and the day before that. Such is the way it goes with exhaustion.

How she wished she could find deep, replenishing sleep. She had been unable to close her mind, her thoughts. Perhaps she was not trusting God? Trying to find a way on her own strength? Fighting for her own answers instead of leaning on Him? *Something for my journal.*

Karin's favorite spot lay mere steps away. Once there she could rest. *Rest. Oh, if only it would come.* Her mind raced and her legs ached. She winced and lowered her head. As a young, vibrant woman, she should not be worn by a two-mile walk as if she were her mother's mother. Something was not balanced in her body. Just thinking about it made her head swim.

The field in front of her gave way to the stream. Karin moved to the left to her tree — a steady oak, weathered by storms and long years. Its strong roots fed from the waters of the stream. Somewhere in its life, something affected its growth and caused it to angle to one side. The curved spot on the trunk made the perfect place for Karin to lean back.

She settled next to the tree and captured a moment of peace. Breathing in, she let the stress of the days and the negative thoughts of the morning exhale from her body. Perhaps another breath would revitalize her being. Taking the fresh air into her lungs, she imagined it fed her body as much as it fed her soul.

After several breaths, she pulled out her journal papers to study and write about the thoughts that plagued her. She let the sounds of the stream and the morning birdsong soothe her as she dove into her work. These papers were precious — so much so, she had kept them close for weeks. They were with her wherever she went, tucked neatly inside her dress at all times. And now they were all that were left to her.

After some study, words poured from her pen and into her journal until her lids grew heavy. Her sight blurred. She slumped forward, working to salvage her energy. *Oh, Lord.* If only she could stay awake a bit longer. Her pen could not work fast enough to rid her of the thoughts that tortured her so.

The time spent in thought and prayer these last few days had been a gift. Karin began to find her way through the maze of turmoil and back to her faith. She closed her eyes and offered silent words of gratitude. It was the first blissful sleep she'd had in weeks.

Earl Petr Bornekov gazed out the window. Clouds opened, and rain poured onto the thirsty earth. He did not celebrate the refreshing of the earth; he was concerned after his daughter. It was past midday, and she had not been present at either of the meals.

Hearing a noise behind him, he turned to see Mary standing timidly just inside the doorway. Her face was downcast. Did she bear bad news?

"Yes?" he said, his voice grating. He tried not to let his anger show.

Mary had been unable to account for Karin's whereabouts. She was only able to report that Karin had left the room before Mary rose to dress her. Who was at fault if not Mary?

"There is still no sign of Lady Karin. The horsemen have returned with nothing."

The muscles in Petr's jaw worked as he attempted to contain his emotions. Vlastik had sent a couple of horsemen to search the grounds. If they had not found her, where could she be?

"That will be all," he said, dismissing Mary with a wave as he fixed his gaze back out the window. A rustle of cloth let him know Mary left the room.

Petr stood vigil in the large library — overlooking the back of the chateau, giving him the best view of the forest line. Did he hope Karin would just appear? If so, he would be the first to spy her.

How could she have disappeared like this? Was she hurt? Dead? Killed by an errant hunter's arrow? Had she run away? Were his overbearing demands too much? Had she been taken? If so, for what reason? Each question led to more.

And so Petr continued to go in circles, ineffective as it was. What more could he do? The only thing left was to brave this torrential rain himself. Perhaps that time had come.

As Petr moved toward the stables, he heard a commotion in the hall behind him. Vlastik came into the study, several young men trailing behind him.

"Petr, come, see how my son has grown into a man! He and his friends have arrived just before this horrid rain," Vlastik said, opening one arm for Petr to join them.

"I would be eager to do so, my friend. But, I fear I cannot." For certain, there was worry etched on his face as he had not the presence of mind to disguise his features.

Vlastik's booming jovial voice dissipated. "What troubles you, old friend?"

"Karin has not returned. She is not to be found in the chateau or the stables. No one has seen her since last night. I am certain she slipped out this morning for one of her strolls, and I fear something has happened to her while walking in the forest."

Vlastik's eyes widened. Had he forgotten the hour? Neglected to keep track of whether or not she had been found?

"If this is the case, we must go at once." He spun to face the young men. "Mount your horses. We must brave the rain for the sake of this young maiden's safe return!"

The young men moved down the hall with great haste toward the stables.

Petr started behind.

"We should wait here in case she returns," Vlastik reasoned.

"I can't sit and do nothing," Petr said. "I must go."

Vlastik nodded. "Then I will go with you." He laid a meaty hand on Petr's shoulder.

"Thank you." Petr put his opposite hand on Vlastik's shoulder.

Karin laid still, her mind and body at odds. She pawed through darkness to reach consciousness, while her sleep-deprived body refused to awaken. Thunder rumbled, and rain drizzled on her face. Stirring, she attempted to waken, but everything seemed almost dreamlike — dark, damp, and dreary. Thunder sounded once more, and the sky cracked with a sound clap.

Karin shuddered. She needed to get to the chateau, but her body wouldn't rouse, and she slipped back into her unconscious bliss.

Voices called out, attempting to pull her toward consciousness.

"Pavel! I found her!"

She sensed someone leaning over her, hands on her wrists.

"Is she all right?"

"Her pulse is weak."

Karin struggled to open her eyes, to tell them she was fine, but they were slow to work. After some moments, she forced her eyelids to obey. A pair of bright blue eyes met hers. Who did these eyes belong to? Trying to sit up, to push away, she wanted desperately to take in her surroundings, but nothing in her body would work.

"It's all right," the voice belonging to the eyes said. "Be still, you are safe."

Another face appeared. "We are friends. I am the Viscount's son. Are you unwell?"

"No." Perhaps an untruth, but at least she managed one word. She struggled to sit up.

"Here," the blue-eyed man said, sliding an arm under her shoulders to help her recline at a slight angle to the ground. His eyes were captivating; it was difficult to pull away from them.

The other man's hands moved over her arms. Was he checking for broken limbs?

It was dark. How long had she been asleep? *No, not night, only raining.* She returned to herself a little more.

Her papers! She reached for them, hoping to crumple them to herself before they could be seen.

"Don't worry, my lady," Vlastik's son said, "We won't leave those."

"No...it's," she tried to explain, but the darkness started to come over her again. "I can't..." The man with the blue eyes firmed his grip on her as she started to slide, and all was dark once again.

Mary moved about Karin's bedchambers, caught up in her own concerns about her mistress — and her future employment — when she heard a commotion at the door. She reached the latch just as the door burst open.

A small collection of men, one of which carried Karin, rushed inside. Turning, Mary was quick to make herself useful, directing the unfamiliar young man toward the bed. He brushed past her as if she wasn't there.

Petr hurried alongside as the young man laid Karin down. Her eyes opened to reveal slits of green. Everyone paused, as if afraid to breathe.

Mary drew a hand over her mouth. Surely the mistress was alive?

"Who...?" Karin managed to croak out with much effort as she gazed at the stranger who had borne her body such a distance. She made an effort to continue her question, but he answered her.

"Pavel," he said, resting a hand on hers, "My name is Pavel."

Seemingly satisfied, she offered him a slight smile before closing her eyes once more.

"Karin!" Petr moved toward her, reaching for her hand as Pavel took a step back.

Mary cleared her throat. "Let us give the lady and his lordship some room to breathe until the doctor gets here."

The younger men nodded and made their way toward the door and out of the room. It did not escape Mary's notice, however that Pavel stole one last, long glance at her mistress's lax form.

Over the next several hours, Karin had more snatches of consciousness. In and out of reality. *What was dream, and what was real?*

A physician examined her. Mary attempted to give her tea. Others talked to her or around her. *All this fuss over a bit of drowsiness!* Karin worked to speak, but words failed. Her limbs refused to obey and lay, as if heavy weights, at her side.

Karin's eventual return to sustained consciousness was slow. It began as if she were climbing out of a pit; little by little, she inched her way toward the light. Then it occurred how strange it all was, how unlike any dream she'd ever had.

At first the light was but a pinpoint, and her progress slow.

Clawing at this invisible mire which held her in place was more effort than she believed she could muster, but as she came closer to the light, the thick substance holding her became thinner and more aqueous. She moved as if swimming, and no longer constrained, it seemed as if the light rushed for her.

Karin's eyes fluttered opened, and her hold on consciousness was firm; the darkness would not come for her again. She sent up a silent prayer of gratitude as she drank in the sights, sounds, and sensations.

One quick glance about the room and she saw that she was in her bedchambers at the chateau. Someone had changed her into a night-dress, and her hair fell loose. The nightshift and her hair clung as if her vision of swimming had been more than illusion. Her eyes adjusted, and what had seemed like incredible light before was now dim. Dark drapes were drawn, and she could only just make out the sunlight in the window beyond.

How long had she been caught in this strange sleep? It seemed like so many hours ago she had been in the meadow. But could she trust her perception of time? She strained to listen for sounds beyond the door. Steps, movements in the hall were evident. But how close or how far was difficult to distinguish.

Testing the mobility of her limbs, she shifted to sit. Her muscles protested, resisting but obeying with some hesitation. And so, with some effort, she worked her way into a sitting position.

The footsteps in the hall came closer. And the door's latch creaked. She could only manage to turn her head in that direction as Mary entered. Her maidservant carried a tray bearing a cup and fresh damp cloths.

When Mary noticed that her mistress was awake and struggling to sit up, she almost dropped the tray, catching it in time to save the cup of hot liquid.

"Milady!" She rushed forward. "No, milady, let me help you!" She grabbed for pillows to prop Karin up.

Karin wanted to protest, but she couldn't deny how grateful her body was for the relief. "Thank you, Mary," she croaked.

"I have your tea." Mary grasped the cup and held it to Karin's lips.

Karin reached to take the cup. "I thank you, but I am strong enough."

"Of course." Mary relinquished the cup but insisted on patting down Karin's face and arms with the cool cloth.

Perhaps this was part of Mary's routine while Karin lay unconscious. Now that she was awake, it was wholly unnecessary, but Mary seemed to be a creature of habit.

"Could you open the drapes? I would like to see the sunlight."

Mary nodded and moved across the room.

"How long have I been like this?" Karin's voice grew stronger. The warmth of the tea helped.

"Seven days, milady."

"*Seven* days?" Her teacup rattled.

Mary rushed over to help steady it.

Karin settled the cup in her lap.

"Yes, you were quite sick," Mary continued, turning away to continue her work around the room. She told Karin the story as if bored, as if she were telling it for the hundredth time. "You were in quite ill when they brought you in, and no one could figure what had happened. When your father called for the doctor, he said it was poison."

"Poison?" Karin brushed a hand across her forehead. Could it be true?

CHAPTER 2

COHERENT

K arin's brow furrowed. Who would poison her?

"They couldn't decide what manner of poison," Mary continued her drawn-out narrative as if Karin hadn't spoken. "They searched for animal marks, but the doctor said some animals leave tiny marks they might not find. And, if you had eaten something, there would not be a mark. The doctor said we would have to wait and let your body fight it with the cleansing tea and medicines. If it could. Your father has been sick with worry. He has been in and out every day..."

Mary chattered on, but the sound of her voice muffled as Karin's mind whirled. This was all rather difficult to take in. It was not possible she had been poisoned, was it? Why?

"If I may, I should go for your father. He will want to see you," Mary said, shoulders stiff, voice clipped. Was she annoyed Karin was ignoring her?

Karin nodded, only mildly concerned about Mary's feelings.

When the door shut behind her, Karin let out a long sigh and thrust her head back into her pillow.

Seven days. Poison. Either one would be a bit much, but to be hit with both at once... Where could the poison have come from? Had someone...? Surely not.

The door was flung open and her father appeared, Mary fast on his heels.

"Send for the doctor," he ordered as he stepped into the room. He moved to the edge of the bed while Mary turned and exited, eyes narrowing ever so slightly.

Petr glanced over his shoulder at the door as Mary closed it.

Karin's body sagged...as always, he was waiting until he was free to express his true concern. Not in front of the servants. No, never.

As the door slid back into its place, Father turned and gathered her carefully in his arms. "Karin, you are well again. We were so worried."

"Yes, Father, Mary told me. I can't imagine what has happened."

Pulling back, Petr settled Karin against the pillows once more. "The Viscount and I have spoken about it more than once, and we cannot understand it. Perhaps another examination by the doctor will provide some answers."

The warmth drained from Karin's face. That had been the one thing she was grateful for—her unconsciousness during the doctor's examination. Still, she nodded.

Father's lips upturned, and she saw a misting in his eyes. "It is a matter for later. My daughter has returned from the abyss." The sentimental display on his features lasted but one moment before he regained his composure. Mary would return soon. "You drank your tea?"

"Yes, Father."

"Good. Are you hungry?"

Her stomach churned at the thought of food and she nodded.

"Of course you are. I will have a tray brought at once."

Footsteps neared the door and moments later, Mary stepped into the room. "The doctor has been sent for, my lord."

Father moved away from the bed and addressed Mary, "Please

see to Lady Karin's comfort and ready her for the doctor. I will have a tray sent up."

"Yes, my lord." Mary bowed.

Father looked at Karin and nodded once more.

Karin had learned how much had to be communicated in these simple gestures. He was relieved she was alive and well.

Then he stepped out of the room.

Mary's gaze rested on Karin. It was time to prepare for the doctor. This would not be pleasant. But it must be done.

By the time the doctor arrived, Mary had bathed Lady Karin, dressed her in fresh garments, and seated her in one of the cushioned chairs to eat.

While she took Lady Karin's dirty nightshift and sheets out of the room, Lord Bornekov had caught her and made it clear he wanted Karin confined to her bedchambers for another day. So Mary attempted to put Karin in a clean nightdress. But Lady Karin wanted none of it.

"Milady, you must see that you would be more comfortable."

"Be that as it may, I must insist on clothes so I can move throughout the house," Karin argued. Must the Lady be so stubborn?

Though Mary feared upsetting her master, Lady Karin's determination won out. As she waited for the doctor, Lady Karin wore a simple burgundy and cream dress, which, while fitted in the bodice, fell loose over the rest of her body. This allowed her freedom of movement.

Two heavy sets of footfalls in the hall warned of visitors. Was the doctor come? So soon?

Mary pulled the door open as the boots upon the stone became sufficiently close. The doctor and Lord Bornekov were steps away from the room.

Ducking her head, Mary moved out of the way so the men could pass her. It was as if she were invisible. As always.

"Doctor Vladjek," Lord Bornekov introduced the man who came to sit next to Lady Karin.

"It is good to see you awake," the older man said in his deep voice.

Mary noted once again his long face and kind eyes. He was taller than the earl, and everything about him seemed long, even the fingers reaching out to grasp Lady Karin's wrist.

"The danger is past, my lord. Your daughter is well on her way to full recovery."

Throughout his examination, he asked Lady Karin questions about what she had eaten since her arrival and what had occurred the day of the incident. She told him of her restless sleep the nights before and how she had thought she was merely sleepy that day.

"Mary," he asked, drawing her attention from her mistress, "Did you notice any marks when you prepared the Lady Karin?"

"No, doctor," she spoke up, her chin rose. "I was careful to look, just as you asked."

"No matter," the doctor continued, turning back to Lady Karin. "I think the poison is of an animal kind. Many times we cannot find their marks. Perhaps you fell asleep, shifted, and disturbed a spider or some such other creature. Perhaps in sleep, it slowed the poison's movement. Had you been awake and tried to walk back, I think the poison would have spread faster. I am glad you were found and helped quickly. She has taken the tea?"

Mary nodded. "As much as I could get into her." *Which was a battle.* Biting the inside of her lip, Mary cursed her own bad luck in having such a stubborn mistress.

"Good work."

The comment was not directed at Mary, however, but toward Lady Karin. As if she had anything to do with it.

"Keep taking the tea to cleanse your body of any lingering poison. Take two cups a day for one week and then one cup each day for one week more. I have another tea if you continue to have trouble sleeping." He pulled out the herbs and handed them to Mary.

Another thing for Mary to concern herself with. And with no added benefit to her.

The doctor then grabbed his few things and put them in his bag.

"Thank you, Doctor." Lady Karin offered him a warm smile.

"Yes," Lord Bornekov spoke up as the doctor stood, "Thank you."

"Please send for me if there is any change for the worse, but I think the danger is gone. Lady Karin is strong, a fighter. Keep her resting for a week. Sun and fresh air would be good, but stay close and calm. I don't want any upsets to worsen her condition. And no long or unsupervised walks on the grounds."

"Yes, Doctor," Lord Bornekov responded.

His eyes cut to Mary. She understood. It was her responsibility to ensure these instructions were followed.

"She is fortunate," the doctor said, as he exited the room with Lord Bornekov. "I had my doubts about her recovery..." The rest was lost as they continued to walk down the hall.

Lady Karin leaned back in her chair and her eyes closed.

"Milady, do you need to return to the bed for some rest?" Mary offered, hoping her mistress would retire.

"No, I think I've slept enough to last for some time." She gave Mary a weak smile.

The maiden nodded, watching Lady Karin's features. What could the Lady's response mean, if it were not an indication of being tired?

Lady Karin caught Mary's eyes. Did she sense Mary's confusion?

"It's just a lot to take in at once," she explained.

"Of course." Mary's shoulders relaxed. What was she to do now? It did not seem as if she could leave the Lady Karin unsupervised. "Are you still hungry? I can go for some cheeses and more bread."

Lady Karin's stomach growled at the mention of more solid food. Her first tray had borne only broth and some bread.

Smiling, Lady Karin nodded. Now that the broth had settled well, perhaps she was ready for more.

"Of course," Mary said, bowing and taking leave.

Mary rather enjoyed these errands, which took her away from Lady Karin for short breaks. Was her mistress having as much difficulty with her? They were still learning each other perhaps. Even so, they would have to find a way to live with each other. The earl was to leave soon and Mary would be charged with Lady Karin's well being. What exactly would her role be? Was she to be her maidservant and nothing more? Or was she to serve in a more supervisory capacity? Her only hope was that Lord Bornekov would enlighten her before that time came.

She entered the kitchen and found a maid.

"I need some cheeses and bread for the Lady Karin," she said, putting on as if she were already tired of waiting.

The kitchen maid nodded and went about slicing cheese.

"And how is the Lady today?" the maid asked. Was this an attempt to engage Mary in conversation?

"The doctor says she will recover," Mary responded, her voice even.

"Did he say what caused this illness?"

Mary made a show of examining her nails. Information was doled out in pieces amongst the servants. This kitchen maid had always been loose-tongued with Mary, so she must be careful with anything she shared. It would, in time, make its way around the whole house.

"He suspects some kind of animal poison," Mary said as if the information was old news.

"You don't say!" The maid set the cheese to the side and pulled down some breads.

Mary nodded, putting on her most serious face. Information was also power among the servants, so Mary wanted to be careful to maintain the illusion she had more to give. It was time to turn the tables on this maid and ask for some. That was how it worked. Tit for tat.

"What do you know of these young men?"

"Not much. They are all friends of the Viscount's son from the university. A couple are quite handsome. I hope they don't mind a tryst with a maidservant." The girl's eyes gleamed.

Now that would be something to talk about. She would have to keep her eyes and ears open.

The maid scooted the plate across the counter.

"Thanks," Mary said, setting it on a tray. "I must get this food to her ladyship," she said as she took the tray and headed out of the kitchen.

The girl called after her, "Of course. Make haste!"

As much as Karin wanted to leave the confines of the four walls around her, she heeded the wisdom of her father for much of the day and stayed in her room. She remained as she was, lounging in the chair. Mary brought books from the library as she requested, but Karin's attention was drawn to something beyond the window.

Gazing at the grounds allowed her mind to drift, sometimes to prayer, sometimes to thoughts of what could have been. It certainly pulled her out of the slump she found herself in. She was alive and grateful to be so, but what life held, she did not know.

A knock on the door broke her reverie.

"Come in."

Mary entered, bearing a tray with her afternoon tea dose.

Karin watched as Mary moved the books and set the small tray on the side table.

"Would you like dinner early so you could retire sooner?" Mary scooted the tea closer to Karin.

Picking up the cup, Karin looked at Mary. Retire sooner? Early dinner? What could Mary mean? "I had thought I would be taking dinner with everyone else."

Mary's face was drawn, her disapproval apparent. "All that excitement? Are you sure, milady?"

"I may need help getting around. But I am quite ready to see more than these bedchambers."

Mary raised a brow. But only said, "As you wish." She moved about the room, fussing over this and that as usual.

Karin had been confined to her chair, so there was nothing for Mary to do. Still she watched Mary's movements. And her features. She knew full well Mary would seek out Father's opinion on the matter. This was why Mary had been chosen among the ladies of her mother's house. Mary was most eager to please the earl and countess, not Karin. Loyal to the Master and Mistress Bornekov, not to Karin.

And so Karin was not even able to trust her handmaiden. Yes, she was truly alone here. And she had good reason to hide and disguise her journal entries with such great care.

Her papers! Karin's face drained. What had happened to those papers? She struggled to regain her composure lest Mary notice her moment of panic. That would only lead to questions. But Mary was too focused on whatever task she deemed important for that moment.

Karin cleared her throat. "I was wondering..."

Mary glanced at Karin.

"What happened to my dress? The one I wore that day?"

"The day of the poisoning?" Mary's eyebrows raised.

Karin tried to mask her impatience. "Yes."

Mary's brows furrowed and she frowned. "Milady, you had been lying on the ground in the rain. The dress was in a state! Mud, grass, and the like. After we removed it, we sent it for cleaning, but I fear it may have been thrown out."

"Were there other things brought back with me?" Karin probed further.

"Let's see... your shoes. But they were in no better condition. I think that's it."

Karin stared at her hands in her lap.

"It's a shame, too," Mary prattled on as she moved back to the bed, smoothing over the linens. "It was a fine dress. I do hope it wasn't your favorite. Although if it were, perhaps you could think upon it and maybe write down some of the details, and someone could remake it for you. In fact, I think I could search out my memory and help you come up with some of the colors and lines. There, that would make it right, wouldn't it?"

Mary's voice droned on, but Karin wondered after her papers. Where were they if they weren't with her? Or with the dress? Did someone have them?

There was silence in the room. Karin looked in Mary's direction to find the maidservant staring at her. Had she missed a question?

"What?" Karin searched her memory. Had Mary said something about remaking the dress if it was her favorite? "That is kind, but no, it was not my favorite."

Mary's eyes narrowed. Almost imperceptibly.

Karin held her breath.

After some moments, Mary stepped toward her. "Finished with your tea?"

"Yes." She held the cup out for Mary to take. The clinking of the cup and the saucer gave away Karin's discomfort with the awkwardness of the moment.

"I'll take my leave then." Mary grabbed the tray and moved toward the door.

Had Mary remembered Karin's decision about dinner?

"I may need a lot of help to prepare for dinner this evening," Karin called after her.

Mary paused. And without turning, said, "Of course, milady. I'll be back."

After you have your little chat with my father.

Petr laughed as the young men urged their horses faster and faster as they neared the chateau. Racing had become part of their day-to-day routine after the afternoon shooting. It provided more sport. The younger men would inevitably pull ahead of the elder, not that this diminished the fun for the Petr and Vlastik. At that point, they would let up and trot the rest of the way, sometimes placing wagers on who would win.

"You have truly been with us today, Petr," Vlastik's booming voice thrilled. "It is a good day."

"I have my daughter back. She is well, and the worst is past." Petr offered him a genuine smile. For the sun shone brighter that day, the grass smelled sweeter, and the birds sang louder.

"The next time we go hunting, you will come then?" Vlastik prodded him.

He nodded. "I promise I will hunt with you each day until I must take my leave."

Vlastik's mouth spread across his face.

Their attention was drawn forward as they neared the chateau. Squinting his eyes, Petr searched to see who had been triumphant. "It looks like your boy Stepan, again, my friend."

The Viscount nodded, pride oozing from his countenance. "He is a gifted horseman."

Petr nodded, urging his horse to move with a bit more speed up the final hill. His thoughts shifted to Karin's recovery. It had been a long week of waiting and worry.

At some point, Vlastik convinced him to go shooting with them in the afternoons. "It will do you good," Vlastik had said. But Petr would not leave the chateau for anything longer or farther. Even then, his mind was always on Karin.

He could not imagine what his wife endured. Daily reports had been written about Karin's condition, and he had sent a messenger to tell her the good news that day.

Slowing his steed as they approached the stables, one of the stablehands appeared and took the reins while Petr dismounted.

Vlastik was not far behind. They walked into the lodge together and into the outer room to change their shoes. The two men chatted about the accuracy of the weapons used that day and talked with the younger men about their younger days.

As they entered the house, Mary approached. Petr fought a wave of dread at the look on her face. Her brows were furrowed and her mouth drawn. Something was seriously wrong.

The other men must have noted his need for privacy as they continued farther into the house.

"Yes?" he asked, fighting to keep the concern out of his voice.

"My lord, Lady Karin would like to join the hunting party for the dinner events this evening," Mary said, the words rushing out of her mouth.

Petr's first reaction was to lash out, upset that Mary was worked up about something so insignificant, causing him unnecessary anxiety. He should treat this as the trivial matter it was, yet there was more. Should he be more protective of Karin's health and insist she take things slow? Or allow her to roam about the house and grounds as she pleased?

Either way, he would not let this maidservant see his worry or consideration for her thoughtlessness. It was her regular reporting which made her valuable. However, he wished he wasn't the one who had to weed through *all* of these "reports".

Letting out a breath, he steadied himself and met her gaze. "Has the Lady kept to her room today?"

"Yes," Mary said, drawing out the word.

"Has she been ill or tired...more than expected?"

Mary paused for a few seconds. Was she considering his question? "I don't think so—"

"You don't think so?" His question came with more impatience than he'd intended. Wasn't she supposed to be looking after Karin?

Mary winced. "Lady Karin spent much of the day reading, but this afternoon she inquired after the day she was brought in. About her dress and shoes. It seemed odd."

"Her dress and shoes? What did she ask about them?" Petr was intrigued.

"She wanted to know what had happened to the things she had with her the day of the poisoning." Mary's eyes flickered toward the ceiling. Was she attempting to remember the words spoken?

"Ah, I see." He frowned.

Silence fell as he took a few moments to consider whether or not she could manage the excitement of this small crowd. He could keep an eye on her. Perhaps it would be good for Karin to stretch her legs.

"She is well enough to join us, I think. I will watch her carefully enough and send for you if she needs to retire."

Mary frowned, her disappointment written on her face. "Of course, my lord."

Karin gazed in the small hand mirror as Mary finished fitting her dress for the evening meal. Mary was in a terse mood. She had not spoken a word to Karin and her movements were jerked and harsh. So Karin did not object when Mary pulled out one of the dresses she did not wear often. The gown was becoming, that was not Karin's hesitation, rather, it was Karin's preference to wear simpler dresses. It would have been her desire to be in something more comfortable. But Mary's mood left no room for discussion, and Karin decided not to create more tension than already existed. With dismay, she realized she was not aggressive enough to have such a strong-willed servant.

The gown was deep blue and hugged her torso after dropping into a wide V-neck trimmed with gold thread. As she watched her reflection in the mirror, she remembered that this dress was one of her mother's special commissions. And it remained one of Mother's favorites. Perhaps that thought would make the hassle of maneuvering in this elaborate skirt that much easier. She would imagine her mother was with her when the weariness threatened to overtake her.

Mary apparently hadn't the patience to do anything as elaborate with Karin's hair, for which she was thankful. The maidservant braided and twisted back the front and sides, securing them with a simple headpiece, letting the majority of Karin's hair flow down her back.

Taking a step back, Mary sighed. She appeared satisfied that everything was in place.

Karin had to acknowledge the complete picture Mary created was quite lovely.

"Thank you," Karin commented in a soft voice.

Mary nodded, still not allowing a smile or word to pass her lips. Picking up the now discarded dress, she moved across the room.

A wave of dizziness overcame Karin, but she refused to let Mary see. Yes, she could be just as stubborn. She was thankful the chair she had vacated long moments before was not far away. The room spun, but she managed to work her way to the chair and land, not with as much grace as she would like, solidly into its seat. There she remained until a knock sounded on the door.

"Come in," she called, attempting to straighten herself.

Father entered. Was it time for him to collect her for the evening meal already?

"Karin?" He made his way to her side. If only she could disguise her pallor!

"I am well, Father. Just a slight headache," she stretched the truth. "I am better now."

He exchanged glances with Mary, who only then seemed to notice that her mistress was in distress.

"Please believe me, Father. I am well enough to venture into the dining hall. I assure you."

Father studied her, his eyes searching her features. After some moments, he heaved a deep sigh. "All right." He extended his arm to help her up. "But I insist you tell me at once if you feel the slightest bit ill."

Karin nodded. "I promise." She reached to take his arm. So determined was she not to let him see how weak she was that she strained her body to its very limits, pulling herself out of the chair. She tried to catch her breath by forcing air to come in and out to a normal rhythm.

Father continued to watch her with concern but said nothing.

The trip from her bedchambers to the great hall was slow, and she leaned heavily on her father. It was tiresome, but she didn't let her father know. She was desperate to be out of that room and longed for conversation on topics beyond her health. Any hint of difficulty, and she feared he may reverse his decision. Besides, the more she walked, the steadier her footsteps became. Still, it would be some time before she would be walking on her own.

As they approached the Golden Hall, a servant announced them, "Earl Petr Bornekov and his daughter, the Lady Karin Bornekova."

Some of the men were seated, some standing, but all were in conversation when she and her father made their appearance. All paused, standing and bowing as Karin entered on her father's arm. Father slid his other arm around Karin's waist to assist her slight curtsy as he returned their bow. Then everyone returned to his or her conversations.

This particular room where they met before dinner was referred to as the Golden Hall. Almost everything in this room was inlaid with gold: the carved mahogany of the doorframes and fireplace, and even the furniture. The gold and dark wood colors were dazzling together. Tables for four were spaced around the room as well as additional chairs for seating.

"Where will you sit, Karin?" Her father looked to a seat near the viscountess. Did he wish her to sit there?

"I would like to meet the men who rescued me. I should like to thank them for the part they played in saving my life." Karin squeezed her father's arm under her hand.

"Of course, of course." Father's gaze drifted about the room, settling on the young men near the grand fireplace.

Moving in that direction, where the three young men stood, conversing at depth about something, Karin steeled herself. She was only beginning to catch a sentence here or there between her concentrated efforts in walking when one of the men noticed her and Father approaching.

The young men also moved closer to the fireside table and chairs, indicating for Karin to sit. She was grateful. Once she was settled, her father introduced the trio.

"This is Zdenek, Pavel, and you may remember Vlastik's son, Stepan." He indicated each in turn.

When she met Pavel's eyes, she knew it was not for the first time. His eyes were a striking blue, the clearest blue of a sky on a calm summer's day. His skin boasted the slightest tan, perhaps as fair as hers when he was not in the sun as much. The sun had also lightened his hair, but it was most certainly blond year-round. Pavel's features were slightly angular in an attractive way, and his jaw was strong. *And those eyes, those striking eyes.* She almost couldn't pull her gaze away, but she did, blushing.

"Gentlemen, my daughter, Lady Karin."

The men greeted her, but their words were jumbled as she fought to focus.

"Karin," her father spoke, leaning toward her, "It was Stepan and Pavel who discovered you in the meadow."

"And for that, I am most thankful." Karin met Stepan's eyes, dark brown. Pleasant, but not as captivating.

"We are glad you are well," Stepan spoke up.

He was a fine young man. She would not have picked him out as Vlastik's son, but now that she knew, she saw the resemblance in their features. Perhaps if she'd known the viscount in his younger days, the link would have come to her quicker.

Stepan and Pavel seemed to be opposite in physical features, but they had similar builds. Stepan's face was round, but not from extra weight like his father's. His nose was more angular, similar to Pavel's, and his mouth was small with a pleasant smile.

The third man in the group, Zdenek, was taller and lankier than the others. He had brown-blond hair, green eyes not unlike Karin's, and an olive complexion. *There must be some Moravian in his ancestry.* His nose was more prominent, and his mouth was made to smile. A pleasant sort of fellow.

"Petr," Vlastik called from across the room, where he spoke with two of the young men. "Come help me settle a dispute!"

"Gentlemen. Karin." Her father nodded at them before taking his leave.

The men sat around Karin.

"May I get the lady something to drink?" Zdenek offered, pulling out a chair.

"No, I thank you. I'm fine."

He nodded and sat.

"It is good to meet you like this," Pavel said. His voice was a smooth baritone, the words pouring out like a thick liquid.

"I'm sure. I must have been a sight!" she said, surprised to find herself blushing yet again.

"Oh no, I only meant that we were so concerned, and we have all been worried about your recovery. It is good to make your acquaintance."

A smile graced her lips. "Of course."

"It can't have been so pleasant a meeting for you either, I should think," Stepan interjected. His voice was strong and kind.

"I don't remember much. And what I do remember is not clear enough to trust."

"I should think that is a blessing." Stepan leaned forward on his elbows.

Karin smiled. How could she change the subject? "I am rather curious about all of you. I was not even aware the Viscount was expecting more guests."

"It is an annual trip for myself," Stepan said. "Pavel has come with me for many hunting seasons along with Radek there." He indicated one of the men speaking with her father, the one with dark curly hair and a beard. "This year, we were able to talk Zdenek into coming along."

"Yes, hunting and sports in a summer palace sounded dreadful, but someone had to keep an eye on these two," Zdenek spoke up.

Karin laughed. She was going to like Zdenek.

"And there are five of you in all?" Karin scanned the room, counting.

"Yes," Pavel answered, but his gaze was on her. "The fifth among us is Lucas. Round two for him."

"And you all come for the hunting?" Karin caught Pavel's eyes again, but soon pulled away.

"And general merriment, of course," Stepan said, eyes smiling.

"And good beer," Zdenek said. He did not smile, but his eyes shone his earnestness.

They all laughed. Yes, she felt much better not talking about her condition or being the focus of conversation. These gentlemen were relaxed and genial. She liked them.

"We had not expected to encounter a lady among us when we arrived," Stepan confessed, his eyes more serious, though his mouth still betrayed his genial nature. "Save my mother, of course."

Karin shifted. "We arrived only days before you. And our trip was not planned much in advance." Would they sense her discomfort and leave the matter alone?

But Stepan continued, "My father has often hoped for Earl Bornekov to come for an extended visit. But I have never known my father's friends to bring daughters or wives unless it is for something more than hunting. What brings you here? Do you hunt?"

"I'm afraid not, my lord. I enjoy riding but have not been on a hunt."

Pavel broke in, "You must come riding with us, then. When your health is more improved. Perhaps we will even convince you to come for a hunt."

Karin offered him a grateful smile. "Perhaps." She appreciated any excuse to look at those eyes.

Stepan did not seem satisfied with her answers, but he did not speak of it further.

A manservant entered the room. "Dinner is served."

Around the room, everyone moved toward the door.

Karin looked for her father. He was not to be found. Had he stepped out for some reason?

The three men at her small table had risen to make their way to the dining room as well.

Zdenek had been seated to her right. He paused. "Are you coming to dine with us?"

"I'll wait for my father to escort me," Karin said, attempting to mask her concern.

He offered his arm. "Allow me."

"Thank you, my lord, but I warn you, I am rather unsteady on my feet. Are you up for the challenge?"

"I assure you I am." He smiled. When he smiled, it filled his whole face.

She grasped his arm and, with a lot of help from her new friend, got to her feet.

Karin's father stepped into the room. His gaze caught hers. Karin laid her other hand on Zdenek's upper arm. Father nodded his appreciation and made his way to the dining room.

CHAPTER 3
SUBTLE INQUIRY

Dinner trenchers had been cleared, and everyone lingered over whatever was left of their drinks. The presence of the young men made for a much more lively dinner than the last time Karin sat at this table. Father was in a jovial mood as well, more so than usual, perhaps because of her recovery. She noticed he had matched the Viscount in drink consumption. The beer and wine were flowing freely. And she saw that Zdenek had only been somewhat joking about this. It was a holiday for them all, she reasoned, and Czech men do enjoy their beer.

But Karin had been enjoying the conversation of the young men, especially Pavel. She had thought her initial draw to him had been only because of his prominent blue eyes and her striking memory of them. But there was something else about him that was magnetic; something about his personality warmed her and put her at ease. She had smiled and laughed more in the last hour than she had in the last month. So diverting was it that much time passed before she started to feel the weight of the day. Though she hadn't done much, it had been much for her over-taxed body. Just thinking about her bed brought on a yawn.

She was in conversation with Pavel and apologized, "I assure you it is not the company or your conversation."

"I understand," he replied. "Perhaps it is time for you to retire?"

Karin would have liked to stay and talk into the wee hours of the morning, but she had made a commitment to her father. Looking over, she saw that her father was deep in conversation with the Viscount and Stepan. And, based on the slight slur in his speech and more boisterous behavior, she doubted he would be the most able-bodied person to assist her.

Pavel's eyes followed her gaze and, apparently, her thoughts. "I would be pleased to escort you, Lady Karin."

"Thank you, my lord. I do not wish to take you from such spirited conversation." She indicated Radek, Zdenek, and Luc, who were even more robust than her father.

Pavel glanced at his friends and laughed a little.

She liked this slight laugh of his; as much as it was stifled, it was still a nice, full sound.

He turned back, fixing those azure pools on her. "To the contrary, my lady, it is for the sake of warm conversation that I wish to steal more moments with you."

She prayed the lights were dim enough he could not see her face color. Karin gazed at him as he watched her, the candlelight flickering across his features. At last, she pulled away and touched her father's shoulder.

"Father, I think it is time for me to retire."

"Oh?" He made a move to stand.

Pavel had already risen, "My lord, please stay and enjoy your beer and conversation. I am not so engaged at the moment and would be glad to escort the lady."

Father gave him a half-smile and nodded. "Thank you. I shall have Mary sent for."

"Thank you, Father."

Pavel held his arm out, his other hand ready to assist. Taking his proffered arm, Karin used her free hand to push up off the table.

After sitting for so long, her body protested the movements, her muscles stiff. His other arm slid around her back, offering additional support. Once on her feet, she smiled and readjusted to grasp the crook of his arm as she said her farewells.

The men stood as she exited. It was a rather difficult feat for some of them. As Karin and Pavel left the dining room, she heard chairs scraping the floor as her father and friends landed. Some not so soundly.

Progressing down the hall, Karin leaned on Pavel more than she cared to, and her steps were slow. "I think my body does not want to work anymore tonight."

"It is all right," he assured her, "Take your time. There is no hurry."

Though her body was in a weakened state, she wondered if part of her light-headedness was from his closeness. Never had she such a reaction to a person before! Pavel had a magnetism that drew her deeper. Into his eyes. Into the mystery that he was to her.

She shook her head. It was difficult to think of anything else, but she had been waiting, wanting for an opportunity to speak about that day. And it was all the better now that she had developed an acquaintance with him.

"You and Stepan are close?" She spoke between breaths.

"Yes, he is a good friend to me," Pavel said, allowing her to lean even more into him as they neared the stairs.

"I don't have visual memory of him that day, but I do remember he was there. Was he the one who came upon me first?"

Pavel took a deep breath. Was he surprised at her question? Would he answer any questions she had?

"Yes." He maneuvered his head to look at her.

She was silent, waiting.

After some moments, he took this as the cue she wanted him to continue. "We arrived midafternoon. The weather was turning, and your father was concerned because your maidservant had not seen you. Lord Bornekov supposed you had gone for a walk and was worried that you had not returned with the rain coming.

"Like any men of sound mind and body, we went looking for you, each in separate directions. Stepan and I both went toward the stream. It was he who came upon you and called for my assistance."

"I remember being awakened. Did I speak?"

"Perhaps..." He tried to remember. "Yes. But whatever you said was not discernable. You wanted to understand what we were saying, maybe explain something to us.... And you were concerned about your papers."

They had come to the stairs. Going down had been a challenge, going up would be a monumental task.

"Yes." Karin wanted to appear nonchalant about the matter *and* remain concentrated on the stairs. "Whatever happened to those papers?"

"Stepan gathered them and, I think, returned them to your father. Perhaps he gave them to your maidservant for safekeeping."

Her heart sank. It was as she had feared. They must have ended up with her father. Was he waiting to confront her? Or had he not read them yet? Set them aside perhaps? Maybe Mary did have them.

"Are you well?" Pavel's concerned voice was close to her ear. He had leaned near. Had he noticed her mood shift?

"Yes," she attempted, having a difficult time thinking with him so close. "It's... I'm tired and still working to piece it all together." It was the truth, if not the whole truth. *So many stairs! It's because of those high ceilings,* she grumbled to herself.

"Give yourself time, Karin." He patted her hand. "You've been through quite an ordeal."

She liked hearing her name fall from his lips. And she felt his care for her, both now and in his recounting of that horrible day —real concern for a stranger.

After much effort, they reached the top of the stairs. She took a deep breath, smiling at Pavel once again, thanking him for his help. Relief washed over her, only to be followed by a stab of disappointment. Her room was close, marking the end of her fine evening. The door to her bedchambers was open, and there was movement within. Mary was already there.

Pavel seemed to notice too. His eyes were on the light spilling out into the hall and the shadow dancing upon it.

"Would it be all right if I settle you in your bedchambers before I go?"

She smiled to herself, grateful that, for once, her handmaiden's ever-present nature was to her benefit. Propriety would not have allowed Pavel to be with her in her chambers unsupervised.

But something gave her pause. "I fear I have already taken too much of your time."

Pavel's gaze was on her once more. How could she not look into those eyes, fairly glittering in the hallway, dark but for the glimmer of flames. "I would feel better knowing you are safe and securely settled."

Karin had a difficult time finding her voice. When she did, it came out strangely soft. "Then I thank you."

As much as she wished they could remain in this moment, they could not. Once again, Karin tore herself away from Pavel's eyes and began moving toward her bedchambers.

Stepping into the room, they found Mary bustling about, turning down the bed, fluffing Karin's pillow, rechecking the drapes, and then back to the bed.

But she glanced in their direction. What had warned her? Their presence? Perhaps the rustle of Karin's skirts?

"Milady, are you well?" Mary's eyes were wide.

What a sight I must be! "Yes, Mary, thank you. I am tired, but well."

"Shall I make some of the night tea for you?" Mary moved to where Karin and Pavel stood just inside the doorway.

"No, thank you. I don't think I will have a problem sleeping tonight."

Mary indicated that Pavel should usher Karin to the chair closest to the bed. He did so, easing her into the seat.

She rewarded him with a smile. "I thank you, for your kind help."

"Think nothing of it. I wish you good sleep and pleasant dreams." He bowed. Then he lifted her hand to his face and pressed his lips to her wrist. And, smiling once more, he stepped toward the door and took his leave.

Mary closed the door behind him and went about her night routine.

Karin barely noticed, even as Mary worked at undressing her. She had made the acquaintance of many young men, but she had never felt so drawn to someone. Something was stirred in her, and the more she was with him, the more tumultuous she felt. It was all so unexpected.

Morning came too early for Stepan. The amount of drink lingering in his body made sitting up a more challenging task than usual. But he dared not dawdle and miss the morning hunt. He would never hear the end of it. Holding his head against the slight pounding, he was determined it would not deter him.

Dressing quickly for the day's games, he slipped into his father's massive study where Pavel and Father were already seated, breaking their fast. Relieved he wasn't the last to appear, he sat. Petr would join them whenever he wakened and readied for the day. Who was to know of the others? Zdenek, Luc, Radek, and Karin would take breakfast in the family cabinet.

As Stepan sat with his plate, gritting his teeth against its clanging, his father pushed a missive in his direction.

"This came for you this morning." Vlastik then returned his attention to his papers.

Stepan glanced at his father, whose attention was drawn elsewhere, and then at Pavel, whose eyebrows raised, before tearing open the seal.

"It is from one of my professors. Professor Evzen. Did you have him, Pavel?"

Pavel shook his head, opening his mouth for another bite of meat.

"He's become a mentor to me," Stepan explained.

Father looked at Stepan. "A letter from the university? We are all in suspense! Stop staring at the penmanship, boy, read it and tell us what's in it!" his father insisted.

The room was quiet for a moment as Stepan took in the contents. "He is updating me on the happenings with Jan Hus," Stepan said, distracted. "It has been decided he should be put on trial."

Stepan's father was nodding. "I had heard something similar myself."

"Imagine that," Stepan interjected. "After all this time, they are going to give the man a trial."

"I don't understand why," Father said, his voice gruff. "The man will never renounce his heresy."

"I wish I were there to hear some of his reasoning. I can't imagine what a fool he's making of himself." Stepan snorted.

Petr stepped into the study, walking over to the fruit. "What a fool who is making of himself?"

"That Jan Hus!" Father said with disdain.

Petr almost dropped his plate. "Oh? What's he up to now? I thought he was imprisoned and cut off."

"They plan to put him up for trial," Stepan said. What would come of it? Surely the man would be imprisoned for life. Or worse. "And it's about time. Right Pavel?"

"It is surprising," Pavel said, his response somewhat timid. His friend did not like being drawn into such tirades.

"That's some news!" Petr turned from the food altogether.

"That's right. And it's news we'll have to dwell on later," Father spoke up. "It's time for us to take to the saddles, men."

Petr gathered a few food items, while Stepan and Father got to their feet. Pavel rose with hesitation, dragging his feet, giving all the appearance of being ill.

"Come now, my friend," Stepan said, as he glanced back. "The fresh morning air will help clear you of whatever bad piece of meat you ate."

Pavel offered his friend a crooked smile as the two exited the room together.

Karin awakened to the sun streaming into her window. It was indeed a glorious sight. She lifted a prayer of thanks, yet again, to the Maker for the provision of another day and for her renewed health. As she shifted to rise, her body alerted her that it was yet in need of recovery.

Slowing her movements, she leaned on the furniture as she made her way to a nearby chair. It faced the window, and she relished the sight of the nature beyond. As slim as her view was from the curtains, drawn almost shut, she still basked in the sunlight that peeked through.

That was how Mary found Karin when she came with the morning tea and breakfast.

"Good morning, milady," she said, balancing the tray as she closed the door behind herself. "You are looking well."

"Yes, thank you. I feel much better."

Mary set the tray to the right of the chair.

Karin picked up the tea, wrapping her hands around the warmth of the cup, taking it in.

Mary went about straightening the bed, fluffing the pillows and blankets. She did not draw the covers up, but readied it as she would for night. Did she intend for Karin to return to it?

"Please do make the bed." Karin was in no mood to argue.

"Perhaps you will need some rest after your excitement last

night." Mary posed her thoughts gently. But that didn't change that Mary questioned her mistress.

"All the same, I wish to feel more normal today. So, please, make the bed." Karin's tone was firm.

"As you wish, milady." Mary's voice was strained.

Karin sipped her tea while, true to form, Mary moved about the room, fussing here and there. At the window, she moved to open the curtains the slightest bit more.

"All the way, Mary."

She didn't protest but did as Karin requested.

Perhaps she has conceded that I will have my way with these things.

Karin didn't notice any of Mary's movements thereafter. Instead, she drank in the sight newly revealed to her—the movement of the trees in the breeze, the grasses as they swayed, and the birds as they searched for ideal roosting. All in all, it was good for her soul.

After several minutes, Mary stood in front of her, blocking the view. "I will return shortly for your tea once you are finished."

It was not a request. Mary was pressing the one issue she would win out.

Karin would be unable to refuse these orders. So she nodded and took a long sip.

When she was again the sole inhabitant of her bedchambers, she fixed her attention back on the invigorating view of the world outside. She was determined to have a stroll to one of the balconies for fresh air. It was, after all, the doctor's recommendation, wasn't it?

As she took in the scenery, her thoughts drifted to her journal and her papers. What had become of them? Mary had no memory of the journal, yet the young men who found her did say they had gathered the papers and returned them. How was it that the journal wasn't returned to her room? Had it been thrown away? Was it in the hands of a servant from the washroom? Would she ever see it again? Or had it, as Pavel suspected, been given into the hands of her father?

Footsteps in the hall shook her from her thoughts. It had to be Mary. Glancing at the teacup, Karin realized she hadn't drank any more of the tea, and it was now cold. Karin gulped the rest and hastily set the cup on the tray, almost knocking it off balance.

Mary was in the room mere seconds later and went straight for the tray. She inspected the cup, and then frowned at the food, which had not been touched.

"I hoped to break my fast with everyone else." Karin met Mary's gaze.

Mary's eyebrow went up. "Breakfast? Milady, it is midmorning."

"Midmorning?" Karin's brows shot up. Though she had been mesmerized with the view out the window, she failed to note where the sun sat. Looking now, she saw that what Mary said was true. "I cannot imagine how I slept that long!"

"You needed the rest. Your body is still weak," Mary said without inflection or feeling.

Perhaps that was true. Suddenly, she became aware of how hungry she was. She grabbed a bread roll and a piece of cheese. "I would like to get dressed for the day when I finish."

Mary nodded. "I'll pull out your things."

Karin laid the cheese on top of the bread and took a huge bite. Her stomach churned its gratitude as she swallowed.

As she continued to eat, her mind wandered to her interaction with Pavel the previous night. She couldn't help but get caught in a daydream, in a reverie of the crystal blue waters that were his eyes.

Pavel watched Zdenek dismounted to better search for signs of their prey. They had followed the trail to this small stream, much to their dismay. The chance they would lose it here loomed over them all.

Stepan grumbled, and he blamed Pavel's distraction for this discouraging detour.

"Why do you continue to lag behind?" Stepan glared at Pavel, an edge in his voice.

"I apologize. My mind is elsewhere." Pavel wished his words were not so timid.

"That is obvious," came Stepan's sharp retort. "I wish you would join us on the hunt."

Pavel nodded and dismounted, coming alongside Zdenek.

Zdenek offered him a knowing look.

Stepan could be so like his father when he was in pursuit of something: focused and passionate. To a fault.

Pavel did not begrudge his friend's irritation. Though Stepan's heat for the chase may be causing him to overreact, he spoke the truth. Pavel's mind would not stay with the hunt.

Even when they were in direct pursuit of the animal, still he found his mind drifting to the previous evening and the conversation he shared with Karin. Her easy laugh and kind eyes.

Shaking his head, his eyes cut in Stepan's direction. Had he been caught in his musings again?

Stepan busied himself supervising the others' efforts.

Pavel let out a sigh. He must keep his mind in the present and push these thoughts of Karin to the side.

Zdenek, Stepan, and Radek searched the opposite side of the stream. Luc took charge of watering the horses. They lost the animal's trail on this side of the stream and supposed it had passed through. Perhaps it would behove him to remain on the same side as the last signs of the buck.

There were rocky places along the bank and, if the animal had chosen that path, his search was futile. But as he continued to move upstream, Pavel spotted what appeared to be hoofprints in the dirt.

"I found something!" He raised his hand, relieved that he was now able to redeem himself.

The other men rushed across the stream, and Luc urged the horses to where they gathered. Stepan, Radek, and Zdenek examined the prints and agreed that it was indeed their prey. Mounting quickly, they resumed the chase.

They continued to track the animal through the thickening forest for several minutes before they caught a glimpse of the prized buck in the distance.

Stepan raised a hand.

Pavel tugged his horse's reins to slow its pace. With any luck, they would remain undetected.

The animal grazed several feet ahead.

Stepan raised his crossbow.

But at the same moment, Zdenek was lining up his shot as well. Zdenek moved to the right and directly into the path of Stepan's aim. Was he angling to get a better shot?

Pavel almost called out to warn Zdenek, but he held his tongue and watched Stepan. Didn't he see Zdenek? Perhaps he could reach out to Stepan.

Stepan opened his mouth just as Pavel reached for him.

Zdenek's bolt flew and zoomed straight for the buck's heart. At the last second, the buck moved and the bolt smacked into the animal's left shoulder, wounding it but also staking Zdenek's claim on the kill.

The buck shot into the cover of the underbrush, but Zdenek was ready and urged his horse into a gallop, chasing after the animal.

Radek and Luc followed suit, racing after Zdenek.

Stepan seemed stunned into inaction. But a few seconds later, pushed his horse into action.

Pavel was close behind.

The buck, wounded by the first shot, was slowed. It was only a matter of time before the chase ended. A couple more well placed bolts from Zdenek's crossbow and the animal fell.

Radek and Luc pulled their horses alongside their friend, congratulating him on his latest conquest. He thanked them for their help tracking the animal. This was the biggest kill since their arrival at the chateau and everyone seemed to be talking at once. Everyone except Stepan.

Pavel's eyes settled on his friend.

Stepan had not spoken a single word.

"Come now," Zdenek said, only then seeming to notice Stepan's drawn expression. "You cannot be so sore I made the first buck that you aren't going to join in the merrymaking!"

"That is not the reason I resist," Stepan said, his voice even. "That kill should have been mine."

"You cannot mean that," Luc said, "We all saw Zdenek's bolt make first contact."

"I was lined up for a clear shot. Zdenek moved into my way."

The men exchanged looks. None of them would have given that a second thought. None but Stepan. Not when he was passionate about something. Any small thing could set him off if he thought he had a principle to stand on.

A collective sigh released among them.

And Pavel understood as well as they. This discussion was only beginning.

"You must know it was not done on purpose," Zdenek said, his words firm.

"You still interfered with my shot and what would have been my kill." Stepan's voice rose.

Zdenek looked stricken. If he could do it over, would he? But, alas, he could not, so he would just have to live through Stepan's frustration. They all would.

Radek moved away from the group.

"Where are you going?" Stepan's frustrated words biting as he spoke.

"To find something to make a tow so we can get this animal back to the chateau." There was an edge to his voice as well. He was the gentlest, most soft-spoken of them all, but it was clear in his tone he did not want to be party to Stepan's arguments.

Pavel's gaze went to Luc and Stepan. "We should too."

Huffing, Stepan dismounted and went after Radek in search of the things they would need to build the tow, while Zdenek prepared the buck to be transported.

The remainder of their time in the depths of the forest was spent assembling and attaching the tow to Zdenek's horse. There was little conversation beyond what was necessary. After they had moved the buck onto the tow, they mounted in silence, Zdenek riding with Radek. They then made their way toward the rendezvous point, where they would meet up with the viscount and the earl.

On any other day, they would have been chatting about the thrill of the hunt, ribbing each other, congratulating each other, but it was quiet. And that made the ride, already slowed by the reduced speed required by the towing, seem like an eternity. They did at length arrive at the clearing.

"Why the solemn faces? Did your prey get the better of you?" The Viscount's booming voice teased.

Then he seemed to notice the tow. He dismounted and walked around the group.

"And what's this? A buck! A seven-point buck! And who? Surely not any of these long faces." His eyes searched the young men.

The manservant who had remained with the Viscount and the Earl to carry their prey had already dismounted and maneuvered his horse next to Zdenek's to transfer the tow.

Zdenek dismounted as well and assisted.

"I think, my lord," Pavel said after some seconds had passed, "That the hunt took more out of us. This honor belongs to Zdenek." Pavel felt Stepan's eyes boring into him.

"I had a lot of help..." Zdenek started.

"Nonsense," Petr spoke up, coming around to examine the prize, clapping Zdenek on the back. "You all may have tracked the animal, but it was your aim which took down the creature. Bravo that you were able to beat your friends to it."

Stepan opened his mouth.

Luc interjected. "Shall we make our way back?"

"I am looking forward to what the cook has in store for us," Radek added.

The Viscount laid a hand on his rounded stomach. "Ah, now *that* is a great idea." He stepped to his horse and mounted.

Zdenek did the same.

But Petr gazed between the men. Had he noticed more to their interactions? Still, he kept his questions to himself.

"You coming, Petr, or shall we send your lunch out here?" the Viscount called.

Petr shifted his attention to his friend and smiled. "Coming, Vlastik."

And so, with the party all salivating for lunch, they were off, leaving the servant behind to get their hard-earned prizes to the stables.

It was nearing the lunch hour when Karin was prepared for the day. She had chosen another simple dress, one of pale green this time. Karin didn't care much for the elaborate dresses her mother preferred, so she had seen to it she had a good selection of these. The fabric was quite nearly the only thing that spoke to her family's wealth. The scoop neck allowed for any assortment of jewels to be displayed about her neck, but she chose a gold chain that bore a modest emerald pendant.

Her complexion had always been fair, but she frowned at her almost sickly pallor, which betrayed her many days out of the sun.

"I think I will sit on the south balcony until the noon meal. I am in need of sun and fresh air."

"There is a fine setting of chairs from which you'll have a wonderful view," Mary commented. Had she decided it was pointless to argue?

Still, Karin understood—this would be a seated venture, not a stroll about the grounds.

It was an unnecessary worry. As eager as Karin was to roam free about the grounds and forest beyond, her body urged her to take small steps in her return to such activity. And it was difficult to find reasons not to listen.

Mary stepped out to call for another servant. Did she not think she alone could help Karin to the balcony? It was another unnecessary worry. A young manservant returned with Mary seconds later.

The journey through the hall, down the stairs, and to the south balcony was long, arduous, but uneventful. Karin received perhaps too much help. But any resistance would be met with protests and more headaches. It was certain that Mary's overprotectiveness was more about appearances than any true concern for her mistress. Not that she didn't care. Karin believed Mary did.

Karin was all too happy when they settled her in a comfortable outdoor settee and, though Mary fussed over her a little bit too much, the manservant took his leave. Mary left soon after and Karin was alone. She would have perhaps an hour before someone would fetch her for the noon meal.

Taking in the view, she breathed in the fresh air deeply. The balcony overlooked the forest's edge on the back of the property. This would be but her first journey to this balcony. Her senses drank in the view, the sounds, the smells, and she said a prayer of thanks for the beauty she beheld and for the breeze which seemed to lift her spirits beyond the treetops. And so she spent much of her time alone in silent prayer — for so many things and for the things she could not put into words.

It seemed mere moments had passed before she heard the unmistakable sound of hoofbeats in the distance. She pulled herself to stand by the railing and watch as the hunting party returned. The young men raced toward the chateau. Perhaps it was a practice they enjoyed regularly. As they came close enough for her to make them out, she noted that Zdenek was in the lead, followed not far by Pavel and Stepan. Radek, who was falling behind, noticed her watching and raised a hand, shouting a greeting. It served its intended purpose. The other young men were distracted, looking toward the house, as if trying to make out what drew Radek's attention. They recovered in short order but not in time to prevent Radek from slipping by.

Was it just her imagination, or was Pavel the slowest to recover? He, too, raised a hand toward her, smiling.

She lifted her hand to wave and felt the need to avert her gaze to disguise the warmth on her face — silly, as he would not be able to see something so subtle from such a distance. Horses and riders flew past the balcony and to the stables, Radek the victor.

What was this strange feeling which came over her when Pavel's eyes met hers? This unexpected fluttering in her stomach? She didn't know what to think, except that she was eager to continue their conversation from the previous evening.

Father and the Viscount passed the balcony. They waved up to her.

She returned the gesture.

Her father seemed rather pleased that she was up and about. Their horses, too, carried them on toward the stables.

Not long after, Mary appeared with another maidservant.

"There are no stairs, Mary. I think I can manage with less assistance. I would regret keeping you from your work," she said to the maidservant.

"Yes, my lady," the girl said before turning and making her way back into the house, going about her own business, tasks which Karin was certain kept her quite occupied throughout the day.

Mary offered her arm.

Karin took it, grumbling to herself. She felt like an invalid, being escorted by her maidservant. At least that was better than having to lean on *two* young women.

No sooner had they reached the door into the chateau than Radek, beaming widely at Karin, met them.

"*Dobrý den*," he said in greeting. "I hope you are faring well today."

"*Dobrý den*, Radek," she replied. "I am... as well as can be expected."

He only then seemed to notice Mary. "May I?" He offered his arm.

"Of course," Karin said, thankful for a less embarrassing entrance to the great hall. "Thank you, Mary. I won't detain you any longer."

Mary moved away from her mistress and down the hall. As she disappeared around the corner, Karin let out a breath and gave Radek a smile.

He acknowledged her gratitude with a grin. Radek motioned toward the hallway.

Karin nodded and they moved farther into the chateau.

"That was a fine trick you played," Karin said, grinning.

Radek chuckled. "Who, me?"

"Yes, you! Do not think me fooled by your diversion."

Radek feigned shock but only for a moment. "Of course not, my lady. It was, you should know, the first time I have won."

"Then I am happy to have been of service."

They neared the great hall, and their conversation became more mundane: the weather, the horses. Their banter ended as they approached Radek's fellow racing friends at the end of the hall just beyond the dining space. The young men greeted Karin in turn, commenting on her renewed health.

Something passed in Pavel's eyes. Karin couldn't quite discern it. A displeasure of sorts? Was it because Radek escorted her? But it was there only a moment, and then it was gone, fading so fast she didn't have much time to think on it.

Father and the Viscount's voices echoed through the hall as they came up the corner stairs, drawing her attention.

"It is good to see you out again today." The Viscount's gaze landed on Karin as they neared the group. "We are fortunate to be graced by such beauty."

The corners of her mouth turned upward. "I thank you, my lord. I am better today."

"We are glad of it," Father added.

"The Lady Karin is truly a worthy distraction, but I insist we stop clumping about and see what hearty respite the cooks have in store for the hungry hunters," the Viscount said as he led the way into the dining hall.

As they entered, they took their seats in turn. Karin found her seat beside her father. Pavel sat beside her. And her pulse raced at his closeness. Would she be able to carry on a conversation with her heart beating as it was? She hoped so.

Looking down the length of the table, Karin wondered after a seat for the Viscountess. Was the Lady of the manor not to join them? Was she unwell? No one else seemed the least bit concerned about her absence.

Servants brought in pitchers to fill their cups, and the meal commenced. Karin held her questions as to the Viscountess's whereabouts. Perhaps she could ask her father on another occasion.

Dinner conversation was light. Karin inquired about the morning hunt, and the men became quiet. However, her father and the Viscount bantered about their adventures. A fox chase was a possibility for the afternoon, but nothing was certain.

Most of the afternoons had been spent riding, playing horse games, and general relaxation, as good hunting was done in the hours before noon. In fact, as she came to understand, the best hunting took place in the earliest hours. Hunting in the afternoon didn't yield much, so it was not common, except for the planned chasing of a fox or rabbit that would be released.

The meal continued with a fine selection of meat, dumplings, potatoes, fruit, and cheeses. It was a hearty meal for the weary huntsmen. Smells coming from the dishes enticed Karin to take note of her rather hungry belly. It was all so good and her hunger so great she found herself needing to pace her meal. Focusing on her meal, she was able to avoid the temptation to stare at Pavel. But it didn't keep her from stealing a glance now and again. Was it her imagination or was he, too, sneaking glimpses of her?

Zelenka knocked with the lightest touch on the door to the Viscountess's room. Her mistress had begged off from the noon meal with the group again, claiming a headache. So Zelenka, a regular servant to her quarters, was delivering a portion to her.

"Come in." She heard through the door.

Without delay and with careful balance, she opened the door, tray in hand, and entered the grand chambers.

No matter how often Zelenka was called to these bedchambers, she could not overcome her awe of the room. The mahogany of the four-poster bed, the desk, and the tables enthralled her with their intricate carved designs. They rivaled everything else in the chateau. Zelenka marveled at the fine linens in rich golds and browns covering the bed and draping the windows. The walls were covered with fine tapestries — scenes of Prague.

And against one wall was a vanity. This was where the Viscountess sat, staring into a mirror.

Zelenka had served this family long enough to guess that the Viscountess did not truly have a headache. When there was a hunting party in the house, she often skipped the noon meals during the week and preferred to have her portion in the privacy of her chambers. What was it that made the Viscountess so averse to the companionship of the others? Did she not enjoy the crowding of the great hall? Was she not one for the noise? Perhaps she simply preferred the solitude.

The Viscountess was a beautiful woman, especially for her age. *Years of beauty treatments have no doubt helped with that.* Zelenka had never been privy to any such treatment but the higher-level servants closer to the mistresses of these high-ranking homes were not all as close-lipped as they should be.

Standing back for a moment, Zelenka marveled at the woman's appeal. The Viscountess had an olive complexion, which betrayed some signs of aging around her eyes and mouth. Her dark hair was full and lustrous. Not many knew how long it was as the Viscountess preferred it pulled up in some elaborate design. But Zelenka had seen it in the evening when the mistress's lady's maid brushed it out. Deep brown eyes peered into the mirror and, something in those eyes betrayed a woman with a deeper side.

There had to be something of a mystery about her. The Viscount had never, to anyone's knowledge, taken another woman. There must be some power she held over him. Perhaps this was her reason for spending so much time at the hunting chateau. Did she encourage this pastime to keep him distracted? And though she seemed to barely tolerate the hobby she came with him year after year, season after season. Was that it? Whatever it was, the secret was held in those dark eyes.

The Viscountess glanced toward the door, pulled from her own musings. Did she sense Zelenka staring? The dark eyes indicated a table nearby. Zelena obeyed, setting the tray down and then went through the motions of setting everything out. Though her fingers trembled slightly, she finished in a matter of seconds. Then she took a step back.

"That will be all." The Viscountess turned back to the hand mirror and whatever thoughts she had been engrossed in.

Though her mistress wasn't looking, Zelenka still curtsied before taking her leave. And though she wasn't ever nervous to enter the chambers of her ladyship, she was always relieved to leave.

Father settled Karin on a comfortable settee overlooking the gardens. She nodded her gratitude. Moments later, Mary came with her tea and something warm for her father to drink. He sat only an arm's length away, but she was still unable to discern what concoction he had requested. As he took hold of his beverage, he dismissed Mary.

They sipped their drinks in silence. Karin's gaze was transfixed on the view she decided was her favorite of the whole chateau.

"I am pleased you are better," Father said, glancing at her.

"Thank you. I hope I will become stronger every day." She took in a deep, revitalizing breath and met his eyes. There seemed to be something more. Something under the surface. What was it?

"Good." He turned his focus to the grounds. "My time here has been much extended, and it has become imperative I return home."

Karin nodded, but he wasn't looking at her; his eyes seemed fixed on something in the distance. Perhaps this was all that troubled him. He had such tidings as these. "I understand. I'm sure Mother is eager for your return."

It was his turn to nod. "Since your health is much improved, I have begun arrangements to leave tomorrow."

Tomorrow? Why had he waited so long to tell her of his intentions? "I see. I wish you good weather and safe travels." She stared into her cup, watching the dark liquid as she swirled the cup but slightly.

Father shifted in his seat.

Was there more?

"There is something I need to speak with you about before I leave." His gaze turned on her.

She looked up.

His eyes were serious.

Why all the mystery? The tension? She held his eyes. He had her full attention. "Yes, Father?"

"I have something to return to you." His words were firm and hard.

It couldn't be...

He reached into his cloak and pulled out a leather-bound book, wrapped with a string.

The color drained from Karin's face. It was her journal.

CHAPTER 4
NEW FRIENDSHIP

The journal had been rifled through, and some of the pages had been torn out. Karin was relieved to have it back but horrified her father had found...

"You can imagine my disappointment at what I discovered hidden in these pages." A darkness came over his countenance.

She lowered her eyes and turned away.

"I thought we had been through all of this." His voice was harsh. "I thought you understood that pursuing the teachings of a heretic could ruin our family."

Yes, they had had this discussion — many times. Some of her acquaintances had exposed Karin to the teachings of Jan Hus, a man who opposed some of the practices of the Catholic Church. If the king's brother, Sigismund, was not so adamantly opposed to Hus, her parents may not have had the need to tear her away from her home, friends, and all she knew. She might not find herself in such isolation from any "corrupting influences". But she could not convince her father. This did not mean she would remain silent.

"I don't understand," she said, her voice finding a strength she didn't feel. "What you call 'heresy', I believe to be truth. How can the truth hurt me?"

Father's features hardened. "What Jan Hus speaks of would bring dissention to the church. You know how fragile a thing unity can be. And the church must be unified to bring stability to the monarchy. Even you must realize that the monarchy and the church are intertwined."

"But Jan Hus only speaks of—"

"You are young, Karin," he said, dismissing her with a wave of his hand. "And you have much to learn, much you don't understand. This Jan Hus and his teachings will not last to see the next king take the throne. To be found supporting such a heretic could destroy your future and any prospects you have! My duty is to the family. Since you refuse to see it, I will help you." His voice became louder, and he stood, now looming over her.

"I believed we had rid you of these devious teachings. Finding that you have hidden them from us obliterates any trust I have. You will remain here while your room is searched. And that will be the end of the matter."

Father moved toward the door.

Would he not let Karin respond? Speak for herself? Of course not, that was not the way of things. Her heart burned.

Her father did pause as he reached for the latch and turned back to her, his voice softer. "Please know, Karin, this is for your own good."

Then he stepped inside.

She touched her face. Moisture fell across her cheeks. The tears she fought had broken through. Laying her face in her hands, she let the torrent come, uncaring of who might hear. Who was there to hear or even care? She was alone.

Karin's father was true to his word on both counts. First, her room was searched while she was detained on the overlooking balcony. Mary's knowing smirk did not escape her the next time they were face to face. Anger swelled in Karin. She had never wanted to strike someone as much as she did in that moment. Prayer stilled her hand. *Lord, help me remember You are in control and that vengeance is Yours.*

However, Karin could not help her own smirk when they were unable to unearth anything. Her father had destroyed all her remaining materials when he had found her journal. So, a look of triumph graced her features when she met Mary's gaze after the futile search.

As promised, Father left the following day. After their conversation, neither he nor Karin were ready to pretend all was well. Their parting was stiff and brief. And though he didn't speak of it again, he communicated his disappointment and let her know she was being watched. So, this was a prison after all.

Though her father was gone, his watchful eye would linger. She was not free to come and go as she pleased, not even free to pray or believe as she saw fit. Try as she might, though, Mary could not censor Karin's thoughts.

Karin understood her father's concerns. Their country was in a tenuous state. Still, she had to be true to what she believed was right. And she had to follow God and obey Him first and foremost. There could be no compromise on this. It wounded her deeply that her father could not, or would not, understand her.

After her father's carriage disappeared, Karin made her way back into the chateau. Her thoughts drifted to those around her. What did they know? The Viscount and his wife—would her father risk telling them the truth of Karin's exile? Or would Father value his reputation too much? Karin wagered the latter. Everything hinged on Father's embarrassment with Karin's behavior. He would not dare expose it to someone of such close connection with the royal family, whose influence and friendship he valued so highly.

What of the young men? Would they would be ignorant to her situation as well? Their association was far too new for her father to trust them with something so private.

Perhaps Mary's knowledge was enough to keep Karin under careful watch. But what had Father told the Viscount to keep Karin under lock and key? That was a mystery indeed. At least for a while, the physician's restrictions would keep Karin close to the chateau.

Karin approached the stairs. Should she attempt to climb them on her own? Her anger might give her the strength she needed to make it. Placing a foot on the first step, she grasped the railing and pulled. There, that wasn't as taxing as she'd imagined. Perhaps she would be recovered sooner than anyone thought.

The second step proved much more difficult. And the third nearly impossible. Attempting the fourth step was more than she could do. Everything in her ached. She wanted to curse her weakened body. But what else was there to fill her days but these mundane struggles?

Karin released a long breath as she leaned on the railing, now stopped on the stairs. Gazing at the ornate carvings on the stairway, she attempted to calm her mind. Perhaps she could continue in a few moments.

After some time passed, she pushed her foot onto the next step. But when she tried to shift her weight onto that foot, she faltered and fell, her legs melting beneath her. She slammed her hands on the solid stairs, the stone stinging her tender flesh. Hopeless—her body, her situation, her inability to control or change any of it. Sinking further onto the stairs, she rested her face in her hands as hot tears rushed down her face.

What if someone should happen upon her? She cared not. The sounds of movement echoed in the halls around her, but no one disturbed her. Why would they?

Lord, please be with me. Give me peace. I don't even know what else to pray for.

Constable Borivoj sat at his desk and mulled over the most recent information to reach his office. There was another incident at the royal family's hunting chateau. Certainly by now, it was beyond calling these "accidents". But, the doctor had declared this most recent "accident" a poisoning of an animal nature.

Borivoj didn't believe that. It was one more — which was one too many — incidents which had occurred at that chateau, creating a cloak of mystery he had yet to pierce. And the doctor declaring them all accidents, it limited his investigative options.

Still, he had decided to keep a ledger on these incidences. Even now, he was searching for the book, which held all of the details he had been able to collect. At last, he laid his hands on it and pulled it free from the stack.

Opening the ledger, he reviewed the incident reports already logged. Then he turned to a fresh page. So, he wrote what details he had, though few, of this most recent occurrence at the chateau.

"Young woman ... poison ... near death ... doctor ruled accidental poisoning by animal source ... unconscious for several days ... full recovery."

Borivoj set his pen down and mulled over the words he had added, comparing them to the other cases. All young women, but this Lady was the first to recover. What was different? Could these other women have been poisoned as well? This had been one of his suspicions all along, but nothing he could prove. What were the chances that all of these women could be found victims of venomous animals? Not likely.

Was there just cause to interview the doctor about this young woman's symptoms? Were they consistent with any known poison? He made a note in his ledger.

"Constable!" a voice called through the prison. "Constable!"

He shut the book and stood to receive whomever was to intrude on his office.

One of his trusted deputies stepped through his doorway. "Constable, we need help! There's been another brawl at the pub, and Ofcharik needs us to calm things before the place is laid to waste."

Borivoj nodded and came around his desk, a hand already on his sword. "Lead the way!"

How had it not worked? The plan had never failed! More than this, it meant the careful planning had come to naught, and there remained a tenuous situation at hand. It meant more risks had to be taken to rid everyone of the threat Karin posed. But what was to be done? What was it about her that she had survived? This was a mystery. The poison had never failed!

Karin was indeed more dangerous than first thought. She was strong.

But I am stronger.

Karin was alive.

But I am a survivor.

Karin was stubborn.

But I am determined.

Nothing would stand in the way of the determination burning inside. This fire had fueled the demise of others who had gotten in the way, and one setback was not going to deter what had to be done.

Just give me some time to think. I may have missed the mark this time, but I always get my prey.

Karin wasn't able to leave the chateau to find peace in the solitude of the forest. Or to get away from Mary's ever-watchful gaze and listening ears. Instead, Karin was sentenced to spend her days in her room, in one of the other public rooms of the chateau, or on the balcony. She chose the balcony most often, as she craved the rejuvenation the fresh air brought to her senses.

One of the young men would see her to the great hall and then to her next destination. As the days passed, a routine developed in which they took turns. Karin could not help but eagerly anticipate Pavel's turn. It wasn't that she didn't enjoy the company of the other men; but she felt a connection to Pavel she could not explain. And, as her strength returned, she asked to be taken for a turn about the gardens behind the chateau following the noon meal.

"It is another fine day, my lady. Are you well enough for a stroll about the garden?" Pavel's smooth baritone warmed Karin's core as they approached the hall where they would turn left toward the balcony seats and right to head to the gardens.

She met his eyes. "I would enjoy the exercise." Her voice was impossibly soft. Was it even audible? What was this spell she was under?

The other young men would take her up to the balcony and then back down the grand stairs off the balcony to get to the gardens. Pavel, however, would take her by another, rather unconventional route. One that did not require her to walk up a set of stairs just to walk down again. While it was true she was not as weak, still avoiding excess stairs allowed her an extended stroll.

Pavel tugged her to the far right hall. A couple of stairs down took them into a long, fairly unexciting stretch of hall with medium-shaded wooden doors dotting the walls. This would not have been a part of the chateau she could have seen otherwise. The servant rooms—kitchen, storerooms, and the like.

But they were never interrupted as they traversed the hall. Perhaps the servants were somewhere else in the chateau at work or simply staying out of Pavel and Karin's way. The end of the corridor had a simple door, which opened into one side of the gardens.

One thing she regretted about her continued return to health was that she would no longer need assistance. It was a blessing to be sure, but she often secretly enjoyed the excuse to have such contact with Pavel. They had comfortable enough conversation, but anything else seemed awkward.

"I have always enjoyed being out in nature," Karin said, breathing deeply as they stepped outside. "Perhaps a bit too much. For a lady."

"How so?" Pavel quirked a brow.

Karin's face warmed and she ducked her head as much as she could. "My mother thinks all ladies should spend less time outside in the dirt and more time learning proper skills." Karin couldn't help but laugh at the memories of herself, covered in dirt after a day of adventures in the area surrounding their home. "My, how I gave my mother fits!" The words slipped out before she could stop them.

Pavel chuckled. "I'm sure you were a precious girl."

Karin paused and turned to catch his eyes. "How can you be so certain?"

He gazed at her, his eyes so clear, she wanted to dive into their blue depths.

"I know you were."

More heat rose into her cheeks, and she pulled away as she started walking again. This man could make her blush! How could this be? "And what of little Pavel?"

Glancing ahead, Pavel strolled beside her. "He had plenty of his own adventures. But for boys, that is our proving ground. Our fathers are pleased to see us on our horses with toy swords, fighting dragons and trolls. Mothers beware!" He smiled at her, his mouth broad across his face.

She laughed. This was his other gift — just as he could color her face with but a glance, he could also make her laugh with ease.

They made their way around the gardens to the grand stairs up to the balcony—the beginning of the end of her time with Pavel. But as they approached the stairs, he held out his arm. She took it, glad for the opportunity to draw closer for a few moments, even if it meant she would have to take on the many stairs.

The staircase was broad and overwhelming, all the more since the lengthy stroll had taken so much out of her. Karin looked up at the chateau as they mounted the first steps. From here, the magnitude of the structure was breathtaking. These stairs, wide at the base, angled inward toward a tall, burgundy, square tower, flanked on both sides by rounded yellow protruding sections of the chateau.

They made slow progress up the stairs, partly because Karin's weakened state, but also because she wanted to extend their conversation. Was there no end to what she and Pavel could speak on? Topics flowed between them. Despite the fact that any compliment he paid her brought color to her face, he was easy to be with and his conversation was enjoyable.

As they reached the balcony, Karin let out a deep sigh and leaned against the railing.

"Perhaps I should not insist on conversing while you make your way up the stairs," Pavel apologized.

"No." She shook her head, catching her breath in gulps. "I enjoy our talks. Truly, it's fine."

"But I am here to assist you, not tax you further."

"You are not, I assure you." She gazed up at him, squeezing his arm, which she held in her firm grasp.

He placed a hand on hers. "Good. I would miss them. Our conversations, that is."

They exchanged a look before she shifted her gaze back over her shoulder toward the gardens and the forest. "I don't think I could ever tire of this view."

"I know what you mean." His voice was softer.

She turned to find him staring at her. Was that what he meant? Lowering her eyes to the ground, she knew not how to respond.

"Shall we?" Pavel indicated they should move toward Karin's favorite seats nearby.

She nodded heart drooping. Must he continue with his day? At least he would see her settled before making his way back toward the chateau. Why she would release the contact with him one second sooner than she had to, she didn't know. But she dropped her arm and stepped to her seat. Situating herself in her seat, she then prepared to smile and say a polite farewell to Pavel.

"May I sit with you for a few moments?" His eyes seemed to sparkle as he asked. Perhaps it was the sunlight shining off his bright orbs.

"Please," Karin replied, attempting to hide her surprise.

He sat on the seat beside her and gazed across the grounds southward toward the forest line. Pavel became quiet and, when he did speak again, his tone was more serious.

"I wonder," he started, the words came out slower. "What brings you to the hunting lodge?"

How to respond? Did she trust Pavel? How much? What brought on this question? Could she share with him? If not him, who? Was she even prepared to tell anyone?

He continued. Did he interpret her silence as meaning she didn't appreciate his question? "We haven't often had the pleasure of female company, save the Viscountess. And, you are not here to hunt." There was a pause as Pavel seemed to consider his words. "I was only curious. Do not think you must answer my prying questions." Pavel looked away with a small grunt.

"No, Pavel, it's all right." She reached a hand toward him, placing it on his arm.

He set his piercing blue eyes on her face.

She drew her hand back with reluctance. Perhaps it was time to trust someone. "My father decided I needed time to think. As I mentioned, I have been a bit more of a...free spirit than my parents would prefer. It is different for me. There are things I have to accept because they are my father's decision, because it is what he says.

"He has decided I require seclusion, time away to think on how I conduct myself. I don't think he expected you and your friends would be here." Her mouth turned upward but slightly.

His face, likewise, betrayed a small smile at her comment. Then his eyes became serious again as they met hers. "Whatever the reason, I am glad you are here."

"As am I." Her voice was quiet but serious, her words surprising even her.

And she found that for several moments, she was unable to pull away from his gaze. So, they remained, searching each other's eyes.

"Pavel!" A voice broke their brief reverie.

Glancing toward the sound, Karin spotted Stepan stepping onto the balcony. He moved to where they sat.

"Lady Karin." He inclined his head toward her.

She threw a smile in his direction. "Lord Dvorak."

Pavel couldn't help but chuckle at Karin addressing Stepan so formally.

Stepan rolled his eyes. "Please, it is 'Stepan'."

"You were looking for me?" Pavel's eyes cut to Karin briefly before settling on Stepan.

"Yes, we are gathering a group for an afternoon chase. Are you interested?"

Pavel straightened, leaning forward even, on the edge of his seat as if prepared to jump up and run after the prey himself. Yet something in him hesitated. Did he not wish to seem disinterested in her conversation?

"Please take him, Stepan," she interjected. Smiling at Pavel's wide-eyed face. "I have long since craved peace and quiet!" She laughed.

"Believe me," Stepan said, "I know what you mean!"

Pavel's features became stricken and his shoulders sagged. Was he wounded by her words? Did he not catch the jest? But the corners of his mouth lifted. He then stood, nodding to Stepan.

Why did Karin feel a pang as he did so?

"It has been a pleasure," he said, meeting her eyes once again. And something else was in his eyes this time. Something she hadn't seen before. A hope of something deeper?

Karin allowed another smile to grace her lips as she nodded. And she watched after him until he was no longer visible. Then she leaned back, waiting to see them launch out of the stables and toward the forest line. All the while pondering possibilities.

Lenka Bornekova had chosen to distract herself with her needlework. She sat in her cabinet, working and trying not to think about events happening so far away. Things that were outside her control, though they impacted her beloved daughter. Even now, her husband made his way home.

And Lenka was eager for news of her *katka* — her little duck — and her recovery. Petr had been faithful in writing of her progress and return to health. But, as he traveled, she had not received a missive in so many days. So, here she sat in the comfort of her personal cabinet, stitching away.

Lenka had warned the servants that she was to be told the second her husband's carriage was spotted on the horizon. Hence, she was not surprised when a breathless maidservant stumbled into the cabinet, forgetting to knock, and disrupting her concentration.

"Forgive me, milady." The maidservant curtsied.

Lenka waved off the apology. "Go on."

"My Lord Bornkov. His carriage comes." She managed between gulped breaths.

Lenka dropped her needle and thread. *He's home! He's finally home!* Though her mind thrilled, her mask remained in place. She recovered her needle and thread, placing them on the cross-stitch board for later.

"We haven't much time. I must ready myself. Call Sharka and have her come to my bedchambers so I might be prepared for my husband."

The young girl nodded, curtsied again, and moved off to fulfill her charge.

Lenka moved as quickly as she dared through the house. Once in her bedchambers, she looked out the window to see the approaching coach. It was but a large dot on the hilly horizon. She had perhaps a half hour.

Glancing down at her dress, she smoothed her hands over the skirt. There wasn't time to change, so this would have to do. Why had she not chosen a more elaborate dress today? It was suitable enough, she supposed. A deep red gown trimmed in a blue-gray fabric at the neckline, sleeve cuffs, and hem, the top of which was tailored close to the body, while the skirt was rather voluminous with a small train.

Sharka joined her moments later, moving to the wardrobe and selecting a gold-colored headdress. Then she stepped to her mistress and helped her affix it in place. The maidservant also set a string of pearls around Lenka's neck and handed her a couple of her favorite rings. Glancing in the mirror, Lenka decided she was ready.

Moving with more speed than she thought possible with the train on her dress, Lenka made her way downstairs. It wasn't long before a manservant was there as well, opening the door for his master. Perhaps it was everything happening with Karin, but as the doors parted and revealed her husband, Lenka's breath caught in her throat. It required all her willpower not to throw her arms around her husband.

Petr strode into the house and straight to his wife, merely taking her hand. Was he not overwhelmed with emotion the same as she?

"It is good to see you, husband," Lenka said, curtsying.

"And you, my wife." Petr bowed his head.

"Please allow me to have drink and bread sent for. Shall we retire to your solar? Or perhaps my cabinet?"

Petr let a smile escape at that suggestion. He enjoyed the privacy her cabinet provided. It was no surprise when he opted for her cabinet.

Lenka glanced at the manservant by the door.

He nodded.

Moving toward the stairs, she led Petr to the room she had just earlier vacated. Petr had always found her private quarters to be more cozy than the others. And seemed to enjoy any opportunity to join her there.

As soon as they were in the cabinet and the door was closed, Lenka wrapped her arms around her husband.

A rush of air escaped him, betraying his surprise at the show of emotion. Still, she felt his warm embrace in response.

"Petr, I missed you!"

"Truly?" He pulled back and looked into her eyes.

Did this display of emotion startle him so? It was true that Lenka was rather reserved. She extricated herself from his arms and took a seat nearby.

"For the last two weeks, I prepared to come to the chateau each day. And each day I reread your letter, and it would dissuade me... barely." The words fell from her lips.

"Because of Karin?" Why was his face downcast? It was not so obvious. Still, she could see his disappointment. Perhaps he thought the source of her emotional show just now was because of Karin, not him.

As much as she regretted it, she could not be untruthful. "I have been so worried, Petr!"

"There were days I wished you were there and days I knew it was best you were not. I started many letters sending for you, but stopped myself. Karin's illness cannot change what we are doing."

Lenka's eyes fell away. "I know you are right."

He sat in a chair near hers, taking her hand in his. "I found more Hussite papers with her."

Lenka's head jerked up. How could Karin have betrayed them again? Knowing what lengths they went to cleansing her of it? Could she not imagine how important this was to her future?

"I am sorry I ever doubted you, husband." She shifted her gaze to meet his.

"I know. I am too." His voice was gentle, sad somehow.

A knock on the door cut their conversation short.

Lenka looked toward the door. "Come!"

Sharka brought in a tray of bread and cheese, which she sat near Petr, and then began to serve mead.

Lenka's mask was back up, and Petr returned to acting aloof. But Lenka's concern after her daughter filled her mind. Whatever would become of Karin if she continued?

CHAPTER 5
ALONE

The days wore on. Karin was never far from Mary's watchful eye. Was Mary noting on her every move? Her every word? There were times she feared Mary could even read her private thoughts. Then she would catch herself. That was ridiculous.

What a strange situation in which the servant controlled the mistress's comings and goings. But Karin felt her strength returning every day. A time would come when *she* would make decisions about what made up her days, a time when she would go beyond the gardens. For now, she would enjoy the company of the young men, but none so much as Pavel.

This particular day, Radek escorted her from the noon meal. Karin decided to retire to her bedchambers. She wanted to sift through her reading materials instead of venturing outside. After they topped the stairs, she excused Radek, insisting she could make it to her room without assistance. So, he took his leave.

As she neared the room, she heard movement and bustling about within. Who was in her chambers? What were they after? Should she be fearful? Or angry? Quickening her pace to round the corner, she crept to the doorway. Perhaps she could peer in and catch the intruder unaware. Her breath caught in her throat. There, in the middle of her room, Mary was hunched over her trunk, rummaging through her things.

"What are you doing?" Karin shoved the door open.

Mary whirled toward Karin, face colored. From the effort of riffling through Karin's things or from the embarrassed of being found out? She reached up to push an errant hair out of her face. "Your father instructed me to make regular searches of your rooms, milady."

What could Karin say about such sanctioned violation? She wasn't hiding anything. And Mary knew more than she did what was in her chambers. But none of that mattered. In that moment, another piece of her was chipped away.

"I regret you had to find out this way. But I am almost finished. If you could just step into the..." Mary couldn't seem to find the next word.

Karin shook her head as she backed away. What was there to say? What was left for her to do? Was there anywhere she could go? But the next thing she knew, her feet raced, carrying her away. To where, she could not say. Just away.

Her feet took her down the stairs, through the house, and outside. Then she picked up speed. Running down the hill and toward the stream, her legs moved as if they would never stop. There was a stray thought, somewhere in the distance, of whether she should be exerting herself. But she pushed it farther. Escape. That was the only thing that mattered. Escaping Mary's ever-watchful eye and the prison cell the chateau had become.

Karin slowed as she neared the tree by the stream, her dear old friend, who had been her early companion. For many hours had this tree, this stream, and her journal kept her company. Her journal... Without warning, her eyes began to water.

Those papers, the only remaining words of Jan Hus, had been ripped from her journal. They had been the final copy she'd been able to hide. Her tears threatened to release as the fullness of the injustice slammed into her, but she dare not give ground. She had shed enough tears.

The tree provided a solid place for Karin to land, out of breath and worn out. Her lungs burned and her body ached. But she felt more alive than she had in weeks. *Thank You, Lord, for giving me the strength.*

Even two days ago, she would not have thought that possible. Indeed, she had pushed her body to its limits.

Karin allowed her body to rest, feeling her heartbeat slow with each passing minute. She had no desire to give Mary another reason to lecture her.

No, she told herself, *Mary doesn't lecture. She prattles on and mothers one to death.* How had Karin the bad fortune to be paired with such a handmaiden? Ah, yes, Mary was chosen to report to Father. *I hope she weighs him with her incessant rambling when she tattles,* Karin thought shrewdly.

Laughing at her own joke, Karin relaxed. It felt good to laugh. And it felt good to be on her own, away from the house and the prying eyes within. Not that everyone's eyes were those of a spy. Certainly not the young men nor the Viscount, who likely cared little about what she did, were watching her movements. But servants talked, and Mary's ears heard everything.

Standing, Karin moved to the stream for refreshment. Drinking her fill, she also splashed the cool liquid on her face, relishing the way the water reinvigorated her senses.

Shaking her skirts as she stood, she moved back to her tree. She best take in the sights and sounds of the world as she could. It was a much better view here. Her bedchambers kept her as a mere observer.

As she approached the old oak, something caught her attention. It was nothing truly, she almost missed it. A strange bump protruding from the ground where the tree branch angled. She glanced about. Was anyone watching her now? Perhaps this was a trap?

She appeared to be alone. No one else knew of this place or its significance. Should she take a chance? Perhaps she had found buried treasure.

Settling on the ground, Karin tested the bump. Solid. Then she used her hands to move the dirt around the object, hoping it wasn't too big. The more dirt she moved, the more she found. It was bigger and deeper than she expected. Dare she keep going? Or give up? Her curiosity had been piqued. She started to paw more vigorously around the exposed edges, digging the object out.

Seconds passed into minutes, but she was soon able to unearth the biggest part of a wooden box. Jerking on the box, she nudged it loose. Perspiration beaded her forehead. She angled herself, planting her feet to leverage more of her weight against the box. As she tugged again, the small trunk came free, pitching her to the side. Karin landed hard on her left hip. Though it was sore, she recovered quickly and moved back toward the box.

She ran her hands over the dirt caked surface. How long had it been here? Why hadn't she noticed it before? What lay inside? Her fingers found the latch. Strange. It was neither rusted nor locked.

Karin held her breath and opened the lid. Peering inside, she found naught but folded papers. Curious. Perhaps it was a love note left at a secret meeting place. Or maybe it was instructions on how to find each other. Maybe it was a treasure map. *I've been confined for too long.* These were grandiose ideas indeed!

After moments of speculation, Karin decided to break the spell of her imagination and reached for the parchment. Her fingers grazed the paper. Lifting it as if it were made of glass, she unfolded it just as gently.

As she looked upon the writing, and gasped. She *had* found buried treasure. *And* a love note? Even more confusing, it was addressed to *her.*

The first page had three words inscribed on it: "For you, Karin." What followed were pages filled with words just as precious to her—

copies of the most recent writings of Jan Hus. She couldn't stop the tears that came. This gift was too great.

Karin had regretted losing her papers, but even then, they were older writings. She had read them several times over. Neither she nor her small circle of friends had regular access to Jan Hus's works. Getting something new was unimaginable.

Who? Who would know? And who would do this? Who would risk it? Her head jerked around, looking for the prying eyes of anyone who might want to take her papers away. She couldn't risk it, couldn't lose them again. Tucking the sheets into the folds of her skirt, she glanced around until satisfied she was indeed alone and safe to view these precious documents. Karin pored over the papers, drinking in each word as she would water in a desert.

Jan Hus and John Wycliffe. It was true Jan Hus was inspired by Wycliffe's writings and by the reforms he called for. Wycliff wanted the Church to return to the condition it was in during the time of the apostles. This would mean a removal of Church hierarchy, taking away traditions and anything else not in the Bible, including practices he found particularly unbiblical—the saints, intercession for the dead, and confession.

And Karin understood why he opposed these things. If she were being honest, she had always struggled with the Church and some of it rituals and traditions. At times, it seemed the Church believed that a relationship with Christ was of only secondary importance. Were they so steeped in tradition that they all but worshipped those actions? And at what cost? Wycliffe was a brave man of conviction. It was easy to understand why he had become a source of inspiration.

Hus, on the other hand, called for less radical changes. He sought freedom for all to preach the word of God and for all — not just priests — to take the sacraments of bread *and* wine at communion. He also declared that no power outside the Church be given to the clergy and that there be punishment for mortal sins. That struck a bad chord with many in power.

How could the Catholic Church justify selling indulgences?

Nothing in the Bible supported such a practice. This was but one of the many questions Karin had. Hus's teachings spoke to this concern. He preached the word of God and called for change in the Church. There were many who followed and many who did not.

How could her father not see the wisdom of this man? How could he not see the error of the Church? *Lord, open his eyes,* was all she could pray as she focused on the papers in her hands.

So lost in the sermon within the pages, Karin lost track of the minutes as they slipped by. Mary would be concerned. And that began to mean something to Karin.

With great care and reverence, Karin placed the papers in the box. Then she went about the task of burying them again. This was the safest thing. This time, however, she did not leave any part of it sticking up to be stumbled upon. It was imperative she be careful with her private things. All the more now than ever. She dared not risk taking something like this into the chateau.

Moving some of the loose brush over the freshly upturned dirt, she was satisfied it would not be noticeable even from a closer distance. Then she began the short journey to the chateau.

Hoping to sneak in as inconspicuously as possible, she came in by way of the servants' hall. No one bore witness to her entry. She made her way down the hall and toward her bedchambers with careful steps. Looking at the stairs, she decided to instead turn toward the grand fireplace. Perhaps she could sit there and gather herself.

As she neared the great hall, Mary stepped out in front of her. Karin nearly slammed into her.

"Where have you been?" Mary's voice was sharp.

"I went for a walk," Karin said dismissively, stilling her hands and attempting to still her thundering heartbeat. She moved to step around her maidservant.

"Away from the chateau grounds?" Mary maneuvered into Karin's way again.

"Do not be mistaken." Karin eyes narrowed. She forced all of the strength into her voice she could muster. "I do not answer to you."

Mary stared at her for a few moments. But Karin did not back down, meeting her eyes and straightening herself to her full height. Was Mary so reluctant to give up her loosely-held semblance of power, however false, that she had carried these last few days? Karin was finished. Her maidservant may report everything said and done back to Father, but she would not be pushed around, and she would no longer feel imprisoned.

With a slight bow, it was Mary who backed down. "Yes, milady." That was the way it had to be.

After those simple words, Mary walked off, disappearing around the first corner she came to.

Karin watched her go. There would not be any real change between them. Mary would still perform random searches of Karin's room. And Karin would need to be careful of her words and actions, as it would all be told to her parents.

Still, there was a wonderful sense of freedom, of taking back her life. She had put Mary back in her place. What had happened to Karin's backbone that it took so long? Karin only truly answered to her hosts — the Viscount and his wife. And they did not seem to expect restrictions beyond those placed by the doctor. This being the case, perhaps she was freer than she assumed. Had her father relied on her fearfulness? If so, he would find out from Mary's next missive that he was mistaken.

The entire thing was impossible. Karin was always watched, so carefully watched. This frustrated every plan the individual in the dark tried to devise. But the one knew Karin would not always be kept so close to the chateau. It did not escape notice that just this afternoon, Karin had ventured beyond the grounds. *Yes, even I am watching Karin.*

Watching... and waiting. The watcher just had to wait. Perhaps her new association with the young men who had come to the chateau, though now a hindrance, could be used as an advantage. Yes, perhaps it could. Just then, a plan began to form. *Patience. Remember, patience is a virtue.*

Two days later the Viscount announced Stepan's plans to visit the nearest village for the afternoon. All who wished to join were invited. Karin watched Lord Dvorak's face as she expressed her interest. The Viscount seemed all too pleased that she wanted to venture out of the chateau. The Viscountess, however, voiced her concern.

"Are you quite sure you are well enough for such an outing?"

"I thank you for your concern, my Lady. I am much better." Karin sought the Viscountess's eyes. Was she so concerned?

"And I can only imagine the poor girl is ready to see something beyond the walls of this hunting lodge," the Viscount spoke up. "Come now, my dear, do not fret. Stepan will take care after our guest."

The Viscountess raised a brow and frowned, but nodded all the same. Once her husband had spoken, she had little choice but to give her assent.

"At least take my carriage," the Viscountess inserted. "Then I can be assured your journey will be in comfort and safety."

"I thank you for your kindness," Karin said. She'd rather not enter the small village in such grandeur, announcing their arrival so ostentatiously, but she could not refuse the Viscountess's offer. So, she would just have to look forward to arriving in style.

Karin was barely able to contain her excitement as the meal continued. Conversation shifted to the outing and what they would find in the small village. She soaked up every detail. What would she see?

In due time, the meal came to a close, and Luc escorted Karin to her room. She thanked him, assuring him she would be ready to depart before long.

However, as she stepped into her chambers, Mary was waiting for her. "Milady, I don't think you are ready for such an outing."

"The Viscount believes I am, and he has given me his permission." Karin spoke simply, her voice even.

Mary glared at her. And for several seconds, they squared off. Would Mary insist on checking with the Viscount herself?

In the end, she conceded.

"Let's pull out something appropriate for you to wear."

"I have some ideas..." Karin started. This was going to be a battle.

Pavel's horse shifted under him, eager to be on the move. The men were gathered at the portico, awaiting Karin. Stable hands pulled the grand carriage around, and everything was in place for her arrival.

"Do you think one of us should ride in the carriage with Karin?" Zdenek asked, looking at the looming coach.

Pavel wanted the chance to spend more time with Karin, but didn't want to seem too eager. So he held back. After a pause, in which no one else volunteered, he opened his mouth. But that was the same moment Stepan spoke.

"I will ride with the Lady," Stepan interjected, dismounting. Once on the ground, he handed his reins to a nearby stable hand.

Then Karin emerged from the chateau.

Pavel's gaze was on her immediately. He noted that she had chosen a more simple dress for the outing. A plain blue-gray over dress with two wide bands over her shoulders that met in a "v" at her waist, displayed the neckline of the black kirtle underneath. Sleeves fell loose over her arms, but stopped at the wrist, not flowing to the hemline as was more common with the finer dresses she wore. The skirt gathered at the waist and flowed down to the ground with only the slightest hint of a train.

Perhaps she didn't want to stand out as much among the village folk. A simple gold cross hung around her neck. Her long, curly, red-blonde hair was left down with the sides braided back and out of her face.

Is this what Karin would look like if she were a well-to-do merchant's daughter? The plainer dress did not diminish her beauty. If possible, it made her even more becoming. Was that not a strange thought? Was it that nothing distracted from her beauty now? Perhaps the myriad of adornments and elaborateness of vesture detracted from her fair face in her finer gowns.

His horse stirred again. Had he been so lost in his musings?

Karin was settled in the carriage with Stepan. A thought that Pavel was not altogether pleased with.

His other friends were maneuvering their horses into place alongside the oversized vehicle.

Pavel followed suit, a little embarrassed once again to be caught so off-guard, as his thoughts were not on what he was doing but on Karin. It was becoming a problem.

Karin walked through the small village of Hradec Kralove, appreciating the many sights and smells. As she made her way around the market, she stopped often to inspect a merchant's wares or to allow a baker to entice her senses with his breads and treats.

They had arrived at the small village perhaps two hours prior. The young men had tired of the marketplace rather quickly and headed for what she supposed was their real reason for visiting this village — the pub. A manservant was charged with her care, but one armload of purchases later, she sent him to the carriage and rid herself of the nuisance. His presence was only for her safety, but she would much rather take the risk and enjoy the place alone than be shadowed. How would the men react when they learned she had eluded their chaperone?

As the afternoon wore into evening, Karin discovered that there was more to tempt her than sights and smells. But sounds as well. At the edge of the market, there was an open structure. Perhaps at one time a stable. A group of musicians and singers found a new purpose for it. They created music within. The melody they played was impassioned. It had attracted other young ladies to gather and move to the music.

Karin watched the dancing. These ladies were not like the ladies of her acquaintance. No, they were merchants' daughters and other village women. She envied them as these women were not bound by the strict restraints placed upon the ladies of the nobility. Upon her. But no one here knew who she was. There was no one to tell her what to do or how to behave. And she could not deny that the music flowed through her as well.

As she realized there was no one to restrain or chastise her "unladylike behavior", it became impossible to fight the rhythm that beat in time with her very heart. Moments later, one of the young women pulled her into their circle of dancers.

There was such freedom in the movement and the music. As she let loose her inhibitions and danced, the restraint and oppression of propriety slipped away for these moments. She became all the more caught up in the rhythm and the words sung of homeland and happiness. In this moment, in this place, she was just Karin.

Pavel watched her dance from the shadows. He hadn't intended to spy on her, but he happened upon the scene as he wandered the market to ensure her safety. Though now that he had found her, he couldn't tear his eyes away. Was this a new side of Karin?

She danced with abandon. It lured him in farther and farther, until he was so close he could touch the dancers, twirling by. As he soon discovered, that was a dangerous place to be. For there were no observers here. Anyone who approached so closely was soon pulled into join the merriment.

A dark-haired, fair-skinned young woman grabbed for Pavel's hands, pulling him into the reverie. Spinning him for some moments, she soon released him into the rabble of moving bodies. It was easy to be caught up in the music. Had Karin been thusly seduced? Yet even as he began to move to the beat, his eyes sought her out.

Moving around the dance floor, he was thrown from partner to partner while the music droned on and the singers continued, untiring. Smiling and breathless, he soon found himself face to face with Karin.

Her wide-eyed expression betrayed her shock. And her cheeks colored. Was she embarrassed? Had he made her somehow censor herself? Did she think her involvement a mistake?

Wrapping an arm around her waist, he took her hand in his. He smiled and stepped back into the throng of dancers before she could object. Her eyes flickered from what appeared to be embarrassment to exhilaration.

While he twirled their bodies, she dipped her head back and laughed. He loved the sound. It too was music to his ears. Pavel was unable to release her and switch partners. And no one seemed to mind their lack of participation. They continued to dance into the night. Just the two of them.

"I wonder what could take Pavel so long," Stepan spoke up.

The other men apparently had not thought about their friend, who had gone in search of Karin some time ago.

But Stepan's concern was starting to pierce his drink-fogged brain. Shouldn't he have been back by now? The others seemed to have forgotten about Pavel's departure altogether.

"I am sure he decided it would best if he remain with her," Radek commented. "Night has fallen, after all."

This too was something Stepan had not taken note of as his focus had been on his tankard and how full it remained.

"He would have told us had he not been able to find her," Zdenek said, but his speech was quite slurred. He had consumed more than his fair share.

Stepan nodded, returning to his pint.

"Speak of the wolf," Luc called out, a little too loudly.

Stepan's gaze flew to the door.

Pavel stood just inside the doorway. He walked with long paces to where his friends sat.

"Were you able to locate Karin?" Was that an edge of worry in his own voice? It seemed so. Suitable, since Stepan felt responsible for Karin. Should he feel as guilty they had holed up in the pub and left her with naught but a servant for company? And even so, Stepan was now not so certain he could rely on a servant to remain with her and protect her as one of them would.

"Yes. And I have accompanied her. She has worn herself out in the market, and is waiting at the carriage. I think it best she return to the chateau."

"You have given up much of your evening," Zdenek spoke, rising. His movements rather clumsy. "One of us can volunteer to go and let you stay and enjoy yourself."

Pavel's brow furrowed.

Stepan followed his hard stare. And he could guess Pavel's thoughts. They had all consumed a little too much, and none of them could be trusted to see anyone home safely.

"It is all right." Pavel clapped a hand on Zdenek's shoulder. "I am ready to retire myself."

Pavel's gaze met Stepan's. Why? Stepping around the table, Pavel came to where Stepan hunched over his drink.

When Pavel neared, he leaned closer to Stepan's ear and spoke in hushed tones. "Please stop the beer for a while before you mount your horses."

Hanging his head, Stepan nodded. Pavel was right. They had judged poorly this evening.

Karin sighed as she leaned on Pavel's shoulder in blissful sleep. It was a sweet sound. Gentle, angelic even. They had not been underway for long, but the movement of the carriage had rocked her into pleasant dreams rather quickly.

Pavel's nerves were alert, seeming to tingle all at once with her so close. But he dare not move away, lest he wake her. So, he sat still, enjoying an even greater closeness than he had earlier that evening. The contact, while they danced, had been exciting. This was more peaceful but, because of the heat of their contact, enthralling all the same.

As she rested, he listened to the rhythmic clip-clop of the horse's hooves and focused on the gentle thumping of her heartbeat against his arm.

A crunching sound echoed through the night.

Crack!

The carriage pitched to the side.

Pavel grabbed Karin and held her tight to his body.

Karin awoke with a start, eyes wide.

"Don't move!" he commanded, wrapping his arms tighter around her as the carriage landed hard, jolting them both.

It continued to roll, slamming them into the side and threatening to throw them out the small window. That would put them in an even more dangerous position.

Pavel kept his body stiff and held on to Karin. He could barely breathe. It was his body that had slammed into the wall and cushioned Karin's.

The car had not stopped moving, and it threatened to roll onto the roof, teetering precariously between roof and side. How much longer could he hold onto her? How much longer could they endure?

CHAPTER 6
DISCOVERED

Some moments later, the carriage stopped. It ended on its side, propped up, perhaps by one of the wheels.

Pavel sensed the carriage was also at a downward sloping angle. They lay on an incline.

Karin and Pavel's bodies had slid toward the ceiling when it rocked before resting, but they lay on the side wall over the window.

Pavel still held onto her. They lay side by side, facing each other. Was the carriage truly settled? Deciding it was so, Pavel relaxed his hold.

His left arm had already released its firm grip. And he couldn't move it. Pain radiated from that shoulder. It had probably been dislocated. The fact that he was lying on his left side did not make things easier. Biting his lip to keep from crying out, he shifted his attention to Karin, still clinging to him.

"Are you hurt?" He moved his good arm up, his hand moving hair out of her face.

She cringed, her eyes were shut tight.

Was it a reaction to the recent bouncing of the carriage or was she in pain?

"Karin," he said, louder. "Karin, are you all right?"

She opened her eyes. They were clear and without tension. And he knew she was not in pain.

He breathed a sigh of relief.

Karin's eyes moved about the carriage. Did she expect it to start rolling again?

Pavel cupped her dirt-smeared face and spoke in gentle tones. "It is over. We survived. Are you hurt?"

She searched his eyes as she shifted, moving all her limbs. "No."

Pavel could not resist the urge to pull her into a one-armed embrace. "Thank God!"

Karin did not react at first. Had he surprised her? Overstepped? But soon enough, she melted into his arms.

He regretted when he had to pull back. The absence of her body's warmth pervaded his.

"Are *you* well?" Her eyes were bright as they searched his.

He didn't want to tell her about his shoulder. But she would become aware of it soon enough. "My shoulder is injured, but it will be fine."

Her eyes slid closed and she let out a breath.

"My lord! My lady!" The coachman came around the outside of the carriage.

"Here!" Pavel called.

With slow movements, he maneuvered to his feet. Then, reaching with his good arm, he helped Karin rise.

The carriage groaned under them.

Karin grasped for Pavel's arms to steady herself.

He grit his teeth against the pain.

She frowned and her gaze flew over his body, focusing on his arm. Did she realize that it was limp?

"Pavel, your arm!"

"It is fine. I promise." Pavel did not want to get distracted. His attention was on their predicament.

The wheel holding up the carriage could give way any second.

What might happen then? He was not sure. It depended on the terrain. Would they lay flat? Or would they tumble down a hillside?

"Come to the window and prepare to receive Lady Karin!" Pavel called to the coachman.

"Pavel, you are injured. You should—" she started as he positioned her under the window.

"I will not hear of it." he said, meeting her eyes.

The carriage shifted again as the coachman climbed on top.

But Karin's gaze was not diverted. She delved into Pavel's eyes, lingering for a moment longer before turning and raising her arms.

As she gripped the coachman's wrists, he grasped hers and pulled her to safety.

When Karin's weight shifted, there was more groaning underfoot. Pavel moved to the corner in an attempt to counterbalance the change, while the coachman helped Karin off the carriage. The man's footsteps return to the window above and then Pavel saw the coachman's hands.

Pavel reached with his good arm.

"Give me your other hand," the man said.

"I cannot, sir," Pavel said, offering no further explanation.

The process of getting Pavel out was more strenuous. With great effort and sweat, the two men worked together to guide Pavel's body up.

Once on top, Pavel saw what danger they were truly in. If the remaining wheel beneath gave way, the carriage would fall down the hillside and any within would be lost.

The sounds coming from the wheel became louder. More crackling could be heard.

Pavel shoved the coachman off the carriage while he jumped in Karin's direction. His only thought was, to move her out of harm's way.

As he jumped, a loud crack filled his ears and the wheel gave way. The carriage, no longer held up by the pinned wheel, slid.

Pavel watched as it hit large rocks, breaking apart as it rolled to the stream at the bottom of the hill.

Karin was at his side almost immediately after he landed. And she saw. She must have watched in horror as their coach made its descent, being crushed all the way down. Her hands clasped his arms tightly as their eyes followed the destructive path the carriage took. Then, she glanced down at him. What did she need? What could he offer?

Pavel let his head drop to the ground, taking in deep breaths. They had made it out. But not by much. He was so relieved he scarcely noticed her fingernails digging into him.

"Pavel?" came her timid voice. Was she worried he had passed out?

He opened his eyes. "I'm all right," he answered her unspoken question. "Perhaps a little shaken."

"What of your arm? We need to get you to a doctor!"

"No." He shook his head. "I assure you even this coachman can care for it."

She arched a brow and frowned. Was she so doubtful?

The coachman stepped over. " That carriage took quite a beating."

"Karin." Pavel turned to her. "Could you tend to the horses? Make sure they are secured?"

Her brows furrowed. But she did not question his request. Instead she nodded and turned. Had he earned such trust from her?

Pavel watched her go. The coachman should be commended. Not only for his capable rescue of Pavel and Karin. But he also thought to free the horses when the creaking started. Now they stood a few feet away. They would not be walking back to the chateau. As Pavel watched Karin, she took the reins and walked the horses to a nearby tree.

Satisfied that she was sufficiently distracted, he shifted his attention to the coachman.

The man's eyes were on him, awaiting instructions. It seemed he, too, knew what needed to be done. Reaching for Pavel's injured arm, he waited for a signal.

Taking in a deep breath, Pavel nodded and gazed up at the sky.

The man put his feet on Pavel's torso and around his shoulder. Then he grasped the limp arm. Pulling hard, the coachman twisted the arm until Pavel heard a loud pop.

Pavel cried out. But just as quickly as it started, it was over, and the pain lessened.

The coachman got to his feet.

Karin slammed into him from behind. "Get away from him!" she screamed as she punched at him and shoved him away.

She fell on her knees beside Pavel, using her body as a shield.

"Karin," Pavel gasped. "Karin, it is all right!" His hand reached for hers as he started to sit up.

She glared at him, wide eyed. Was she shocked to hear him defend the man who just attacked him?

"He fixed my arm," Pavel tried to explain. "I'm sorry we startled you."

Karin's eyes fell on his left arm, no longer dangling by his side. She shifted her attention toward the coachman. "I'm sorry...I ..."

"Do not concern yourself, my lady," The coachman brushed off his jacket.

"Thank you," she said, sighing.

How worn she must be. She had been tired before this ordeal, and it must have taken a lot out of her. Perhaps sheer determination was the only thing that had kept her going for the duration. But even that must have been wearing off.

"I think we best get back to the chateau," Pavel said, hoping to turn her attention elsewhere.

Karin nodded. Was she as eager for her bed as he was for his? Or was he more interested in just getting out of this place?

With a little help from Karin, Pavel got to his feet. Then they moved toward the horses. The coachman mounted one. Karin and

Pavel climbed onto the other. Then, with slowed steps, they made their way back.

When Karin awoke, the amount of light seeping into the room indicated that the sun had already crept over the treetops. She was accustomed to rising before dawn, but the events of the evening kept her out later than usual.

And then Karin had been nearly unable to sleep. Her mind filled with thoughts of the day and of Pavel. The more time she spent with him, the harder it was to resist this pull, this attraction. The more she learned about him, the more she liked him.

Karin sat up and swung her legs over the side of the bed. As she rose, her body protested. Her muscles ached from the accident, but she was thankful she suffered no worse than some soreness and bruising. It could have been much, much worse.

Padding across the floor toward the window, she then opened the drapes wide so she could gaze over the trees and mountains in the distance. It was a beautiful day, one which held every promise in the world.

Karin's thoughts shifted to her interactions with Pavel the evening before. How long had Pavel watched her? She had been so caught up in the dancing, she had not noticed. What had he thought?

He must have looked on her with favorable eyes, as he had joined in. The moment his hands connected with hers, it seemed as if she were flying. His touch grounded her and made her soar at the same time.

Sitting on a nearby chair, she relived the moment in her heart. And then, as much as she didn't want to dwell on the other events, she couldn't forget how Pavel saved her life. Or what it had been like for him to hold her so tightly. Had it been his embrace or the danger of the moment that had caused adrenaline to shoot through her?

Did Pavel think of her the way she thought of him? There were times when she was sure of it—when they shared a look, a moment, a touch. Other times, however, she was not sure of anything. It was all so confusing.

Footsteps shuffled beyond her door. Was it time for Mary to prepare Karin for morning mass? Karin soaked in the final moments of silence before the door opened and Mary entered bearing a tray with Karin's morning tea.

"Milady," Mary greeted her mistress as she stepped into the room. She set the tray on a side table next to Karin and went about straightening the bed.

Karin drank the tea, grateful for the warmth.

Once the bed was settled, Mary pulled out the items needed to dress Karin: chemise, kirtle, and gown. As soon as Karin finished her tea, she stood and allowed Mary to start her routine.

First, the linen chemise went on, hugging close to her body. Next came the form-fitting, red-orange kirtle. The gown was golden-yellow with a fleur-de-lis pattern of the same red-orange as the kirtle. Mary pulled Karin's hair back, twisting and securing it with pins as she worked.

As usual, this took place in silence. Everything had been tense between them for days. It wasn't altogether unpleasant. Not too long ago, Karin would have been plagued by Mary's rambling. Now it was perfect silence, albeit a little strained. Soon thereafter, Mary pulled away. Had she completed her work on Karin's hair?

Karin's reflection offered her a smile. "Thank you," she said sincerely. "You manage my hair quite well."

Not everyone could make Karin's curly tresses obey the way Mary could, and it was something Karin appreciated.

Karin moved into the larger cabinet where she would break her fast. Foods were being spread out for the guests from the nearby rooms—breads, jams, meats, cheeses, and fruit. The same as every morning. Breakfast would be taken with Zdenek, Luc, and Radek.

Zdenek was already seated, eating. Where were Luc and Radek?

Though the hour was later, it was not altogether uncommon for she and Zdenek to breakfast without them. They were the early risers.

Selecting a few things from among the foods offered, she then smiled at Zdenek as she sat.

"*Dobry den.*" She lifted her meat knife to begin her meal.

"*Dobry den,*" he replied, raising his knife to her.

"I trust you slept well."

He nodded. "And you?"

"I did. Thank you."

Their conversation continued with early morning pleasantries. Though Zdenek was early to rise, Karin had discovered that he tended to be more reserved in the morning.

Luc might be later getting to breakfast, but he came with rapid speech. So, she and Zdenek always ate in relative silence until Luc arrived.

Radek was more introspective. There would not be much conversation from him no matter the hour of day.

As Karin and Zdenek sat in silence, the door burst open and their friends rushed in. Instead of gathering food, they made their way to Karin.

"Lady Karin, are you well this morning?" Luc asked, the words spilling from his lips.

"I am." What did he know?

"There is talk of a carriage accident." Radek's words were just as fast, but still subdued.

The coachman. Pavel wanted to wait to share the news with the Viscount before anyone else. So Karin had not shared the tale.

"Carriage accident?" Zdenek said, seeming to struggle for the words. Had he consumed too much drink last evening?

"Yes," Karin started. "One of the wheels gave way."

"And yet you were unharmed?" Radek asked eyes wide.

"Apart from some soreness and bruises, yes. Thanks to Pavel. He saved my life."

"You are lucky to be alive," Luc said. He stared at Karin, but it was as if his thoughts were not there. It was as if he gazed through her. Was he imagining the accident?

"For certain," Zdenek agreed.

"Enough talk of this!" Karin chided. "You two had better get food if you wish to eat before mass."

Luc and Radek looked at each other and then rose, making their way to the food.

"I know you do not wish to speak of it anymore," Zdenek said in a quiet voice, leaning in. "But I am glad you are well."

"Thank you." She smiled at him. "So am I."

Everyone made their way toward the chapel. Attached to the chateau, the small chapel was as beautiful as any other room. Rising high, the ceilings featured crisscrossing dark wood beams. The small room was filled with pews of the same dark wood. One end of the room featured the high altar, priest chair, and sacraments.

Karin filed into the pew occupied by Stepan and Pavel, sliding in next to Pavel. She greeted them with a smile as the room fell silent.

A lector stepped forward to begin his recitation as the priest and altar servers entered. Once the priest arrived at his chair, he led the assembly in the sign of the cross.

"In the name of the Father, and of the Son, and of the Holy Spirit," the priest said.

The congregation crossed with him with a chorus of, "Amen."

The priest then launched into his greeting, but Karin had a difficult time keeping her mind on what he said. Her thoughts continued to stray to the previous evening. Was it due to Pavel's closeness? Back to the dancing and to the incident with the carriage. It was those moments of closeness with Pavel that she found herself dwelling on — and the way that it stirred something in her. Even now, quite aware of his arm brushing against hers, a surge in her nerves caused her skin to pucker.

Karin closed her eyes. She should not be thinking of such things at this time. Her mind should be on God. *Father, forgive my distraction. This is Your time.*

Focusing once more on the priest, she became aware that he was halfway through the Confiteor, nearly to the assembly's response. She did, in turn, contribute, before the priest concluded with a prayer of absolution.

As he closed his prayer, they sang the Kyrie Eleison—one of Karin's favorites. What more could one ask of God but "Lord, have mercy"? When she lifted her voice, she sang from her heart, seeking God's mercy upon her soul. They moved next into another hymn and then to the Silence—a time to pray and become more aware of being in God's presence.

Next came the scriptures and then the homily. Karin expected with the climate of Bohemia that there would be direct challenges to Hus's teachings. She was not disappointed. Wishing she could leave, or ignore the priest's words, she sat, her hands drawing into fists and her heart beating harder as the man continued his rant.

The priest's voice grew louder, and he became more impassioned. "These heretics who believe anyone can preach..." He paused as if he had to gather his own anger. "God speaks directly to the pope. It is he who determines who shall preach and what we are to preach."

Karin looked at her hands in her lap. There was movement, ever so slight, beside her. Was it her imagination, or did Pavel tense as well when the priest spoke thusly? Yes, his hands were balled into fists, though at his sides and, though almost imperceptible, his jaw was clenched.

Could it be? He? A Hussite?

Her thoughts flew to her tree. The box. It was him. Had to be.

With a boldness she didn't think she possessed, she reached over and covered his hand with hers.

His eyes cut toward her.

Karin's skin tingled. Heat sparked between them.

His eyes softened and he tilted his chin but slightly.

And so, with no words spoken between them, they acknowledged their connection as followers of Jan Hus.

Karin drew her hand back into her lap before anyone was to notice. But how could she still her heart, her hands as the service continued? Her mind raced with her desire to speak with Pavel. There were so many questions. When? How?

Her desire to look at him was overwhelming, but she avoided his eyes lest she give in to these questions. The wait was torture. But when would they find time to speak?

Pavel touched her hand.

Karin's gaze drifted toward him.

He inclined his head toward the aisle.

The congregation moved toward the priest to receive communion. She turned, following the motions of the ritual, but her body was ever more aware of Pavel's. So near, yet so far.

At last, it was time for the Concluding Rite, and they were dismissed. The group moved in silence, almost solemnly, toward the greater chateau.

How was she to meet with Pavel? For certain she could not request an audience with him in private. But they would not be able to speak of their connection with the others listening. Not even in ear's reach of the servants. Mary would find out.

And so, as they left the chapel she avoided his gaze. What could she say? Perhaps if she tried to speak, everything else would spill out.

Stepan stood in her way. And he spoke. Something about his relief of her well-being. She had a difficult time following the nuances of his attempt at conversation.

Still, she smiled and thanked him.

Then his brows furrowed. "My lady, are you well?"

She met his gaze. "Perhaps not." Karin drew fingers to her forehead. "I think I may be in need of some rest."

"Of course." He held out his arm.

Slipping her hand through his elbow, she allowed him to guide her toward her bedchambers, eyes focused on the floor.

Where had Pavel gone? What was he thinking? Would there be a chance they could meet?

Karin walked from the chateau with as much outward calm as she could muster. She had to force herself not to hurry. What would happen if she were found out after telling Stepan she needed rest?

Making her way to the forest's edge, she arrived at the tree line and could not hold back any more. She broke into a run. When she arrived at the stream's edge, she was alone. Had she expected Pavel to be there? Why?

Dropping to her knees, she began to unearth the box. Perhaps he left a message. Digging with furious intensity, she paid no mind to her hands or dress. She freed the box with less effort than before and pulled it open. The same papers lay within. Nothing more.

What did it mean? Would Pavel leave her to wonder?

Karin lifted the papers out, studying the words penned on the front. "For you, Karin".

Thunder sounded. She looked toward the sky. Not a cloud. Listening closer, she realized her folly. It was not thunder, but the rapid fall of hoofbeats in the distance.

Louder and louder, closer and closer they came. Was it Pavel? Or did one of the others come to seek her out? Had someone seen her leave the chateau? What to do with the box? The papers? She had not the time to bury it, so she tucked the papers into the folds of her skirt.

Pavel and his steed broke through the cover of the trees. Reining in his horse, he slid down as he came closer, landing just short of where she stood.

Karin's eyes stung as she met his gaze.

His breath came in gasps.

She held out the papers. "This! This was you?" Tears now brimmed her eyes.

"Yes." He put hands over hers, pulling the papers down so her face was unobstructed.

"How did you know?" her voice cracked.

"I was in the gardens the day your father..." His face contorted. Was he angry? He seemed to have great difficulty finding the words to continue. "The day before your father departed, I heard what he spoke to you on the balcony... when he raised his voice."

The tears flowed then. She had been convinced she was alone, that no one could understand. And not five feet away had been someone who heard. God had been good to her.

The papers slipped from her fingers as Pavel pulled her into his embrace, pressing her head to his strong shoulder.

After a few moments, he pulled her to the dip in the tree branch and settled there, now sitting.

Her sobs subsided, and her eyes moved from his shoulder to gaze into his eyes. Their faces so close, the intense heat was all that was between them.

Cupping her face, Pavel wiped her tears with the pads of his thumbs. He pressed a kiss to her forehead and then, with the slightest hesitation, he leaned in and tenderly pressed his lips to hers.

She responded, opening herself to him, gripping his arms like a lifeline.

He broke the kiss for but a breath. Pulling back just enough to look into her eyes. As if he sought assurance that she was agreeable.

Did her eyes beg for him to kiss her again as much as her heart longed for them to? They must have because his lips tasted hers again. And he dove deeper, with a kiss that held more hope and promise.

Sliding one arm around her back, he cradled her torso, holding her to himself. With his other hand, he reached for hers, intertwining their fingers.

When they broke apart, both of them were a bit breathless.

Pavel pulled her into his embrace, hugging her to his chest. As much as he relished the feeling of having her in his arms, he was concerned about her virtue, about the appearance of impropriety. What had he allowed to happen? They should be chaperoned.

But would her father allow it? Could they hide their allegiance to Jan Hus? Would he want to? Until he could answer those questions, their relationship must remain secret. So, there would not be hope of a chaperone.

Father, give me wisdom. Lead me not astray.

Not a scratch... not even one scratch. Karin sat at the dinner table, enjoying her conversation and dumplings without one scratch. How did this happen yet again? All of the carefully laid out plans, and she escaped her fate once again. Just to look at her — happy, hopeful, blissful, and ignorant in her youth — aroused all the more anger in the one who watched with deadly intent. The watcher, who would not rest until the master plan to rid the chateau of Karin's presence forever had been seen through, would not give time to be discouraged by failed attempts. No, that energy would be put into the next plan. As long as Karin was breathing the same air, there would always be a next plan.

Professor Evzen sat to write his prominent student an update. As the son in a family closely friended to the royal family, who would one day rise to the station of Viscount, Stepan had become an important piece. Evzen had been impressed with Stepan, both as a student and as a young man. He would be a powerful viscount when his time came. That was nothing to scoff at. To be in his good graces could only be to one's benefit. So, Evzen counted himself fortunate to have found a place of favor with the young man.

Even as much as Stepan viewed him as a mentor, it was Evzen's every intention to maintain close contact so his place may remain secure. Stepan seemed all too interested in the happenings with Jan Hus, so keeping him updated would serve Evzen's purpose.

There was no real news to disseminate at that time. The trials of Jan Hus were a farce. Anyone with foresight could have seen that coming.

Evzen had initially been torn about Jan Hus. When Hus had been dean of philosophical studies, teaching the ideals of Wycliff, a banned subject, it was easy to take an opposing side. Then the man became rector and had the court's favor, so Evzen had to play the other side, all the while catering to Stepan's dislike of the man.

Now with Hus on trial, it was a lot easier to play to Stepan's opinion of the man. Many of Evzen's peers at the university still sided with Hus. And the academic in Evzen could agree that there was truth to Hus's words.

Even so, Evzen had made his choice. He would side with the royals and curry favor with them. That was safest. So he began his letter to Stepan.

Stepan urged his horse ever faster as he approached the chateau. The trees opened to the grounds, he chanced a glance toward the balcony. Was Karin watching? His breath caught when he spotted her lone figure there. Focusing his attention to the horse beneath him, he squeezed his heels into the animal's flank. Could the destrier possibly give him more speed?

He almost always won these races, and he would not disappoint Karin this day. Yes, he would win this one, too. For her.

The horse snorted and grunted. Perhaps she gave him everything she could. An arm's length ahead of his closest competition, Luc, the temptation to look toward the balcony again to glimpse Karin became overwhelming. But he dare not take his eyes from his destination nor his mind off the horse for even one second, lest he be overtaken.

As they passed the balcony, his eyes cut in that direction to see that Karin had risen and walked to the railing. All the better to see his victory!

Stepan did not let up, pushing his horse once more. The animal gave him a last burst of speed, pulling him decisively ahead. Rushing past their agreed-upon finish line, he pulled on the reins, slowing the horse and raising his arms with a loud shout.

The horse turned as Stepan's legs commanded. And he bowed to Karin, arm extended. Now all would know the victory was for her. Even from a distance, he saw her smile as she waved to him.

Stepan moved his horse into the stables, blood rushing through him, heart thumping wildly. From the race or from the exchange with Karin?

He had grown quite fond of her these past weeks. In the stolen moments with her, he found conversation to be easy and pleasant. Her grace and resilience impressed him. She had faced many challenges in the short time since coming to the chateau. Yet, she had overcome. Stepan could not have helped but watch her. Of course, he had been struck first by her beauty. Long since, however, his admiration had deepened.

Handing off the reins to a stable hand, he then rushed into the chateau to find Karin. Stepan moved with a speed previously only granted to his horse through the halls.

Stepping onto the balcony, he found Karin returned to her seat. He paused, taking a moment to even his breathing. It would not do for him to be panting when he approached.

"*Dobry den*, my lady," he said as he came alongside her chaise.

She wore one of his favorite colors. The light blue gown with a scoop neckline, hugged her torso nicely until it met the skirt at her waist. Light blue was interrupted only by a gold damask pattern.

"*Dobry den,* Stepan. And congratulations. Well done!" She looked up at him, placing a hand over her brows.

Did the sun shine in her eyes? He sat on the chair next to her to ease her vision.

Smiling, she nodded.

He loved the way the upturn of her lips lit her face.

"What brings you out here?" Karin faced the tree line once more.

"Does a young man need a reason to desire the company of a lovely young lady?"

"Is that it? When I find a lovely young lady, you shall be the first to know."

Did she think him a tease? He leaned forward on his elbows. What words would move them forward, but not offend? How could one move beyond a light-hearted friendship toward something more?

"Was your hunt successful?" Karin faced him again, still squinting in the brightness.

He nodded. "A couple of quail, some birds."

"We will have a good dinner."

It was his turn to smile. As his face fell toward his boots, he caught a glimpse of something in his periphery. Shifting his focus toward it, he noted the book facedown on her lap.

"I apologize. I did not mean to disturb your reading." He rose, preparing to excuse himself.

"No, it's all right." She laid a hand on his arm.

Did she wish him to stay? His gaze landed on her hand, making contact with his arm. Perhaps there was more, could be more, between them.

He sat. "Is it a good book?"

"No." She shook her head, the gentle laugh rumbling in her throat. "No, it is not. It is rather boring."

Leaning his head quizzically to the side, his brows furrowed. "Boring?" Why would one continue with a book they abhorred?

"It is not so bad. The story is intriguing, but I care not to read as much about geography and history. I am much more of an action person. Rather than so many details, I wish the story would move along."

"The same for me," he clasped his hands together. "I don't wish the story to be muddled with extraneous conversation and exhaustive, irrelevant information."

Her lips spread in a wide grin. "So we are agreed?"

"Agreed," he nodded once.

They shared a small laugh between them.

Yes, there must be something more here. Something that could... would grow.

Pavel came to meet Karin on the balcony. He watched as she placed a hand on Stepan's arm and how they conversed with ease. Something unpleasant welled within him. Something hard and pained.

Though his relationship with Karin had changed, that did not diminish the fact that she had developed friendships with the other young men. This he had to repeat to himself a few times. Still, he couldn't help the dark cloud which seemed to settle as he watched.

It would be best if he walked away from the scene. Turning opposite, he remembered his arranged meeting with Zdenek. They planned to inspect the carriage wreckage. Perhaps that would keep his mind off this gloominess that loomed over him.

Luc wandered around the cabinet in which he broke his fast each morning, examining the artwork of the tapestries. Though he sat in this room each day, he had never taken the opportunity to study the work of the artists' hands.

He had dabbled with many forms of art himself and wished he could make it his career. But this was not possible. As the sole heir, his family relied on him to become something more... productive and affluent. So, he sought instruction in the law. Yes that was more distinguished. And the university he attended was quite prestigious. It was all rather grand.

But it was not where his true passions lay. Truth be told, not many of his peers had real zeal for the law. Many were there for the same reason as he—an esteemed career which afforded a comfortable living. However, he doubted any of them were in as desperate a situation as he.

While he moved from tapestry to tapestry, admiring the weave and the color palette, a maidservant approached him.

"Pardon the interruption, my lord. You have a missive." She held a tray bearing a letter.

"Thank you," he said, taking the folded paper.

The maidservant curtsied and left as quickly as she came.

He watched after her and then his gaze swept the room. Was he alone? Finding a seat nearby, he tore at the seal. His parents' seal.

Dearest Lucas,

We hope this letter finds you well. Are you enjoying your time at the royal hunting grounds? Making good connections, we hope. You are fortunate to have made such fine friendships with such men as you have. Do not take this for granted, as fortunate friends are always an asset in life.

All is well here. Your father continues in his treatments, but his prognosis remains the same. We are glad not to have to worry as we once did, as you are so well off in your studies.

Your sister's courtship continues to go well, and we hope the nobleman will soon make an offer of marriage. If so, then our fears will be laid to rest.

Only a little longer, Lucas. Our secret must be kept for only a little longer. Then our future will be secure.

CHAPTER 7
DANGER

Pavel and Zdenek took great care as they moved down the hill to the wreckage below. It was difficult to discern if the rubble had been disturbed, as there was not much remaining that resembled the grand carriage. But Pavel only sought two things: the wheels and the wheel mounts. He and Zdenek parted and moved around the debris. As he picked through piles of wood and metal, trying to make out anything he could, his stomach turned at the thought of what might have happened to him and Karin.

After a while of searching the remains and the surrounding area, he and Zdenek found enough pieces of the wheels, but the wheel mounts were not to be discovered. Piecing together the wheels as best they could, Pavel hoped to get a better idea of what happened before they were smashed.

A couple of the wheels were in fair condition. The others had been broken to bits. Perhaps the wheels in good shape had rolled free of the carriage before it plunged down the hill. Pavel examined one of those. Was this the one that left the carriage first? From all appearances, it seemed this wheel had broken away from the carriage by force—the force applied by a large mass landing on it as it rolled down a hill, for example. No, this wheel was not to blame. The other wheel yielded something curious.

"Zdenek, look!" Pavel called him from his work assembling the pieces of the other two wheels.

Zdenek peered over Pavel's shoulder.

Pavel shifted to give his friend a better view of where the wheel would have joined the wheel mount.

"What does that seem to be?" Pavel laid his finger on a strange crisscross mark on the wood. It would not have been made by the crushing pressure of being fallen on or by the weight from the carriage as it was drawn. Zdenek would come to the same conclusion he did—these were the marks of a blade.

"It can't be!" Zdenek drew in a sharp breath, eyes wide.

Pavel caught his eyes.

Zdenek had only come with Pavel, as he said, to keep him level-headed. Pavel's friend did not believe there could have been foul play. But that changed.

Pavel nodded. The nature of this near miss gave him cause to wonder...and question. Was Karin's near-death experience upon their arrival at the chateau not as accidental as it seemed?

"We have got to inform the —" Zdenek's voice rose.

"No." Pavel's voice was firm, certain. "We do not. Someone did this, and I do not want him to think we are watching now."

"We cannot keep this a secret."

"We can, and we will." Not only did Pavel not want to give warning to this person with a murderous heart, he also thought of Karin. No good could come from her knowing these incidents were not accidents. "Think, Zdenek. If not for my sake, do this for Karin. We will reveal all in time. Grant me a few days to find more evidence."

Zdenek fell quiet, looking to the ground as if it would yield his answer.

"I will trust you," he said after some moments, raising his eyes to meet Pavel's. "But only a few days."

Pavel nodded, relieved to have that time. "Let us examine the other wheels and see if they were also touched."

One of the other wheels, most likely the wheel on the same side as the one marred wheel, had the same knife marks. If Pavel were to wager, he would bet that both wheels were supposed to give at the same time. Pavel and Karin would not have had a hope of survival next to the incline had that occurred. The one wheel hanging on the rock was their salvation. Surely God's hand was on them.

As they prepared to leave, Pavel took a last look over the wreckage, which could just as well have been the place where his and Karin's lives came to an end. His stomach lurched. He was ready to leave this place.

"Let's go," came his simple request.

Zdenek's gaze rested on his face for a moment, then he nodded.

They climbed the hill to their horses in silence. Pavel could not muster words when his stomach turned so. And the hair on the back of his neck stood on end. He paused.

Was someone watching them? Had someone trespassed on them? He scanned the area with careful gaze, taking in the most minute of detail.

"Something amiss?" Zdenek called from farther above.

Pavel held up a hand. He finished his search and shook his head. It was nothing but his own nerves playing tricks with his mind. "It is my imagination."

Zdenek nodded and continued the rest of the way up the slope.

Pavel followed, but he could not shake the feeling. Not until they were a couple of leagues away from the site.

What Pavel had only guessed, and what Zdenek did not know was that someone watched them. Watched and waited.

Constable Borivoj had heard about yet another incident within his jurisdiction, and he had come to do his own investigation.

The meal came to an end, and Karin's gaze moved toward Pavel, heart aflutter. It was his turn to escort her. This would be the first time they would be alone since the new development in their relationship. Excited chills tingled down her spine. Would he find a moment to kiss her again?

"Lady Karin," Pavel started, as he stood. "Are you ready to retire?"

She nodded, afraid to speak, almost unable to breathe.

"Please," the Viscount interjected, "allow me." He rose and walked to where Karin sat. Reaching toward her, he pulled her chair out as she stood.

"Gentlemen." She nodded and curtsied. But her gaze rested on Pavel. What could this mean? What could the Viscount want?

Pavel's eyes held hers. There was a tranquility about him, as if he wanted to communicate a sense of calm.

There was little time to glean such, as the Viscount escorted her out of the great hall without so much as a pause to catch her skirt lest she trip.

The Viscount led her through the halls and toward the stairs. He attempted to make conversation. "How do you find your accommodations?"

"I must say I am well pleased." She forced a smile onto her face. If only her nerves would believe it.

"Good." He nodded. "And I have been well pleased with your return to health."

"Thank you, my lord." They began to mount the stairs.

"And I wish to celebrate it." His eyes were bright as he shifted to catch her gaze.

"That is most kind." She worked to keep her face from contorting into a confused expression.

"I shall host a ball in your honor. Would that be agreeable?"

Nothing could be farther from Karin's preferences. But this *was* a great honor he bestowed upon her. How could she not submit?

"I do not wish you to trouble yourself on my behalf."

"Think nothing of it." He waved a hand. "Your father is like a brother to me. He would do the same in my place."

They reached the top of the stairs, and Karin could think of no way to object and maintain propriety.

"Then I thank you for your kindness, my lord."

He nodded. "It is decided then."

They walked the rest of the short distance in silence. What would the ball bring? Would her father and mother come? Would she dance with Pavel?

Realizing she had ignored the Viscount, she turned her attention back to him. Thankfully, he seemed to be deep in thought as well. In moments, they approached her bedchambers. And she held back a sigh of relief that this was where the Viscount would part ways with her.

"I thank you for your assistance, my lord, and for your many generosities bestowed upon me."

He waved it away again. "A pleasant evening to you, Lady Karin," he said, as he released her arm.

Karin dipped her head in a slight nod and curtsied before making her way through the door and into her room.

Viscount Vlastik Dvorak watched her go. Perhaps he was older now, but he was not blind to the happenings between the young people under this roof. Yes, he could see the spark forming between this lovely young lady and his son. And he could not be happier.

Stepan approached him and let on as much. To be sure, the Lady Karin met with the Viscount's approval. He would be thrilled to approach Petr on his son's behalf. Perhaps they would have a good, long laugh about it. From the birth of their children, they had joked that Karin and Stepan would be intended for one another but nothing had been made official.

Truth be told, the Viscount had hoped for this exact thing when he offered to house Karin for such a time as her parents needed. Why they required she take time away from her home was still a mystery, but it mattered not. Vlastik had been thrilled it coincided with Stepan's favorite season for the hunt.

And so his plan, it seemed, had worked to perfection. Smiling to himself, he imagined the look on his friend's face. The smile stayed with him as he retired to his study.

Pavel stretched the bowstring back as far as it would go, feeling the strength in the weapon as he pulled it taut. He, Stepan, and Zdenek were testing different bows; gauging weight and general feel in preparation for their next outing.

Their morning hunts were spent on horseback with a crossbow, but that afternoon they would be traveling on foot and would take on the challenge of the more traditional bow and arrow.

They perused the Viscount's rather extensive collection of hunting equipment to find pieces which would best suit them. Stepan had the added advantage of greater familiarity with the selection.

A loud *wham* disrupted their concentration. They exchanged glances. What had made that sound? It seemed to come from outside. Perhaps the large front door had been flung open.

Zdenek seemed to have the same idea, as he moved to the window. His eyes widened and his mouth became drawn.

Pavel and Stepan's gazes clashed and they moved toward the window.

A servant girl, who couldn't have been more than seventeen, was thrown out onto the dirt road. She recoiled from the strong voice and words coming down on her from her overseer. The girl's olive-colored skin was bruised and swollen from a beating, and much of her dark hair had been pulled free of a ponytail and now hung around her face, disguising her features.

Pavel peered at Stepan. What was happening here? Should they step in to defend the girl? He was prepared to, but it was not truly his place. Rather it was Stepan, or his father, who should speak against such treatment.

"The girl is a Hussite," came Stepan's simple reply. His eyes fixed on the scene below. Was that disgust in his voice? And why did he speak as if this fact alone explained the abuse?

"And this implores such treatment?" Pavel spoke with a boldness unlike him, the emotions that welled within him were heated.

Stepan glared at him, confusion naked on his face. "She is also a thief," he added. "The Constable will be here soon to collect her."

Pavel knew it was a fabrication. If the girl had been found with stolen goods, they had been planted. The Viscount and, by extension Stepan, were loyal to the king's brother, Sigismund. Thus, they would, of course, share in his special hatred for Jan Hus and his followers. But Pavel never would have expected such extreme apathy from the men Pavel thought he knew.

Another sound interrupted his thoughts. This one from the hall.

"Here you are!" Karin's lilting voice came from behind.

Pavel closed his eyes, wishing her away. He did not want her to see the happenings below. But it would be unavoidable as she saw that they were transfixed on the events outside the window. It would break her heart, as well it should. How would she react? Would she give the truth of her loyalty to Jan Hus away?

Zdenek spoke, moving away from the window. "Karin, what brings you to seek us out?"

Pavel prayed Zdenek's attempt to deflect Karin's attention from being exposed to the girl's plight would be successful.

"What are you all looking at?" she asked, unmoved by his efforts at distraction.

"It is nothing," Stepan said in earnest as if he truly failed to see the problem. Could he not? Was he this cold? This inhumane?

She walked toward the window.

Pavel tried to stop her, taking a step forward to block her.

But Karin caught his eyes. Could she see it had struck a chord? Did she already know him so well?

As he gazed into the depths of her green orbs, he knew he would not be able to keep her from it. She was determined to find out for herself. He did not stop her again as she moved past him.

Closing his eyes, he prayed she would have the presence of mind not to expose herself or him. Perhaps if she saw, she would understand how dangerous it was, how important it was to be careful, and how low Hussites were viewed in the homes of those loyal to Sigismund.

As she came to the window, she gasped. Karin's hands went up against the opening as if to reach out to the girl.

"What ... what is ... ?" was all Karin could manage.

"She is a Hussite and a thief," Stepan said in a firm, flat voice without feeling. "The Constable will be here soon to collect her, and we will be rid of her."

"Is this how you treat all thieves?" Karin dared to ask.

Stepan met her eyes. He stepped toward Karin and his voice became timid. "She fought back when the manservant tried to remove her from her quarters."

It was not true. As Pavel glanced around the room, he would wager that the others knew it too. What could they do but accept it?

Pavel noted the tenderness in Stepan's voice as he moved ever closer to Karin. It would have been easy for Karin to mistake it as concern for the young girl, but it was for Karin's benefit. Why?

As Stepan neared Karin, Pavel's eyes narrowed and he found a new source of anger rising in him. No, he did not want Stepan any closer to Karin. He could not allow it. His hands balled into fists and he fought the urge to lash out.

But as Stepan came within an arm's length of Karin, she moved from the window, backing away from Stepan or from the scene, who could discern?

Silence fell for several moments.

Stepan looked after Karin. He seemed wounded.

Pavel watched the distance between Stepan and Karin, the anger within him cooling as that space grew.

"Did you need something, Lady Karin?" Zdenek asked. Was it a hope to change the subject?

"No, I ... I just ..." She placed a hand over her mouth. Was she unsettled? Queasy? "Please excuse me." She turned and rushed from the room, grazing Pavel's legs with her skirt as she left.

His heart sank.

"I will see that she is well," Pavel said, excusing himself. He did not care what the others might think. Not in that moment.

Once in the hall, Pavel found it difficult to catch her. Karin quit the room with as much speed as she could muster. And kept going. Pavel lengthened his stride in order to close the distance.

"Karin!" he called as he approached lest he startle her.

She turned. Unshed tears pooled in her eyes. "Pavel, that was horrible! We have to do something ... we cannot just ..."

All too aware of their surroundings, he pulled her into the empty study behind him. Only then did he pull her into his embrace, holding her to himself.

She quieted in his arms, leaning into him.

"If there was something I could do for her, I would." His voice was just above a whisper. "But I cannot."

"It is a lie! Only because she is a Hussite!" Hot tears fell from her eyes. Pavel felt them through his shirt.

"I know. Everyone knows," he whispered near her ear.

"It is not right." She was quieter, calmer, but still incensed.

"I know, Karin, it is not." He stroked her hair.

"What are we going to do?" She clutched his shirt tighter.

She no longer spoke of the servant girl, she wanted to know about their safety.

"We will be careful. And Karin?"

"Yes?" came her small voice.

He pulled back so he could catch her eyes.

"If this ever comes to something bigger... I do not know, perhaps war breaks... being in this place or in the home of any other family loyal to Sigismund... to be found a Hussite will not mean irons, it will mean the sword. Do you understand?"

A small sound escaped her.

He hoped she did understand. If there were war between the two, Hussites would be considered traitors in the eyes of the royals, and traitors were executed.

Still unable to speak, she nodded at him.

He pulled her back into his arms and held her as tightly as he dared, feeling the full force of the ferocity of his love for her.

Deputy Frantisek busied himself with the Constable's new recruit, Jakub. He trained him on the many processes of the office. As they went through the routine cell checks, making sure they were clean, secure, and ready for the next unfortunate soul who crossed the line of the law, he tested Jakub's observation skills.

"Did you hear about the happenings in the village last night?" Frantisek asked.

Jakub returned a blank stare. "Another batch of brawlers get thrown out of the pub?"

"Not everything we do involves dealing with drunks," Frantisek said with modest scorn in his voice. Although, he had to admit things had been rather slow since Jakub joined up. Constable Borivoj had also kept Jakub from the real investigative work until he became more acquainted with him.

"A party from the royal family's chateau visited Hradek Kralove and was almost killed on their way back when their carriage collapsed on the hill to the east."

"What? How?" Jakub's eyes gleamed. Having joined only a few

weeks ago, he became rather bored with breaking up drunken fights. He was chomping at the bit to hear a real case.

"Not too many answers. But they were on the edge of the road closest to the big drop-off when one of the wheels collapsed. My understanding is that one, maybe two, of the party were inside, and they just got out before it slid off the side of the hill and smashed to pieces."

"Has the Constable assigned anyone to investigate?" Jakub asked, hopeful.

"Investigate what?" came the booming voice of the Constable as he entered the jail. Had he already returned from talking to the local magistrate?

"The incident of the carriage collapsing on the way to the royal family's chateau. I understand the occupants barely made it out." Frantisek turned to face the Constable.

Borivoj stomped closer, his eyes hard on Frantisek. But they also seemed to ask him to continue. Should he? Dare he not?

"I heard about it this morning from one of the servants restocking the larder at the local butcher. He was gossiping with the other servants."

"Hold that thought." Borivoj stormed into his office.

Frantisek didn't move a muscle until he heard Borivoj summon them. He obeyed, moving in that direction, Jakub by his side.

Borivoj was opening a notebook and grabbing at the nearest quill. "Did you catch this servant's name?"

"No, but he might have been part of the cooking staff. I could point him out." Frantisek swallowed hard. Why didn't he pay more attention?

"Hmmm," Borivoj mumbled as he scribbled the note. "Did he say who was riding in the carriage?"

Jakub piped up, "I heard three, maybe four men...and a woman from the chateau were in the village."

Borivoj waved his hand.

Would Jakub have more information?

After a moment in which he didn't seem to realize he should continue, Jakub's words rushed out, "Frantisek was showing me the local pubs, and the barkeep at the larger one on the corner pointed out the special party. There were four men seated and a fifth — so, maybe it was five men — came in and spoke to them for a few moments before leaving. I overheard them mention that a young woman was with them." Jakub looked back and forth between the two men. "Is that helpful?"

Deputy Frantisek watched him with a slight nod. "We always need to observe. You never know when something may be important. What do you think, Constable?"

After Borivoj finished scrawling the details into his ledger, he left it open to dry while he took a few minutes to muse over this new information.

"I do not know," he said after some pacing. "I have heard several things over quite some time. There is not anything solid to proceed with, but I have kept notes. Anything involving the nobility, especially those connected to the royal family can be... delicate. So you must keep word of this to yourself." He gave them each a stern look. "That is all I can say." With that, he closed the ledger and dismissed them.

After they had left Borivoj's office, he closed the door.

Jakub continued to walk into the jail while Frantisek held back. Was it now? Could he address this with the Constable now?

"What is the matter?" Jakub said, turning toward Frantisek.

"Nothing. Just another matter I need to discuss with the Constable."

Jakub sighed, heaving his shoulders. It was clear he knew he was being left out.

"I need you to sweep out the cells."

Jakub gave him a reluctant nod, moving in that direction.

Frantisek shifted his attention back to the Constable's strong door and gave it a light knock. "Constable?"

"Come in," Borivoj called.

Frantisek entered, making sure to secure the door behind himself. Walking closer to the desk, he stopped just short of Borivoj. "Constable, is there something else going on?"

"I'm not sure." Borivoj chose his words with great care, examining his deputy's features.

"I understand that some things need remain secret, but how can I have your back if you do not let me know what is happening? How many years have we served together?"

Borivoj seemed to be contemplating how much, if anything, to share. "Frantisek, have you heard of other accidents involving the Viscount or the chateau?"

"On rare occasion...what have there been...maybe three?" Frantisek replied. Was the Constable leading him somewhere? Had he decided to trust Frantisek with something of a delicate nature?

"Eight. And spanning almost ten years," Borivoj said.

It couldn't be. But he did not doubt the Constable or his numbers. Still...ten years? There was one thing that confused him. "You have been here many years, but this dates back before your tenure."

"The third time I heard of an incident at that chateau, I got a hunch there might be something more to these accidents. So, I started collecting notes," he said, pausing. He gave Frantisek one of his hard stares. "You must realize the delicacy this involves. If there is something happening at the royal family's chateau, we must have an solid case before we ask the slightest question, or the king would have our guts for garters."

Frantisek sat down. He was starting to see why the Constable was slow to include him. "What do we do?"

" Keep collecting facts and listen for any news . Don't even think of starting an investigation. You hear how Jakub got wind of last night's incident from a gossiping servant? Believe me when I say gossip flows in *all* directions. If we start asking questions without proper cause, news will travel fast." Borivoj nodded in the direction of the door where, not far beyond, Frantisek knew Jakub had gone back to checking the cells as directed.

"He doesn't know the ropes yet and might trip in his eagerness to solve something. We must leave him out, or he will ruin any chance of uncovering something sinister."

Frantisek gave a silent nod. He understood. "Can we even inspect the remains of the wreckage?"

"I have already been there and collected what notes I could. I found one wheel intact, and it was clear it had been cut by blade."

"Then—" Surely that was enough!

But Borivoj cut him off. "I know this may seem to be the opening we need. But we must tread with careful steps, and I am thinking about how to proceed with this proof."

Frantisek nodded. He would do as Borivoj said. Mind his step and watch the boundaries. But he would keep his eyes and ears open.

Karin had not packed a gown appropriate for a ball, so the Viscountess ordered that a gown be made. And so measuring and fitting sessions filled Karin's days. These sessions seemed to last forever. The initial planning and measuring took place in the Viscountess's private cabinet, a place where Karin had yet to be invited.

"It will be good for us to spend time together, I think," the Viscountess said as the seamstress, introduced as Anastazie, set out fabric selections. "Your days have been full of isolation and young men. Not that time with attractive, fit young men is a tragedy." The Viscountess laughed.

Karin could not help but smile, her face warming as her thoughts shifted to Pavel's physically fit and attractive physique. "No, my lady."

"Please, I want you to call me Pavla," she said.

"I don't know if I could do that," Karin said, surprised at the Viscountess's suggestion.

"But I insist." The Viscountess touched her arm. "It pains me we haven't become better acquainted."

"You have a grand house to oversee," Karin said, "I understand."

"You are too kind," the Viscountess said, her words thick like syrup. She glanced toward Anastazie.

Karin's gaze followed. The seamstress had finished laying out fabric choices.

"Now, enough of that. Let us come and pick out your colors to start with."

The Viscountess led Karin to the couch to look at the rich greens, blues, reds, and golds. One by one, the Viscountess held them in front of Karin, putting them down in one of two piles. One pile was the fabrics about which she shook her head, and the fabrics in the other pile were the ones she would cock her head to the side about and make a quizzical face. Karin figured "no" and "maybe," respectively. But when the Viscountess picked up a deep forest green, her face lit up.

"This is the one," she said more to Anastazie than to Karin.

Was Karin's opinion irrelevant?

"The dress designer needs a fabric from this selection as well." Anastazie indicated a subset she had laid out. Those fabrics coordinated with the one the Viscountess had already chosen.

The Viscountess made a quick selection, a dark green heavy satin with a gold damask pattern. Not what Karin would have chosen, but she dared not speak out against her hostess.

Anastazie motioned for Karin to stand before the mirror to be measured.

The Viscountess took a seat nearby and signaled a servant to serve her a beverage.

The dressmaker undressed Karin to her chemise. It was not the first time Karin had been measured, but it was a bit odd to be in naught but her chemise in front of the Viscountess and the strange seamstress. Her family had used the same dress designer her whole life. But there surely was no reason to be embarrassed, so Karin pushed those thoughts to the side.

It would be different as well that she was to have no say in the gown. Even the dresses commissioned by her mother bore something of Karin's opinion. Still, she would not speak back to the Viscountess if the older woman wanted to plan a gown for her.

Karin and the Viscountess spoke little while Anastazie worked. They exchanged talk of the weather, shared words about the young men in the house, and talked of the current fashions.

"It is good we are becoming better acquainted," the Viscountess said, sipping her drink as she watched Karin move this way and that for the seamstress.

Karin had great difficulty discerning the truthfulness of the Viscountess's statements. The woman reminded Karin of a fairytale character with a golden tongue. Did everything from her lips sound overtly charming?

Karin was all too grateful when Anastazie assisted her back into her garments.

The Viscountess ordered a drink brought for Karin as well. Once Anastazie finished, the Viscountess bade Karin sit with her for a few moments. Then she spoke with the seamstress.

"Beata has the dress design we agreed on?"

"I saw the design this morning," Anastazie said, gathering the fabrics.

"Good." The Viscountess's smile was perhaps a little too wide. She waved her hand and Anastazie scurried from the room.

"What were we speaking of? Ah, yes, we were becoming better acquainted." The Viscountess shifted to catch Karin's eyes. "I have not yet solved the mystery of what brings you to the chateau."

"My parents wished for me to have time away," Karin said, shrugging as she raised the cup to her lips.

The Viscountess's eyes narrowed as they continued to study Karin. Why did it seem as if they bore into her?

"Come now, my dear." The older woman placed a hand on Karin's. "You can trust me. I am nothing if not discrete."

"Forgive me, my lady, but I have told you what I can." Karin fought the urge to inch away from the Viscountess. She wished to create distance between those deep eyes and herself. "Perhaps your husband might share more if you but ask—"

The Viscountess pushed away from Karin's hand and looked opposite. "Clearly you do not wish me to know." Her tone had darkened.

"It is not so simple." Karin's own voice was rather timid.

As quickly as she had twisted away, the Viscountess turned back, all smiles. "I am certain. Should you ever choose to trust me, I will always have an ear bent in your direction."

"Thank you," Karin said, a bit unsure. What had come over the Viscountess to cause such a change? Was there any way to know?

Karin stared at the cup, now resting in her lap, and wished for a reason to excuse herself. There might be cause to call up her outing with the young men. Perhaps if she chose her words well, it would make her excuse seem more reasonable.

"Please forgive me. I have forgotten the time, Viscountess. I promised to join the men for their afternoon outing. If you will excuse me," she said, standing.

"Of course, have a fine time," the Viscountess said, her tone dismissive.

Karin curtsied before exiting. She hated lying. The truth was that the men had said they would wait for her appointment to be concluded. But Karin found cause to stretch the truth. *Forgive my deception, Father.*

Making her way down the hall, she almost felt as if she were escaping. Had the measuring session been so bad? Or had she just been so uncomfortable in the Viscountess's presence? She could not be certain. But she was eager for fresh air and the invigorating exercise of a ride.

Moments later, Karin was secured in her saddle—as secured as she could be. It irritated her that decorum dictated she ride sidesaddle. The fact that her sleeves were as long as her gown did not help. What was the likelihood they would get tangled in the horse's legs?

"Ready?" Stepan called out. His eyes sought Karin's. Did he need confirmation from her alone?

She nodded.

Everyone took off.

All except Karin. Her horse, a caramel-colored mare named Whiskey, wasn't so eager. And she couldn't fault the hesitation. Something made Karin uneasy on the horse.

Pavel lingered, keeping a modest pace with Karin. Did he sense her hesitation?

After some moments, they reached and maintained a fast trot, but it was not near quick enough to catch the others. Were the young men attempting to show off for her sake or would the spirit of competition been present regardless? Anything done on her account was lost.

Her focus remained on the horse underneath her—keeping control of Whiskey's movements and maintaining her place in the saddle. Something was not right. Whiskey seemed skittish, and the saddle... something was not right.

Karin and Pavel breached the edge of the forest only to find that their friends were well out of sight and hearing. She wished them well on their race.

Did Pavel regret that he was unable to join in? After her tales of her days in the saddle, she flushed as she imagined what Pavel must think now. Did he suppose she had exaggerated? Or perhaps out right lied?

"I am sorry I am keeping you from your friends." Karin risked a glance in his direction.

"Do not worry so. I can think of no where I'd rather be." His words were warm and his eyes set upon hers.

Whiskey shifted and she jerked her attention back to the mare.

"Are you well, my lady?" Pavel drew his steed closer to hers.

Karin cut her eyes toward him.

His features betrayed his concerned.

"Yes." She forced a smile onto her face. "I am well. I assure you I am quite comfortable upon horseback, albeit I would rather not be side-saddled." The warmth of her face deepened.

Nor could she help but notice the smile which spread across his face. She was relieved that he chose to see the humor. There were not many women of her station who would openly admit a desire to ride like a man. But, having watched women fight their attire at such an awkward riding position, and having done so herself, left little doubt that she could tolerate such impediments so often.

His gaze caught hers and she found appreciation there. Perhaps it was something he could like about her—that honesty. For she knew no other way to be. Her thoughts were broken as she realized he spoke.

"...think may be something is amiss."

"Pardon?" Her face flushed anew.

"Do you think there may be something amiss?"

"The horse or perhaps the saddle," she said after some moments. "I do think something is out of place."

He turned his horse to the right, entreating Karin to follow. "There is a stream not far. We can water the horses and check your saddle there."

Pulling off the path, they maneuvered the horses through the trees and closer to the stream. What would they find? Would there be an answer to all of this? Or would it prove to be all in her mind?

Once the horses were drinking, Pavel dismounted and came to assist her. Reaching up, he held her waist as she steadied herself with hands on his shoulders. He hoisted her down without much effort, but his hands lingered. As they stood, faces a breath apart, he did not pull away. Nor did she want him to. Drawing her closer, he captured her lips.

Pavel's kiss was every bit as wonderful as Karin remembered. Her hands slid the length of his arms and rested on his shoulders. It was too much. His hand moved up to angle her chin, allowing him to deepen the kiss.

They remained locked in each other's embrace for a time that could not be measured and was but fleeting in her mind. Karin dropped her head to his shoulder. He pressed another kiss to her forehead. Was he as lost as she? For she could hardly see straight when he was near.

If only we could stay like this forever. She dared not whisper these words aloud. Whatever this was with Pavel, it was too new for her to speak such things. And, while the actions he took toward a lady implied much, she was not willing to risk anything by breathing her hopes of the future.

When Pavel pulled back, Karin sensed his hesitancy. Was he so reluctant to end this moment?

"I will check your saddle." His words were breathed. After stepping away from her, he walked around the horse, pulling on various straps. "Karin, who saddled your mare?"

"One of the stable hands."

Pavel was now on the other side of the horse, hunched and looking at something not visible to her.

Karin stepped behind the horse, careful to keep a hand on the horse's body lest Whiskey become spooked and kick out.

"What is amiss?" Karin asked as she came around.

"These straps are loose." He pulled at the strap which held the saddle to the horse. "This saddle would have slid to the side had you pushed the horse faster. You would have been thrown."

Serious blue eyes met Karin's.

Pavel stood. "I am surprised that even at a trot you managed to keep the saddle upright. No wonder you had such difficulty."

Karin's eyes were wide. "Pavel, I checked the saddle before I mounted. Those straps were secure."

"Then how could this have happened?" He tightened the straps, focusing on securing them.

"I do not know. There were others who came to check my saddle."

"Who?" He stepped toward her, his work completed.

"Another stable hand, Luc, Stepan. Everyone was only trying to help."

"Someone was not." His eyes were serious.

Karin didn't want to guess which of the three might be responsible for this.

"We should head back." Pavel moved toward the stream.

"No." Karin reached out and laid on his shoulder.

He halted, turning back toward her.

She took a deep breath. "I am having such a pleasant afternoon, and I so rarely get out of the chateau. You have remedied the problem. Perhaps can we continue with our plans."

Pavel's eyes rested on her. Was he weighing his decision? After some moments, he nodded. "All right, we'll continue to the rendezvous."

She smiled.

His eyes darkened again. Was he so concerned after her? "But stay close."

Nodding, she clasped her hands together at hip level.

Pavel helped her mount, checking her saddle once again. After a couple of pulls and tugs, he seemed satisfied she was as sound as she could be. He mounted his steed, and they were off.

Now, with Karin able to move faster, they arrived at the rendezvous point in a matter of minutes.

The chosen meeting place was the same spot the men would converge to while hunting if they should be split up. A small clearing among the trees, it was raised on a higher plain. The trees around the clearing had thinned. Anyone close could be spotted from some distance away. It was not an ideal position to hunt from, but it made a perfect meeting location.

As Karin and Pavel neared, she saw the others. How long had they been there? Their horses appeared antsy.

Zdenek spotted them first. "Where have you been?"

Karin opened her mouth, ready to tell them all that had been discovered of her saddle, but Pavel interjected.

"We stopped to water the horses."

She glanced at Pavel. Would he say nothing further?

"And," Pavel's tone lightened, "the lady likes to stop and smell the flowers."

Karin shrugged, smiling.

"Even so, our horses are quite ready to stretch their legs," Radek said as his horse stirred.

"Do you think you can avoid the daisies for a while, my lady?" Stepan said, a broad smile across his face.

"I shall do my best, my lord." She shifted, preparing to maneuver Whiskey into a faster pace.

The horse responded immediately, moving onto her hind legs.

Karin kept a tight grip on the reins lest she be bucked off.

"Whoa, Whiskey," she soothed.

It was no use. The horse had been disturbed. Whiskey became more agitated, moving this way and that, as if wanting to fell Karin.

She held on still. The manner of injuries sustained by people thrown from horses were well known. Then, without warning, Whiskey took off into a full gallop.

Karin cried out, grasping the reins and pulling back as hard as she could. While she was not an inexperienced horsewoman, she would not have considered herself proficient either. Controlling a spooked horse was not among her skills. And, try as she might, she could not contain the horse. Cursing her sidesaddle situation, she held tight to the reins, certain she would have greater control if seated astride.

In the midst of her terror, hands grasped for the reins. Who?

Stepan. The fastest of the young men, he would be the one to rescue her. Try as he might, he could not reach them and Karin could not release her own grip.

Stepan's horse moved impossibly closer to Whiskey. His body nearing hers. An arm wrapped around Karin's waist.

"Jump toward me!" Stepan yelled in her ear.

She shook her head. Surely she could not.

What would he do? Continue with his plan and trust that she would do as he commanded?,

"One ... two ... three!"

Karin leapt toward him as he pulled her body from the spooked horse and onto his steed.

He then slowed his horse, his chest heaving under her ear, his breathing rapid and hard.

She landed haphazardly on the horse, somewhat side-saddled, facing Stepan, clinging to him.

"It is all right. It is over." He soothed, holding her in his firm embrace.

The other young men appeared around them. A chorus of spoken relief sounded amongst the group.

Her eyes sought Pavel, but she was unable to discern his features. There was relief for certain, but something else flashed in his eyes. Was he jealous? Upset that she clung to Stepan? She released her grip and moved to dismount.

"Don't, my lady." Radek held out a hand. "Stepan, you must take her back to the chateau."

"Yes," Zdenek agreed. "Don't let her out of your sight." He maneuvered his horse closer to Stepan's and assisted in shifting Karin to turn and sit more securely in front of Stepan.

"Zdenek and I will search for Whiskey and meet you back at the stables." Radek turned his horse in the direction the crazed horse had run.

It was agreed that this was a sound plan. And so, they parted ways.

While the riding party was out, Viscount Vlastik Dvorak received a visitor—someone whose presence was not unwelcome but disturbed the staff all the same. Needless to say, though the Viscount dismissed all servants forthwith and had the cabinet doors closed, gossip flew as to the possible reasons for Constable Borivoj's visit.

"Please, do sit," the Viscount said, waving a hand in the direction of several comfortable seats as he took a large chair for himself.

Borivoj chose a chair closer to the Viscount, wanting to engage him at eye level with ease. "I thank you for receiving me, Viscount."

"Of course, Constable, of course. Tell me," he said, picking up a cup of some hot beverage from a tray a servant set nearby before all were banned from the room, "what brings you to this part of Hradec Kralove? Not police business, I hope."

"This is more of a...friendly visit." Borivoj was careful as he chose his words. It would not serve him to alarm the Viscount. He must downplay his investigative intentions as much as possible.

"Good, good," the Viscount's shoulders relaxed and he leaned back. "That is the manner of visit I prefer to entertain."

"I must confess," Borivoj warned, "My visit is not without its matters of business to attend to."

The Viscount's brow rose. "I would suspect you to be lying if you did not make such a confession. And I prefer to dispense with those things first. So, let us see to that."

Borivoj had only just lifted his own cup to his lips but nodded and lowered the drink. "Of course." He squared his shoulders. "I am certain you are aware of the carriage accident on the road between this chateau and Hradec Kralove."

The Viscount studied Borivoj, but remained silent.

"I understand two of your guests were involved."

"Dreadful business." The Viscount leaned forward, brows furrowed. "I am relieved you are investigating the matter."

Borivoj watched the Viscount. Allowing silence to fall between them. Would the Viscount speak again? Give away information he should not?

After some moments, the Viscount interlocked his fingers. "I fear I was remiss in reporting the incident. We were astonished, you understand, and seeing to the recovery of our guests."

"Of course," Borivoj measured his words. He did not dare move lest he give away anything of his thoughts. This was the time to study the Viscount. And the man began to shift in his seat. Was he becoming uncomfortable?

Borivoj wished he had his ledger to make real-time notes. But that would push their meeting beyond the realm of a "friendly visit" and raise the Viscount's defenses for certain.

The stillness between them became awkward. Would the Viscount become so uneasy he would declare an end to their conversation? Perhaps it was best if Borivoj kept him talking. Maybe even dole out some information and guage his reaction.

Leveling his gaze on the Viscount, Borivoj pressed on. "I discovered that one of the wheels, perhaps more, was damaged with a blade."

"Someone tampered with the carriage? You mean to say this was no accident?"

"That is how it appears, my lord."

The Viscount's eyes widened and his mouth dropped open. Was he truly so surprised?

"But who would do such a thing?"

"I do not know, but I intend to find out." Borivoj met the Viscount's eyes. "With your permission, I would like to perform a search of the chateau to seek out any inconsistencies here..."

"The chateau? You think it possible one of my guests... ?" The Viscount's mouth clamped shut, then opened and it seemed from the movement of his lips that he attempted to find words, but failed.

At last, he rose. "No." He turned, giving Borivoj his back. "It's not possible." Spinning toward the constable again, his eyes flashed. "It must be someone in the village. That is where the carriage was just before the accident...incident."

Borivoj remained silent as the Viscount moved to the window, gazing out across the grounds. Was he so resistant to the possibility of placing suspicion on one of his guests?

When he faced the constable again, his features were set. "You must start in the village. None of my guests are capable of such a thing."

Borivoj drew in a breath. What could he say to reason with the Viscount? The man couldn't think he knew his guests so well. But as Borivoj opened his mouth, the Viscount continued.

"After you have performed a thorough investigation in the village, perhaps we can talk more. Until then, I cannot open any of my guests to your suspicions."

Just as Borivoj feared. But what could he do? A hacked wheel did not give him cause to search the chateau, the people under the protection of the royal family. The Viscount was right—the tampering had happened while the carriage was in the village. And that was where the investigation had cause to go.

Still, Borivoj couldn't shake the feeling that the deed was linked to the chateau—eight incidences and six bodies were not the stuff of coincidences.

But none of this mattered.

His hands were tied.

Stepan dismounted and raised his arms to Karin. She allowed him to assist her to the ground as she scanned the area. After entering the stables, Pavel and Luc had disappeared. The only other soul present was the stable hand preparing to take Stepan's horse. Now that they were on steady earth, even he vanished.

"Please allow me to see you to your chambers," Stepan said, his voice full of emotion. His eyes glistened as he held her gaze. Was he so concerned?

"I would rather sit for a moment," she said, indicating a nearby bench. Her legs were like porridge beneath her. Would they hold her if she stepped forth?

Stepan reached for her hand. Had he noticed her uneasiness? He slid an arm around her back and led her to sit.

When he rose, he was pulled by Karin's hold on him. Had she clasped his hand that firmly? Loosening her grip, she offered him a weak smile.

His mouth did not turn in response. It remained drawn, his eyes serious. The muscles in his jaw moved.

"I beg you, my lord. Do not worry yourself so. I am well enough."

"Still, I insist a doctor is called."

"Please do not trouble the doctor. I am only shaken."

Stepan's eyes rested on her face. She must have been a sight—hair unruly from being whipped in the wind, face scratched by small branches while on the out-of-control animal.

His gaze softened. Perhaps he would heed her words.

She let out a breath.

Stepan's hand rested on her shoulder, the gentle touch seemed as something beyond their companionable friendship. "You will be tended by a doctor. You suffered quite a fright."

Peering into his eyes, she sought answers. Was there more behind his gesture? If so, what? As for the doctor, she could do nothing but accept. This was from the son of her host, the man who had just saved her life. So, she nodded.

"Shall we continue into..." Stepan raised an arm toward the chateau.

"I would be most grateful for a moment of rest."

His brows came together. "Will you be all right until I return?"

"Yes." She kept her voice even, calmer than she felt. Did he not think she could manage to sit in the stables without creating mischief?

He turned and, with some hesitation, headed for the house.

Karin sat just as Stepan left her. She stretched her limbs and closed her eyes. As she prayed, she found a peace, a balance that restored her calm. When she opened her eyes, the stables were still empty and silent.

Where had Pavel gone? Back to the chateau? Was he not concerned about her? Was he angry? Should she go after him? Or let him come for her?

As the minutes passed, she found that she could no longer remain as she was. Perhaps it was best she return to the chateau. But could she trust her legs? Standing, she tested her weight on her more strengthened muscles. All seemed well. A step forward, hand outstretched toward a nearby post, her balance did not waver.

With the use of her legs returned, she should find Stepan and plead that the doctor not be brought. She moved toward the far side of the stables.

Hands grabbed her and pulled her into a stall. Her back was pushed against the rough wood of the wall. She opened her mouth to scream but her vision was filled with Pavel's bright blue eyes.

He pulled her into a tight embrace. An arm wrapped around her shoulders, his hand stroking the back of her head. The other arm held her to him. His face was in her hair, her shoulder. For several moments, he just held her.

When he spoke, it was as soft as a breath. "I was so afraid. Every-thing....it all could have been over in an instant...if anything happened to you."

His words warmed her from the inside, like slipping into a warm bath. She soaked in his presence, his arms, his touch, his words. "It's all right. I am well."

He held her for several moments more before pressing a kiss to her hair, then to the side of her face, then briefly to her lips, pulling back far enough to look into her eyes.

"I don't want to hide anymore. I want everyone to know how we feel."

For a few wonderful seconds, Karin believed it was possible. Then reality crashed upon her. Nothing about such a pronouncement would be appropriate. Or received well.

"It is impossible." She raised a hand to his face.

Pavel placed a hand over hers. He gazed deeply into her eyes, never wavering. "Not when your father returns. I will ask him for your hand."

"What are you saying?" Her eyes widened.

"Karin, I want to marry you. No matter what happens, I want to know that we'll be together."

It was all too wonderful for her to take in, so it spilled out through her eyes. With great tenderness, he wiped her tears away.

"Are those happy tears?" His voice was so soft.

"Yes! Of course...yes!" She threw her arms around his shoulders and kissed him.

"Karin?" Stepan's voice came from just inside the stables. Would they be found out? Or could they bide their time?

With regret in her heart, she pulled away.

Pavel ducked farther out of sight.

Karin stepped out of the stall. "I am here, Stepan, moving about. I am feeling much more myself," she said, pacing toward him. Could she draw his attention away from the horse stall? "As I told you, I only needed a few moments of rest. And I am well."

"Hmmm," His brow rose. "As I see. However, I still think you should be seen."

"If that is what you wish." Taking his arm and turning them toward the chateau, she afforded a glance over her shoulder in the direction of the stall.

Soon, Pavel. Please let it be soon.

Pavel watched them go, trying once more not to let the twinge of jealousy overtake him. He remained in the stable, trying to calm himself from the happenings of the last hours—the spooked horse taking off with Karin was one of the scarier things he had experienced. In that moment, he had prayed that God would trade his life for hers. And in this moment, he was thankful God saw fit to spare them both.

The distant clip-clop of hoofbeats brought Pavel back to the present. He stepped out of the stall. Zdenek, Radek, and Whiskey neared. From all appearances, the horse was ready to race off, pulling and fighting against the thin straps of rein that bound her.

Zdenek and Radek employed what tactics they could to control the possessed horse and their own.

Pavel rushed toward them. He would help. But how?

Whiskey bucked.

"Whoa, Whiskey!" Zdenek called out, "Whoa." He pulled hard on the straps that strained to their breaking point.

Now as they were just outside the stables, Zdenek and Radek slid off their horses.

Pavel grabbed for Zdenek's horse's reins, and a stable hand grabbed for Radek's.

Once those horses were in their stalls, Pavel returned to Zdenek and Radek's side. With his friends holding the reins taut, Pavel and the stable boy attempted to soothe Whiskey.

Pavel laid a hand on her neck, rubbing as much as he could while speaking in soft tones. Moving his hands over her neck and chest, he tried to calm her.

Whiskey stilled somewhat but continued to shift.

Pavel continued to coax Whiskey to stop moving while the stable hand checked her hooves. Perhaps something had become lodged there.

The boy glanced at Pavel and shook his head.

Moving his hands over the horse's body, Pavel worked on the saddle's straps. As it was removed, he spotted a sharp burr under the back of the saddle. It was stabbed into the horse's flesh. Had it been situated there under the saddle? Waiting for Karin to but shift her weight as she urged speed from the animal?

He jerked the burr out.

Whiskey stirred and then calmed.

The stable hand took the reins of the now docile horse and walked her to a stall.

"How unfortunate for Karin," Radek said.

Pavel glanced at Zdenek. Was his friend thinking the same as he?

Zdenek's eyes were dark and his face drawn. Yes, he knew too.

This was no accident.

CHAPTER 8
THE BALL

Karin afforded herself a long look in the mirror and could not help but admire the picture she presented. The dress the Viscountess had designed suited her quite well. Dark green velvet set against her pale complexion and strawberry-blonde hair was a stunning contrast.

The dress created a wide "v" over her front, revealing the kirtle's neckline. As elaborate as any other part of the dress, the kirtle was made from the dark green heavy satin with a gold damask pattern to it. A low waist and a scoop neckline, which hung low enough for her to display an ornate necklace, was flattering to her shape.

Karin's hair had been twisted and braided up off her shoulders. A pair of gold-inlaid drop pearl earrings adorned her ears, and Mary clasped a matching necklace behind her neck.

"I think you are ready, milady," Mary commented.

Karin nodded.

As if on cue, there was a knock on the door.

Karin rose as Mary crossed the room to open it.

"It is time for the Lady Karin to be announced." The manservant's voice carried into the chambers.

Karin moved forward and stepped into the hall, nodding to the manservant.

He led her from her rooms to the grand staircase in silence.

Stepan waited at the top of the stairs. He, too, was dressed in all his finery.

He turned. Had he heard them coming? His eyes widened as his gaze landed on her. And did his breath quicken? Or perhaps he simply suppressed a sneeze?

"My lady," he managed, "You are exquisite this evening."

"Thank you." Her face warmed under the intensity of his stare. "You are rather handsome yourself."

He reached forth, offering his hand.

She slid her fingers into it.

Raising her hand to his lips, he turned it and pressed a kiss to her wrist. Why did he do that?

His eyes never left hers.

It became more difficult to think. Was Stepan interested in—?

Stepan turned and led her down a couple of steps. Then stopped.

Why must she be in all these constricting clothes? She couldn't breathe. Were Stepan's eyes still on her? It was as if she could feel them boring into her. Dare she look?

The manservant had descended ahead of them. Was he to announce them? What was he waiting for? As the man continued his downward progress, so painfully slow, Karin believed she would faint before he reached the bottom.

However, he halted a few steps short of the landing. Raising his staff, he thrust it toward the floor. A loud bang sounded.

Then silence.

All eyes were on them.

"The Lady Karin Bornekova and Lord Stepan Dvorak," he announced.

Stepan had set foot on the next step down as soon as the manservant started speaking.

Karin gripped his arm and moved alongside him. What should

she anticipate from this ball? The crowd greeting her? She glanced about for Pavel in the sea of faces, but she could not find him. There were too many people.

The crowd parted as she and Stepan stepped to the floor. Stepan led her to the center of the room's open space and spun her in a single circle. They would share the first dance of the evening, starting off the celebration as host and guest of honor. Music played from somewhere on the other side of the room, and Stepan moved to the cadence of the instruments.

Were all eyes on her? She and Stepan were the only dancers. And then at the second round of the song, others joined them on the floor.

Relief flowed through Karin when she was no longer the center of attention. So much had it disturbed her that she hadn't been able to pay much mind to Stepan as they whirled around the room. Did she smile enough? Had she conversed pleasantly with him?

"It is a bit much, is it not?" Stepan smiled.

"Yes," she admitted. "But I appreciate everything your father has done for me," she was quick to add.

He waved her off, reminding her of the Viscount. "I am certain. But I am also curious how a woman who is so deserving of all this seems so uncomfortable receiving it."

She searched his eyes at the compliment. "I thank you, but I am afraid I have no answer. Perhaps because I am not often the object of such admiration."

"Something we must remedy," he said, his voice husky as he drew closer. But just as soon as he did so, he pulled back and led her toward the far side of the room.

Karin wondered after these words, these actions. These compliments did not seem as if they were delivered in friendship. What was she sensing from Stepan in his words? Or was she seeing something that wasn't there?

Her gaze wandered from Stepan to the crowd around the room. Pavel continued to elude her. Where was he?

"Some refreshment, perhaps?" Stepan held a beverage toward her.

"Yes, thank you." She took the cup, but avoided meeting his eyes. Lifting it to her lips, she had only begun to sip when Zdenek appeared.

"I insist I have the next dance with the loveliest lady at the ball."

"If you must," Karin smiled at his words. She surprised herself with how eager she was to be released from Stepan's presence.

Zdenek led her to the dance floor, not giving her much chance to set her drink down.

Her young men came each in turn to dance with her. Strange, how she had come to think of them as *her* young men. But, they were each special to her.

The ball had been progressing for a couple of hours, and Karin had danced with all the young men of her acquaintance...except Pavel. He continued to evade her. Why? Had she upset him?

Taking a deep breath, she found a seat. Perhaps it was just as well. For she was tired and in need of respite. Yet her heart weighed heavy and a thickness rose in her throat. Would he not come to her? She smoothed her hands over her skirt and fought the sting in her eyes.

The hair on her neck tingled. A warm breath feathered near her ear.

"Come now, my lady, you would not forgo your favorite?"

Karin turned to meet Pavel's eyes. Was he not concerned what others would think of his closeness? For in that moment, she did not. "Indeed I would not, my lord."

Sliding a hand into his, she let him lead her onto the floor. Her feet were tired, but she was thankful for every moment she had in Pavel's arms. And for this, the tears continued to threaten.

As they moved through the steps of the dance, she relished each time their hands connected. The way his eyes held hers. And how his arms surrounded her. It was not dissimilar to the way the other men moved through these steps with her, but it felt different with Pavel.

They moved together to the music, and it was exciting. He held her a little tighter than he needed to, a little closer than he should have. But she didn't care. Not one bit.

The music drew to a close and the dancers stilled, moving to the sides. Karin laid a hand on Pavel's arm and worked to catch her breath. Placing a hand on hers, Pavel secured her attention as he led her onto the balcony. She glanced over her shoulder. Had anyone noticed their parting?

Their friends were on the other side of the room, apparently deciding whom to dance with, jabbing at each other. No one seemed to notice as she and Pavel quit the room.

Breathing in the fresh, cool air, Karin was grateful for the break from the crowds, from the warm room, even from dancing.

Pavel moved them to the edge of the railing overlooking the gardens below. For several moments, Karin enjoyed the quiet and the soft breezes from the east. As Pavel did not speak, she did not either. What was there to say?

At length, Pavel broke the silence. "You are breathtaking this evening, my lady."

She shifted to look at him, not caring she was blushing. "Thank you."

He rested his hand on hers already on the railing. Was there more he wanted to say? Did he hold back? So much of what she wanted could not be said. Must they content themselves with what could be communicated in a look, a few harmless compliments, and the touch of one hand on another?

"There you are," Stepan said, coming out of the festivities.

Pavel took a step away from Karin.

"Karin needed some fresh air," Pavel said. It was true.

"Ah." Stepan was closer to them now. "You both missed Zdenek trying to ask that brunette to dance. It was truly sad, Pavel. But I suppose not altogether so terrible... she accepted the dance. I think all bets are open as to what happens next."

"Shall we?" Stepan held out an arm for Karin.

"I *am* sorry, Stepan," Karin fought to keep her voice light. "But I think my feet have had enough for the evening."

"Then we shall find a seat from which to enjoy the rest. There will not be much more. I promise."

Karin was reluctant to leave Pavel's side, but took Stepan's arm, looking back at Pavel as Stepan drew her away.

Pavel raised an eyebrow as if to ask her a question. Was he being coy? Implying she might enjoy Stepan's attentions?

She gave him a stern look.

His face opened into a smile.

Then she directed her attention forward. Pavel would find out how unwise it was to tease her!

Lenka watched as her husband finished a letter to his daughter, telling her of his return. She loathed the thought of Petr returning without her. How long had it been since she had seen her *katka*? Once again seated in her cabinet, Lenka worked with diligence on her cross-stitch. As the tension tightened her shoulders, she returned her focus to the thread.

Petr's return to the chateau had been a scarce subject. He must know it was a sore matter for Lenka. Still, she could no longer keep her peace.

"How long will you be gone?" Lenka kept her head down, eyes on her stitch work.

Petr glanced up from his letter and paused. Must he think on it? "I do not know." He then returned to his paper.

A letter had come from the Viscount, requesting Petr's presence to discuss a matter of great importance involving Stepan and Karin. He did not say anything further on the matter, but he did not need to. Lenka knew what it meant.

"It seems as if you will soon announce an engagement." Lenka worked her needle with great intensity.

"I believe that is true." Petr glanced in her direction, smiling.

Lenka looked up to meet his eyes. "Do you not think I should to be there for such a day?"

"Should you be there?" Petr rose. "I think, dear wife, there is some confusion." He walked to where she sat. Leaning over her, he cupped her face with one hand. "Do not worry yourself. I plan to send for you before we make such an announcement public."

She met his gaze. "Send for me?"

"Do not think I would stand alone on such a happy day." Petr laid the backs of his fingers on Lenka's face, running them gently down her cheekbone. "No, you will be by my side the day we announce our daughter's engagement. It is a day we have both sacrificed and worked for. We will stand together on that day."

Her lips tugged upward as a tear made a trail down her face.

Petr wiped it away and pressed a kiss to the place it had been.

"The end is in sight," he said, his face breaking in a smile.

Pavel watched Karin. She was not eating much of her lunch. Caught in conversation with Zdenek and Luc, she gave him little consideration. How to direct her focus back to her meal?

He nudged her.

Her green eyes were on his. It almost caused him to forget his reason for summoning her attention.

"Do you have no appetite, my lady?"

Karin leaned back and moved the food around on her plate. "I am simply distracted...listening to Zdenek recount his first hunting trip." Then her eyes were on him again. "Have you heard this story?"

The corners of Pavel's mouth turned upward. "Many times." It was a rather diverting story.

"And why praytell are you so interested in my eating habits?" A brow arched as she leaned toward him.

"Perhaps it is that your disposition in the afternoon upon a missed lunch affects me." He forced his features into a serious expression and leaned nearer.

Karin's cheeks colored, and she leaned away, glancing around the table. Did she fear someone might notice their closeness? Shouldn't he concern himself thusly?

Pavel's gaze cut left and right, confirming what he already knew —everyone was too involved in their own conversations to notice.

There was movement in the doorway to the far side of the great hall. Pavel watched as a man, by all appearances a courier, entered with a folded paper. The young man made his way straight for the head table.

The Viscount barely acknowledged the man. He reached out and took the missive. Though the Viscount afforded the young man little more than a glance, the courier bowed and slipped into the back-drop, having been dismissed.

Ripping at the seal on the paper, the Viscount set eyes on the words within. After what could have only been a few lines read, he rose, his chair legs scraping the floor.

A hush fell over the room.

"The news has just arrived," the Viscount announced, "The the deed has been done. We are rid of the menace."

Pavel reached under the table and grabbed Karin's hand. Could he keep her calm?

Her gaze flitted about the faces of those around her, but there was no recognition in her eyes. Only confusion on her features. Did she not understand the Viscount's words?

A breakout of murmurs surrounded them, but Karin's response was Pavel's only concern.

"What does he mean? What menace?" Karin said. Her voice was louder than Pavel would have liked.

Pavel leaned toward her. Their faces so close. But he cared not for how it may appear. Only that he be as discrete as necessary. Would she? "He speaks of Jan Hus." His voice broke.

The man he had known and respected was gone. Just like that. A man who had been his professor at one time, someone whose ideals Pavel believed in and followed...and now his voice had been silenced.

"The trials to decide whether or not to execute him on charges of heresy..." Pavel quieted. Could he speak the words? "They made their choice." He wanted to retreat within himself, but he couldn't. Karin needed him right now. And he had to keep her calm. Reaching out with his other hand, he pulled both of hers between his. Could he draw her attention?

Her gaze upon him, green eyes flashed with new understanding. The color drained from her face and her mouth fell open. One of her hands slipped free and flew to her lips.

Karin's eyes slid closed and moisture appeared at the corners of her lids.

"Look at me!" Pavel commanded under his breath.

Her eyes opened, glassy and sad. And her breaths came rapidly. Would she become light-headed? Still, she obeyed him, keeping her gaze on him.

"You cannot let them see, Karin." His eyes searched hers. He worked to keep his voice as gentle as a caress. "Do you understand? This is not the time."

She nodded, swallowing against a tightness in her throat. He saw the struggle to do so. The tears that threatened dried, but her breathing was still sporadic.

Pavel held her gaze, taking deep breaths in and out, silently inviting her to breathe with him. After several rounds of soothing inhales and exhales, her shoulders fell.

He sent up a prayer of gratitude. Then he scanned those sitting around the table. Everyone was caught in their conversations—in celebration or inquiry. No one seemed to notice Karin or her distress. For that, he was thankful.

This was only the beginning. The followers of Jan Hus would not sit by. What would this mean for him and Karin?

Stepan could not stifle his smile. Who wouldn't with such a turn of luck? Jan Hus had been executed. Perhaps he would be able to return to the University...if his father allowed. There would be no more of Hus's inane teachings and and end to the controversy on campus surrounding his ideals.

The students and professors as a whole had become enamored with Hus. It made Stepan's stomach turn. Few retained their senses throughout the sensationalism which swept the campus. For certain his friends had kept their heads straight. At least in his father's house, if they found a Hussite, they could deal with them as the traitors they were.

A letter had arrived an hour earlier from Professor Evzen, but Stepan knew what it would contain—details of Hus's last days and the execution. It was not for lack of wanting to read these delicious details that Stepan carried the letter rather than reading it immediately; rather it was because there would be a better time and place. He would need to bide his time with Karin in the house.

Her reaction to the treatment of the Hussite servant girl gave him pause. She was a sensitive soul and needed to be shielded from the harsh realities of the world.

His father could have been exhibited more tact the day before when announcing the demise of Jan Hus. Karin had been at the far end of the table, but Stepan noted her reaction. She was quite beside herself at the reality of executing criminals. Pavel had helped ease her, and for that Stepan was grateful. Still, he was determined to protect Karin's eyes and ears from such harsh things.

As Stepan neared his room, he passed Pavel in the hall.

"I have been looking for you. Are we on for an afternoon ride?" There was a spark in Pavel's eyes.

Stepan nodded. "After I have a chance to read my missive from Professor Evzen."

"More reports?" Pavel's brows furrowed.

Stepan nodded. "I suspect some details about the execution."

"Ah," Pavel said. Something in his features changed, but it was difficult for Stepan to discern his thoughts.

"Would you care to—?" Stepan started.

"No, I...um...I wanted to take a short ride before," he said. Why was Pavel having such difficulty finding his words?

What was happening to Pavel these last few days? He had been distant. And disappeared without notice.

"As you wish." Stepan quirked a brow at him. "But this is the best news to come our way, my friend. You will see."

Pavel nodded, looking off down the hall.

Why was Pavel's gaze so forlorn? Did he think of Karin's upset over the news of the execution? Of course he would be.

"Are you concerned after the Lady Karin?" Stepan softened his voice. "No lady should have to deal with such concerns. I wish my father had been more thoughtful of her presence."

"Indeed," Pavel's gaze met Stepan's once more, his words were slow, measured.

"It is a shame she saw that treacherous servant thrown out. I truly regret the entire incident. Karin is so innocent. For her to be exposed to such dreadful occurrences...I must better shield her."

Pavel nodded, the movement rather slight. "I do fear that Karin, as so many women of the nobility, will be forced to suffer seeing and hearing the things we must deal with. Is there any way to protect them?" Why was his voice so timid?

"Our women of stature do a fine job providing a sense of refinement and culture, but I fear they don't realize the true teeth the world carries." Stepan clapped Pavel on the shoulder. "It is up to us, the next generation of nobility, to elevate the fairer sex above these ghastly things. You and I can make that happen. Come, I think I shall join you for that ride. It is a fair day to chase the wind."

Stepan stuffed his letter into his pocket. There would be other times to read it. Perhaps that evening, he could devour it by candle in his chambers. Pavel was right. It was an excellent afternoon for riding.

Two days later, a letter arrived for Karin. As she slid the folds of the paper open, she saw the penmanship—her father's. She excused herself from her conversation with Radek and Luc and took the letter to her bedchambers. Once she was settled in a chair, she reopened the letter and concentrated on its contents.

After the opening pleasantries and well wishes as to her continuing improved health, the letter spoke of her father's imminent return to the chateau with good news. She could scarcely believe it!

Was her time of confinement coming to an end? Was that the good news? Was this due to the execution of Jan Hus and the civil unrest following in the wake? Was Father concerned for her safety? Did he think it best she remain under his watchful eye? Or did he think her less of a threat without someone to follow? Nothing was certain, as there was so little information given in the letter.

But what of Pavel? Would the end of her time here be the end of their relationship? No, he said he wanted to marry her. So her father's arrival would mean Pavel would ask for her hand! The thought caused a swell of warmth to fill her. Wasn't this the very thing her parents wanted? A marriage to a nobleman of good breeding and standing...something that would be advantageous for them. What reason could they have to refuse such an offer?

Her parents did not need to know he was a Hussite. No, that was something they could discover once she and Pavel were wed. Just thinking of the possibility of their joining made her heart leap. How would she contain this joy? This thrill at the thought of becoming Pavel's wife? Would it always be like this? The excitement, the acute awareness of her heart's beating, and of the beauty around her? Just a few more days, and they would not have to hide.

Karin's intended purpose was not for the Viscount, the watcher sighed. But anger still burned deep within. She could not live. The watcher despised the young woman. Had she not become more insufferable? More unbearable with each passing day? Karin would not become connected to any member of this family, least of all become the future mistress of the house of Dvorak. It would not stand, would not be tolerated.

If only the same young man the watcher tried to protect was not busy thwarting such well-laid plans, the deed would have be done. But this young man could not be faulted. He did not know how devious Karin was. How could he? For he only saw what she wanted him to. She had entrapped him in her web. Shrewd. The watcher could see it all, even if he could not, and it would not be allowed to continue.

Karin would be dealt with.

Karin pulled her cloak tighter around herself as a breeze brought with it a chill. How long should she wait for her beloved? But she knew, she would wait all night for even the hope he would appear. Seated on a bench in the garden, far from prying eyes, among the beautiful blossoms she had enjoyed on numerous occasions, she waited.

The stars enraptured her, pulling her gaze heavenward toward the many twinkling lights above. Pavel and Karin had never attempted such before—sneaking out to meet in the late evening. But Father would be here the following day and, with him, the promise of many more things to come.

Karin needed to see Pavel, to speak with him. Alone. So, at the evening meal, she had slipped a note into his hand when she was certain no one watched. In the note, she asked him to meet her here after nightfall.

Hands fell over hers, crossed and on her upper arms. They rubbed her arms, generating warmth there and also in her core.

Turning, she confirmed with her eyes what she knew in her heart —it was Pavel.

"It is rather cool this night." He sat next to her, losing contact with her arm. She missed his touch at once.

"But it is beautiful." She raised a hand toward the stars. Her gaze followed. "So clear. It is almost as if you could reach out and pluck them from the sky."

Pavel made a sweeping gesture as if to gather many stars at once. "For you, my lady."

Smiling, she could not help but shiver as another chilled breeze whipped by.

Pavel wrapped an arm around her. "You are cold, my lady." His words were soft and warm near her ear.

"Not anymore." She gazed into the azure pools of his eyes. Just beyond him, she caught sight of a star streaking across the sky. "Look!"

Pavel turned, following the direction of her hand. But it was too late for him to catch a glimpse.

"A shooting star," she explained when his eyes met hers again.

"Then you must close your eyes and make a wish." Pavel whispered.

She let her eyelids fall. Her heartbeat thundered in her ears. The heat coming from his body soaked into her. He was so close.

What should she wish for? She couldn't seem to put a thought together. All that existed was Pavel and this moment.

Soft lips pressed against hers.

She let out a sound and tilted her head to deepen the kiss. This, this is what she wanted.

After a few moments of bliss, he pulled back.

Without opening her eyes, she said, "It came true."

His mouth met hers again for another, lighter kiss. Then he pulled her into a warm embrace.

"Pavel?" she said against his shoulder, now opening her eyes and gazing across the gardens again.

"Yes?" he whispered into her hair.

"My father is coming tomorrow."

"Oh?" He stroked the hair falling down her back.

"I too am weary of hiding. Will you speak with him soon?"

He buried his lips in her hair. "Yes. I will arrange to speak with him as soon as he will receive me."

She moved ever closer to Pavel, rubbing her cheek against his chest. "How will I endure the wait?"

Pavel clasped her tighter and then loosened his hold, keeping her in the cocoon of his gentle embrace.

Was he, too, eager for an end to these secrets? Was he anxious for the talk with Father? How could she reassure him? Could she?

Moving her face against his shoulder, she relished in this moment. And prayed it would be the first of a lifetime.

One thing was certain—after tomorrow, there would be no more hiding.

CHAPTER 9
HOPEFUL

P etr prayed for his journey to be over long before he spotted the familiar shape of the chateau and the burgundy and yellow of the structure. It had rained much of the trip, and it seemed impossible to remain dry with the direction of the rain. The portico was a welcome sight.

Once in visual range, only a matter of moments separated him from the drier interior. His coach pulled under the overhang and the door of his carriage was opened. He stepped down and found his daughter prepared to greet him. Had she been watching for him? She stepped forward and embraced him. Was she not bothered that he was drenched?

"Father, I am glad you have returned."

"Thank you." He stepped back, displeased to note that her dress was now damp. "I am pleased for your continued recovery."

She nodded, moving toward the entrance to the chateau. It was likely she was more aware of the chill in the air now, having soiled her dress from their embrace.

Moving into the chateau, he was grateful to get out of the cold, rainy weather. He wanted to be shown to his room forthwith for dry clothes, but Vlastik would want to receive him. So they moved toward the same receiving room they had waited in weeks ago. Thankfully, the Viscount did not keep him waiting long.

"My dear friend, you will catch your death of cold in those wet clothes!" Vlastik admonished Petr as he laid eyes on him.

"I assure you I am quite all right." Petr resisted the urge to wipe at his nose.

"Nonsense!" Vlastik continued, his brows furrowed as he led Petr father into the chateau. "I insist a hot bath be prepared at once and dry clothes be put out." the Viscount all but shouted to a nearby manservant. "And show the earl to a fireplace for heaven's sake."

The young manservant seemed at a loss. Perhaps he did not know whether to wait for the hot bath before preparing the dry clothes or put the earl in dry clothes forthwith while the bathwater was heated. It wasn't long before he moved toward Petr. Had he made a decision?

"Follow me, my lord." The man led Petr up the stairs, away from Vlastik and Karin.

The manservant took Petr to his previously inhabited bedchambers. A fire was stoked with all due haste. Two servants together stripped him of his wet clothes as another young manservant prepared a hot bath. It wasn't long before all was ready.

Sinking into the tub, Petr welcomed the heat of the water to warm his chilled body. As he returned to normal temperatures, he could relax. It was short-lived, however, as his thoughts soon shifted to Karin.

What had her time here been like as he was away? From all of Mary's letters and reports, she had kept herself free of any objectionable materials.

And why had Vlastik summoned him if not in hopes of making official some plan to wed their children? Perhaps he could gain an audience with his friend that evening lest his curiosity keep him from the sleep he so needed.

Would everything finally fall into place?

Karin had not been able to sleep. She was too eager for what her father would say to Pavel. Surely he could not refuse her this happiness. Why would he? Pavel was a good man from a noble family, a fine match for her. A baron's son. How could her father refuse his daughter to make such a connection?

Still, something in her feared the worst. Such nonsense. There was nothing to indicate that her father would deny her, but her worries kept her from peaceful rest. As sleep continued to elude her, she gave up any hope it would come and rose just before dawn.

Dressing for the day in silence, she longed for the solitude of a walk by the stream. Pavel had arranged to meet with Father before the hunting activities. Would their meeting happen within the hour? Regardless, Karin's secret place beckoned her. So, she made her way to the stream. Still, it was just as difficult to quiet her thoughts. At last, leaning her head back, she closed her eyes and prayed.

Father, help me place all in Your capable hands. You know my heart's desire, and You know I only want to serve You with my life. I ask that You, in Your gracious loving kindness, grant Pavel and I this happiness of serving You together.

Karin prayed the words over and over, beseeching God in the silence, as in her torrent of emotion she knew not what else to pray. How long she lingered or how many times she uttered those few lines of prayer, she did not know.

Her face warmed. Could it be? She opened her eyes. Yes, the sun had crept over the treetops. The hour for the men to rise for breakfast and prepare themselves for the hunt had come. Pavel and Father would be deep in conversation. Shouldn't she return?

Standing, she whispered the words of her simple prayer once more, pouring her whole heart into her supplication. Then she shook her skirts clean of any clinging grass and made her way toward the looming walls of the chateau. She tarried only to gather some of the beautiful wildflowers growing along the way.

Climbing the hill, she spotted a figure moving from the massive structure to the stables. Who would be out so early? A servant? No, the figure was finely dressed. She narrowed her eyes to hone her vision. Could it be...Pavel? Fair hair, tall, somewhat muscular physique...the figure certainly looked like him.

Karin quickened her step and changed direction toward the stables. Several minutes later, she closed the distance, still she was practically jogging by the time she reached the entry to the smaller structure.

Once inside, it took only a matter of seconds to find the man readying a horse.

It *was* Pavel.

Dropping her basket, she rushed to him.

"Pavel? What is it?" Her words were breathless. She gasped from the exertion of her hurried walk.

Without turning, he continued to prepare his horse. Why would he not look at her? And she knew. Something terrible had happened. They were not to be married.

If it were not so, he would have taken her in his arms right then. They would be the happiest people in the world, speaking words of love to each other.

How? Why? A new kind of heat filled her. It burned between her shoulder blades. How could he? How dare her father deny her this! "What, Pavel? What did he say to you?"

Still no answer. But he paused.

Karin grabbed his arm. He would have to push her out of the way or stop and answer her.

"It is not to be." Though he did not continue to work the straps of the saddle, he still wouldn't look at her.

"*Why*? Why would he refuse us?" Her voice broke. There were tears in her eyes, hot, angry tears, and she gripped his arm. Why wouldn't he face her? Though she pulled at him, he wouldn't budge.

"Karin, you are promised to another!" His voice was firm. And he turned, his eyes on her at last.

Then she saw why he had avoided her gaze. There was sadness in his eyes. Was it as painful for him as it was for her? She allowed her mind to absorb his words. Would she be married to someone else? Have children with another? Belong to someone else? Not to Pavel?

"No..." She shook her head, looking at the ground. It couldn't be. Turning her face to look at him once more, she continued, "I have never heard any of this. Why would my father not tell me? It cannot be true!"

"But it is, Karin," came his simple reply, his face downcast.

"No!" The anger welling in her found it's way out. Her words gained strength. "How can he care so little for my happiness?"

Pavel faced the horse, his body still turned in that direction. Yet he made no further move to ready the saddle. "This marriage has been set and cannot be undone."

Karin drew in a ragged breath. "Who..." She could barely speak the words. "Who am I to marry?"

He closed his eyes against the truth. "Stepan."

"Stepan?" She widened her eyes.

"It is a match made from your birth. The Viscount will not disregard their agreement because we are in love."

For the first time, Karin imagined a future without Pavel. It was almost too much to bear. Had it only been a few days ago she had been able to picture her future at all? Yes, the day he asked her to marry him. The future had seemed so bright then, filled with images of Pavel and the happiness they would have in a life together. Now those images were shattered, and there was nothing but darkness before her.

Pavel brushed past her, bringing her back to the present. He continued to ready his horse. Was he leaving then?

"Pavel, where are you going?" She reached for his arm.

He halted. "I cannot stay." Meeting her gaze once more, she saw that his eyes were glazed with unshed tears.

Could it be? She would not say goodnight to him this night or any other? Or see him the next day? It was too much.

Tears ran down her face.

"I cannot stay here. See you each day, be near you, all the while knowing I can never have you. I fear my heart would be beyond repair."

"No," She shook her head, barely able to see him through her tears. With grasping fingers, she reached for him, clinging to his shirt, his chest, as if he were a lifeline.

A crazy plan struck her. "I will come with you!"

Wiping at her eyes, Karin moved to grab another saddle. "We will run away together."

Pavel strode toward Karin, coming up from behind and wrapping his arms around her, stilling her movements. "We cannot do that. Where would we go? Where would we belong?"

"Who cares? As long as we are together." She shifted in his arms. Was she so determined to saddle a horse? Could he stop her? His hold on her was not tight, but she did not break free. Did she not truly want to?

"It would not be right." He turned her to face him. "I will not shame you and your family. It is not God's plan, Karin." Gazing into her green eyes, he risked the loss of his heart forever.

"How can it be His plan for us to not be together?" There was weakness in her voice. And sorrow in her eyes. It nearly broke him.

"I don't know, but it is." He pulled her closer for perhaps the last time, allowing himself to linger in that embrace for longer than he should have. It tempted him to stay, to fight for her, to take her up on her offer of elopement—anything that would give them the happy ending they longed for. But it would be an illusion.

Still, he could not help but catch her lips for one last kiss, and he tried to convey all of his affection and love for her in that last contact so she would never forget that there was someone who had cared for her to such depths.

Karin's hands clung to his shirt as if to never let go.

He moved his hands over hers, intertwining their fingers before maneuvering her hands so he could press a final kiss to each one as he released her lips with a pang of regret. If only he could disguise the moisture in his own eyes as he pulled away.

"I must go."

Karin's shoulders shook with sobs that threatened to break free. "Please," was all she could manage.

Mounting with one swift move, he focused on directing the horse. If he peered into her face one more time, would his resolve melt into concession?

"Pavel!" she pled as he shifted his horse.

But he couldn't look back. He would never leave if he did.

He urged the animal into a trot, then a cantor. And mere moments later, all sense of the stables and the chateau was far from his awareness. But he could not pull it...pull her...from his heart.

Petr watched much of the exchange between Pavel and Karin from the window of the study where he and Pavel had met several minutes before. Regret poured through him. He did not relish the pain his daughter must feel, but what he did was best for her and for their family. And that is what fathers do.

It was obvious that she cared deeply for this young man, and it pained him to see her as she crumpled to the ground upon his departure.

But young love was fleeting. Perhaps she could find a lasting love with Stepan. What Petr may or may not know about Pavel's standing or family was irrelevant. A binding agreement had already been made with Vlastik, an agreement which had not been entered into lightly, an agreement which the previous night he expressed his intention to fulfill. Petr's hands were tied, regardless of Karin's feelings.

She would come through this infatuation in time. He was sure of it. All the same, his heart ached for his daughter as she fell to the ground, body wracked with sobs as Pavel rode away. And, as much as he wanted to give her this private moment, the members of the house would be moving about any moment.

Karin must be retrieved lest the whole house be made aware of the situation. His decision to go after his daughter at once was also hastened as it started to rain. She, however, did not stir. Instead she remained, lost in her own world, ignorant even of the rain coming down upon her.

In Petr's desperation, it seemed to take forever to make his way through the halls of the chateau and out of the stables. As he knelt by Karin's side, lifting her face to his, he became aware of the extent of Karin's pain. Her eyes reflected a hollowness.

"Karin, come inside," he spoke in a volume to be heard above the wind and rain, but hoped it was gentle enough to coax his daughter.

She looked through him, unresponsive to his request other than to move her chin from his grasp and drop her head into her hands.

Petr leaned over her, moving close to her ear. "Karin, I know you are upset. You will come to understand in time. But there is no reason sitting out here in the rain. You are making a spectacle of yourself!"

No movement. No sign of life except the heaving of her sobs.

Petr cursed this stubborn streak. Gathering her in his arms, he prepared to carry Karin into the house. He was surprised that he did not met with resistance. She was limp.

Moving toward the house, rainwater dripping from Karin's dress, Petr did not stop until he arrived at her bedchambers.

Mary was waiting, straightening the room. Upon spotting her master carrying Karin, she halted.

Petr, however, did not pause. He launched into a series of instructions with a tone that communicated the need for immediacy. "The Lady Karin needs a warm bath and fresh clothes. She is unwell."

"Shall I send for the doctor?" Mary stepped into motion behind Petr.

"That will not be necessary. She has a bit of a chill from being out in the rain."

Petr sat Karin on a chair while Mary rang for assistance.

Mary then moved toward Karin and began to unlace her dress.

Karin remained still, motionless, as if in a trance. It could have been happening to someone else, for all the reaction she gave. She did not so much as flinch as Mary pulled at her wet clothing, exposing wet skin to the cool room.

That was the last thing Petr noticed as he left Karin to her privacy.

The Lady Karin kept to her room in the days that followed. There was much talk among the inhabitants of the chateau of a relapse. Only Mary and Petr were permitted to enter her chambers. So it was just that—talk, speculation. Not only was Karin keeping to her room, but she remained bedridden in those days as well. This was not known either.

Her caregivers could not make sense of it. She had not a fever nor sign of ailment. Yet she remained unyielding to any and all attempts to coax her out of her room. For the most part, she remained wholly unresponsive.

Karin woke each day with no desire to get out of bed. Not even the dawn streaming through the window could brighten her mood. Her heart ached, yes, but it was more. The world no longer held promise; it was a dark place. Everything was so bleak, as if the darkness were something physical that could smother her. Many days she wished it would so she would not have to feel the way she did.

She could not find the motivation or the strength to pray. This may have been the worst of it—to have no one to turn to. In the weeks prior, when she had been in such a hopeless situation, she always had prayer. When all else had seemed grim, she found solace in prayer. But there was no light to be found there—nothing, it seemed, could penetrate this dreariness. And so it continued to envelop her, day after day.

At long last, Father summoned a physician. But nothing was determined to be amiss physically. Though upon closer examination, the doctor did have an answer.

"Your daughter is suffering from what is called 'melancholia'. It is caused by an imbalance in the body. She must get plenty of sunshine each day. Many cases of melancholia respond well to music and dancing. And you must make sure to keep her out, among people. Helping her find things which she enjoys will be the only way to help her restore balance."

Karin heard all of this, but these things did not interest her. She looked to her father.

He shook his head. Did he, too, think the task insurmountable? What would he do? Would he attempt to follow the prescribed plan?

The doctor reached into his bag, rummaging for a few seconds before he pulled out a package of herbs and handed them to Mary. "Brew these into a tea twice a day and have her drink it slowly."

Mary nodded.

"Should I send for the girl's mother?" Father asked.

Would that make things better? If Mother was here? Or would Mother's concern make this worse?

"I would recommend not. She needs companionship, yes, but I think she may need more of a firm hand."

"Of course, doctor."

The doctor laid a firm hand on Father's shoulder then moved toward the door.

"Thank you again, doctor," Father interjected. And the two stepped through the door and beyond the reach of Karin's hearing.

Karin had worn out her ability to follow their conversation either way. She had not a care for whatever would happen. Turning her head away, she longed for sleep to overcome her.

Zdenek, Luc, Radek, and Stepan had lost all sign of the animal they were tracking. Stepan glanced at his friends. They, too, appeared none the worse for it. No one seemed interested in picking up another trail. Should they return to the chateau? Continue to ride through the woods in silence? Neither seemed likely to quell the swell of anger within him.

"Have you received word from Pavel?" Luc spoke into the thick silence. No one had dared speak of Pavel since his sudden, unannounced disappearance.

"No," Stepan said, keeping his focus on something in the distance. What was in Pavel's thoughts? Why had he not spoken to Stepan? Did their friendship mean so little?

Turning toward Luc, he found three sets of eyes on him. "I had expected some manner of explanation..." Stepan paused. He wanted to offer some words on Pavel's behalf, but he had none. Pavel had neither informed him nor discussed whatever matter had arisen to cause him to quit the chateau in the manner in which he did. And to not have sent word added insult to injury.

"Something of great importance must have pulled him away." Radek's features were set, solemn. Must he always seek out the best in everyone?

"And what of this strange illness which has gripped Lady Karin?" Zdenek voice was low, laced with concern.

"I, too, am distressed by it," Stepan replied, frowning.

"Is it not a relapse of her earlier illness?" Luc quirked a brow. He always kept one ear tuned in to the household servants' gossip.

The others fell silent. Were they each as Stepan—caught between their thoughts and emotions? Worried about both Pavel and Karin?

Luc's gaze flickered to Zdenek and his mouth rose on one side, a rather crooked, mischievous smile. "What of the girl from the ball? Eva, I think, her name was."

As much as his heart weighed, Stepan's eyes cut toward Zdenek. Would his face color?

"Zdenek?" Luc continued, "Have you had opportunity to call on her?" Though he spoke to Zdenek, Luc's gaze flew between Radek and Stepan.

And then it happened. Zdenek's face became bright red. What would he say?

Zdenek hesitated. "I..." He licked his lips as his words trailed.

"It does seem no one could place you afternoon before last," Radek said, looking at Stepan and raising his brows.

"Oh?" Luc's voice rose, glancing at Zdenek.

His face deepened to another shade of red.

Radek's shoulders shook as laughter seized him. Then he cleared his throat. "What Zdenek does with his time is his own."

"Thank you," Zdenek said. His eyes were on Radek, his mouth upturning slightly. Could it be gratitude for at least one understanding friend?

"Especially if he wants to call on pretty young ladies," Radek said, before a fit of laughter escaped him.

Zdenek frowned at his friend.

Stepan joined his friends in their merriment at Zdenek's expense. It was hopeless.

The following morning, Mary threw open the curtain upon entering Karin's bedchambers.

Karin recoiled from the harsh light. She groaned and drew her covers closer to her face, shielding her eyes from the intrusion on her senses. But it was all for naught—Mary removed the duvet. A struggle over the covering ensued, but Karin's weakened arms were no match for Mary's strength.

When Karin met Mary's eyes after the battle, she expected to find triumph or pity, or even perhaps a smug look. But the eyes which met hers were sad, sympathetic, and even regretful. It softened Karin's resolve and gave her the courage to sit up.

What had the doctor said the previous day? Her memory of his visit seemed rather blurry. Still, Mary went about readying her. For what? Would she be forced from the room? Where would she go?

Sunlight. The physician had spoken of sunlight. Would Mary take her to the balcony? How that would have excited Karin before. How hard had she fought for her trips to the balcony during her previous recovery? But now, it frightened her. The bed was a safe place, and getting out of it would be stepping forth into her life, a life she did not want to face. Couldn't she just huddle into the warmth and safety of the bed? Refuse, once again, to face her life? Or would Mary, and even Father, fight her reluctance?

Just one step at a time. Now that she sat in the bed, she needed to make it to the chair nearby. This chair was the same in which she would sit while Mary prepared her garments each day. It was safe, wasn't it?

Karin stole a glance in Mary's direction. She busied herself selecting the things she would dress Karin in.

Her gaze moved over toward Karin. Was she making sure Karin didn't fall back into the bed? Or perhaps because Mary wished she could find the words to encourage Karin?

Mary pulled out one of Karin's favorite dresses—a comfortable burgundy dress made up of simple lines from a rich fabric. Next, Mary pulled a light kirtle from her trunk and began preparing them both.

Watching Mary go about her business, Karin allowed herself to become lost in the monotony of her movements, to be distracted from the overwhelming task of getting out of the bed. While forcing her mind to stay latched onto the ministrations of Mary's hands, Karin set first one foot, then the other, on the floor.

It felt rather strange to stand after so many days of being in bed. There she stood, supporting her own weight. And nothing terrible had happened. She did it!

Karin's next goal was the chair and, labored step by labored step, she moved ever closer. It was no easy task to reach it, but this, too, she accomplished.

At last, she released her weight into its capable structure. The chair almost toppled as she dropped into it.

Mary spun. Had the clattering noise been so loud? Seeing Karin in her dressing chair, Mary offered a small smile before turning back to her work.

This was perhaps the first fully pleasant exchange between them, and it was the first stirring of hope within Karin in several days.

Deputies Frantisek and Jakub had spent the better part of their week inquiring around the village. Had anyone seen any strange goings-on around the grand carriage, which had been in the village the week prior? It was all for naught. No one could give Frantisek any information—at least, no useful information.

A laundry woman said she may have seen someone near the carriage, but she did not know what the person was doing. The description of said person was average height, average weight, and brownish-blonde hair—perhaps.

"It was dark," she explained to Frantisek.

How was he to follow up on that? Better yet, how was he to take this information back to the Constable? Frantisek wanted to have *something* to take back to Borivoj, but it seemed as if he would return to the prison with nothing again—nothing but this witness statement that was less helpful.

Borivoj would want Frantisek to follow up on it the next day, and he would have to figure out how to do so.

Jakub was all eagerness at the start—a *real* police investigation. By now, even he was wearying on their questioning of each villager to return with no real information. So much for training him in investigations.

Turning at the baker's shop, they made their way back to the prison. Upon entering, the sound of boots clomping on the floor echoed. Was the Constable pacing? Borivoj had assigned them to this task, so he'd had to cover all other calls.

Frantisek and Jakub walked to the Constable's office door.

Jakub peered at Frantisek. His eyes were wide. Was he nervous about their report?

Frantisek knocked.

"Come in," the booming voice called.

They entered the smaller room as Borivoj sat behind his desk.

"Anything today?" Borivoj pulled his ledger book toward himself.

"Not much," Frantisek said. "There was one woman who said she remembered the carriage and may have seen someone around it at some point."

"That is something," Borivoj said, making a note. "Did she describe this person?"

"Man. Average height, average weight, brownish-blonde hair."

Borivoj wrote it down and then glanced up. "That could be anyone. It could be you."

Frantisek nodded.

Borivoj let out a long sigh. "I suppose it is someplace to start."

"You cannot be serious!" Frantisek's voice rose. He calmed himself, lowering his tone. "She could have seen someone looking to steal something. Or someone passing by. Or just one of the servants in the party."

"It is still worth looking into," Borivoj said. "Besides, it is all we have."

Frantisek nodded. He had known he would be following up on this vague description anyway, so he would do well just to accept it.

Petr heard movement on the balcony below. He watched as Mary escorted Karin to a seat in the sun. Mary tucked a blanket around Karin. Was she so concerned as to her mistress's comfort?

"Thank you, Mary," Karin's voice was small.

It was difficult to make out her words from the floor above. Was a new understanding developing between Karin and Mary?

Petr was pleased. He had found this corner balcony—a place where Karin could get sunshine in peace and quiet. There was no reason for her to spend time among the others in the chateau. Not yet.

It had been difficult, but Petr kept the concerned noblemen at bay with simple reports of her progress. Perhaps it was overprotectiveness, but Petr was not willing to risk what Vlastik or Stepan would think if they were to see her in this state. Or worse, what if they were to find out about her brief attachment to Pavel? This was best.

Now that they started her treatment, sunlight and a more stringent routine, she was already much improved. Each day, Petr and Mary would bring Karin to this forgotten balcony and leave her with her thoughts. Little did Karin know, her father watched over her from a window one floor above.

The door to the balcony opened. Did Mary forget something? Had she come to check on Karin's progress with the tea?

As the figure stepped through the doorway, its broad shoulders and solid form belied that it was not Mary.

One of the noblemen? Had someone discovered Karin's secluded spot and trespassed upon her quiet?

The straight brown hair shifted as the man moved a step toward Karin. Stepan. It had to be.

Petr spun. He must make haste and insist on Karin's privacy.

As he turned, he came face to face with Vlastik.

"My friend," Vlastik said in a calm voice, holding up a hand.

Were Petr's features so telling of his ire? He pulled in a ragged breath.

"Do not keep my son from your daughter."

"Karin is not well..." Petr clamored for words as he moved to step around Vlastik. How was he to explain the situation? What would convince Vlastik to let him pass?

Vlastik moved to block him again. "I understand. And I hope you know we are all concerned for her, no one more so than Stepan. Do not let pride guide your decision here, friend. I do not think my son is discouraged by your daughter's illness, quite the opposite. So do let him speak with her, if only for a short time. We can keep watch from here."

Petr's breathing was as rapid as his pulse. But he dare not refuse his host such a request. In that moment, his options were closed off. He must hope Karin had enough sense not to speak of her relationship with Pavel.

CHAPTER 10
A NEW HOPE

Gazing across the side meadow, Karin closed her eyes and let the wind whip strands of hair across her face. Trying to envision a future seemed a futile venture, but still she looked to the days ahead. Would she ever remain in this dark place? Or would the sunlight eventually penetrate it?

The door creaked open behind her. Was Mary come to collect her already? Or was Mary out to check on her?

She glanced at her cup. Karin had not been faithful at drinking it. The herbs were rather bitter, and it was even more unpleasant once the warmth had gone. Lost in her thoughts, it was easy to let her tea get cold.

Lifting the cup to her lips, she drew in a couple of long sips. There now, some progress. Perhaps Mary would not be so perturbed.

But the footsteps drawing near were heavier than Mary's and the breathing was deeper than Father's. Had someone else come? Who?

Her chair angled away from the door, she could not see who approached. Should she be concerned? No fear rose within. Because she had no need? Or because she cared not for her own safety?

At length, she turned, more from curiosity.

"Stepan." Karin met his gaze. How long had it been since she had laid eyes on him? On any of the others?

He stepped closer so she did not have to turn quite so much.

"Karin." His features were drawn. Was he concerned for her? "How are you?"

His worry was endearing. Did it stir something in her? Yes, there was a gentle, subtle warmth in her chest.

"I have difficult days and days that are not so...trying."

His eyes seemed to be the source of the warmth.

He nodded. "And today?"

How was she to answer? Each day seemed so much the same as the last. One melting into the other. That would not serve him.

She waved a hand toward the only other seat. "Please, sit."

Stepan obeyed.

The corners of her mouth tugged, but she could not make them move upward. "Today has begun to brighten."

Stepan's lips broadened and a slight blush touched his cheeks.

Was there, deep down, a hint of the old Karin in that moment? She so enjoyed the company of these young men and how their attention and consideration had made her days of isolation easier.

"We have all been so anxious," he said. Then he hesitated before confessing, "*I* have been anxious after your well-being."

His words caused a chill to shoot through her. The sting of heart-break was too fresh for her to entertain another's interest.

It would make her father happy, she thought darkly. Was she overreacting? Perhaps Stepan was reaching out as a friend. And she needed friends.

"Thank you." Karin looked toward the chateau grounds.

Silence fell between them.

What should she say? What did she have to give?

"I appreciate you coming to—" Karin started while Stepan said, "I do not know if your father told you—"

A smile touched her features at their awkward timing. It was a genuine smile. The first in so many days.

"Please, you," Karin said with a brief nod.

"I did not know if your father told you about Pavel. The timing of your... " Was he struggling to choose the right word? "Illness...perhaps prevented you from knowing that he has quit the chateau."

Karin's gaze shifted away from Stepan once more at the mention of Pavel. Now she fixed her gaze back over the grounds. She did not hear all he said. It had not occurred to her how others would find Pavel's sudden flight. Closing her eyes, his face was before her. And her heart was sad. All semblance of warmth left her.

"No one had a chance for a proper farewell." Stepan's voice cut into her thoughts. "He left early in the morning. Perhaps there was some urgent business at his father's house. I cannot imagine he would leave in such a way under any other circumstances."

Karin closed her eyes and fought tears threatening to overcome her. Her pulse thundered in her ears so loud she could not hear Stepan.

His hand fell on her arm.

How much time passed in the silence?

"Karin, are you well?" His tone was gentle.

Turning to face him, she tried to push down her warring emotions. "I am just tired."

"Shall I call for your maidservant?" His voice was filled with concern.

She placed a hand on his. "No, thank you. She will be along soon. Please sit with me. Tell me of Zdenek, Radek, and Luc."

He seemed uncertain. Did he fear for her health? Did he think calling for Mary would help?

After some moments, his features relaxed. "I do have a story of Zdenek." His mouth quirked into one of his more devious smiles. "Do you remember the young lady from the ball? Eva? "

Karin nodded.

Stepan continued with a tale of Zdenek's overtures toward courtship. How strange that these noblemen viewed her as friend and yet still a lady worth pursuing. The relationships she had formed with these men were rather unique.

The door creaking drew both of their attention, cutting into Stepan's story.

Mary stepped out to the balcony and moved toward the pair.

Taking another long sip of her now cold tea, Karin swallowed and cringed. The cup was not drained, but it was close to it.

As she neared, Mary peered in the cup and frowned.

Karin shrugged. Why would she bother? Why would she care about Mary's thoughts?

But Mary's eyes softened. She gathered the cup and tray.

Karin swung her legs over the side of the lounge, and Mary collected the blanket from Karin's lap.

"I fear I must take my leave." Karin directed her gaze toward Stepan. " I have enjoyed our conversation."

Stepan rose and offered his arm to Karin.

She accepted it, offering him the same small smile she had come to manage.

Now on her feet, she paused to squeeze the arm that she held. Karin then released him and moved toward the door.

"Karin," Stepan called after her.

Turning, she sought his eyes. "Yes?"

"May I join you again tomorrow?"

The corners of her lips tugged, this time into a smile. "I would like that."

He bowed.

She tilted hers and, with Mary in tow, moved into the chateau.

Petr peered at his friend, who had long since seated himself across the room.

"Yes?" Vlastik asked, eyes meeting Petr's.

"Karin is back in the chateau." Petr turned back toward the window. What words had been spoken between Karin and Stepan?

"What do you think?" Having given up his vigil by the window, Vlastik had no idea what had transpired below.

Petr's focus drifted downward to the balcony where Stepan still stood.

Stepan continued to gaze after her for a few moments. Then his head shifted so that he looked toward the grounds. Was he deep in thought? About what? Did he suspect anything?

Petr had seen glimpses of the old Karin in her exchange with Stepan. Should it encourage him? There was a moment when Karin had become distressed, but it had been fleeting. Stepan had recaptured her attention, and her smile. Something Petr had sorely been missing.

"I think it was best," Petr admitted.

Vlastik sighed. "I knew it would be."

Rising, Vlastik crossed the room, moving to stand next to his friend. "I think if you continue to let Stepan visit your daughter, then we will have *two* happy children when we announce that plans for their wedding are already in place."

Petr nodded. What had Pavel told Karin? Had he disclosed this? The betrothal that was in place? What exactly had Pavel and Karin said to one another?

Karin gazed over the countryside as she picked at the food on her plate. Having finished her meal, she was enjoying the banter between her father and the Viscount. She glanced in Stepan's direction. His smile betrayed his amusement.

Soft brown eyes met hers. And they shared a stifled laugh.

Their fathers were close friends, but their conversation could get quite colorful when one of them remembered something with the slightest difference. It was almost as if no one else was at the meal at this point, the Viscount and Petr were so engaged with each other.

"Excuse me, Father," Stepan interrupted their repartee. "I think after this wonderful meal, I need to walk a bit. If you will excuse me."

"Of course." The Viscount didn't seem too set on Stepan's request. He turned toward Petr, opening his mouth. Would these jabs never end?

"Karin, would you care for a walk?" He stood and offered her his hand.

She allowed a smile to grace her features as she reached for it. "I would."

The Viscount and Petr exchanged a look. Karin wanted to roll her eyes. At least they had halted their quarrel.

"Are you quite certain they are not in need of a chaperone?" the Viscountess spoke to her husband. "It is not proper for a young lady and young man to..."

The Viscount shushed her. "They will be all right. Stepan will not wander far. We will chaperone from here."

"Petr, you must speak some reason to my lord husband. After all, she is your daughter."

"As you see, my lady, there is no speaking reason to your husband. Certainly not from me."

"Now, listen, Petr, if you will but remember..." the Viscount started.

That was all Karin heard as she and Stepan moved farther away. She held a hand to her mouth to contain her laughter. Glancing at Stepan, she saw him doing the same.

They moved deeper into the forest. Karin would inquire about various plants she admired and Stepan would point out tracks of animals. Twice, they chanced upon a clear view of an animal in the distance.

He is a gifted hunter. It is lucky I will never be his prey.

Continuing their walk, Karin was thankful Stepan did not use his full stride. Rather he paced his step to hers. Their conversation was comfortable and easy. They had developed a solid friendship. Was this not the best basis for anything else?

With Pavel, everything happened so fast. And everything between them was so heated. With Stepan, she did not feel the same nervousness, or the same magnetism. Which was better? She did not feel for him the way she had for Pavel—she was not in love. But, perhaps what they had could develop into love.

Stepan's words grew louder as his hunting tale continued.

Karin's face warmed. She had lost track of what he had been saying.

"What? I'm sorry. I must have—" she started.

"Shhh!" Stepan's voice was harsh. He cocked his head to one side. It seemed rather odd.

A laugh bubbled in Karin at what a strange picture Stepan made.

He jumped toward her. "Get down!"

What? Was there danger?

He shoved her to the side and toward the ground, landing on top of her.

Karin let out a *hurumph* as everything in her lungs rushed out. Gasping for breath, she struggled for air. Could she not breathe? She clawed at her neck.

Stepan's weight lifted and shifted to the side.

Her hand grazed something. And pain slammed into her. There was heat, a stinging in her shoulder. Touching the source of the pain, she felt a gash in her upper arm. She pressed a hand over the wound and clenched her teeth against the pain. Her breaths rushed in and out, seething through her teeth.

What had injured her? Was there some sharp rock that could have caused it?

"Are you well enough to move?" Stepan's face was over hers. There was an urgency in his voice.

"I think so." Karin sat up. Did he not care about her wound?

He jumped to his feet and held out a hand to her.

She allowed him to lift her.

His eyes moved over her from top to bottom. "We need to clear the area before whoever that was takes another shot."

Did he still not see the blood coming from her arm? Still, Karin nodded, her world spinning. What was he talking about? Someone was shooting at them? She didn't have time to think before he tugged on her, pulling her behind him as he shuffled through the trees.

Stepan pushed her to continue as fast as she could. It was madness. But he was quick to assist her at every turn.

Karin focused on blocking out the pain. She followed him, wishing he would let her pause. Her breathing was uneven and burned.

But he did not. So, she kept her eyes to ground, mindful of anything that may trip her.

As they neared the spot they had departed from, he slowed his pace.

Thanks be to God! She glanced toward him. His face was quite pale. "Stepan, what's wrong?"

He shook his head. But his breathing was worse than hers! What good would he be to her a heap on the ground?

She opened her mouth to insist, but felt him slow even more.

"There is a stream nearby I know well."

Karin nodded. Perhaps she would tell him of her injury once they made it to the stream.

Moments later, she heard the sound of water rushing over stones. And soon after, they arrived.

"Please, drink. You need it." His voice was firm, but not as demanding as it had been. And she found no reason to argue.

Falling to her knees, she scooped water toward her mouth. "What happened? Why the rush? Did you not see that I have been wounded?"

He had not the space to answer before she spun on him.

Then the pieces came together. Stepan was twisted toward his left side, examining his own arm, which was now home to a hunter's arrow.

How had she not seen? Not known? He had kept her to his right side. Why had he hidden this from her?

The arrow pierced his arm, now sticking through. Had the blade been what grazed her arm? He had fallen on her. When the arrow came through, the head would have fallen on her arm.

How childish was she! So worried after her own wound when he incurred such a serious injury while protecting her.

"Stepan!" She maneuvered to examine the arm.

He jerked the impaled limb back and away from her. "Please, Karin, you don't need to see." His eyes were wide and darker against his pallor. "I don't want you to see."

Why? Why hide it from her? "I want to help you."

"It is a hunter's wound. My father can tend to it well enough when we rejoin the others."

An ache filled her chest.

"Let me see your wound." Stepan reached his good arm toward her.

She shifted to give him a better view. A trail of deep red trickled down her arm.

"We need to stop this bleeding," he said, his tone offered no room for argument.

Leaning toward her, he bent down and tore a strip from the hem of her dress. As he tied the cloth around her arm, cinching it tight, she sneaked a peek at his arm.

He had spoken true. She did not need to see it. The wound opening was a mess of the darkest red, pulsating out of his arm...and flowing all the more as he moved.

The world spun. Her stomach flipped.

An arm wrapped around her waist, holding her against warmth. Stepan?

"It is all right. Just breathe...in and out, in and out." As she followed his direction, the world became more stable. Her hands gripped the front of his tunic.

"Stepan?"

"Uh-huh?" He lifted a hand to stroke her hair.

"Whom was the arrow intended for?" Her voice was timid, the words breaking as she spoke.

His arm once again fell to her back, hugging her to him. It comforted her.

"Who's to say it was for either of us? It may have been a stray hunter's arrow meant for some poor animal."

How could he dismiss the incident so easily? What was he holding back? Why would he have been so quick to clear the area if not for danger?

Still, she did not press the matter. He only wanted to protect her.

"We need to get you back to your father," she said after several seconds. The longer they waited, the more blood Stepan would lose.

Stepan looked off in the direction they had come. And his features fell. Was he unsure about the short trip? What did he fear?

Karin rose, taking his hand and pulling his good arm over her head. Then she laid it over her shoulders.

Stepan paused, opening his mouth. Was he preparing to protest?

"That arrow would have struck me had you not gotten me out of the way." Her voice was firm as she searched his eyes. "At least let me help you."

Stepan eyes remained on hers. Their faces were so close. Would he attempt to kiss her?

She turned her head and focused. It would not be right. Keeping her eyes on the ground, she spoke, "We best make our way back."

Stepan shifted beside her. Was he preparing for the walk?

After some moments, she stepped forward and urged movement from Stepan. And, leaning on her, he did make progress.

It would be slow, but Karin was determined to get them the few yards that remained to where they would find their fathers and help for Stepan.

It was time. There was no avoiding it. All other efforts had failed, and this was what it had come to. *She* had insisted it must be done, and tonight was the night.

The young man whom Karin called "friend" walked as if afraid the slightest sound would awaken the entire chateau. He moved down the hallway in the cover of night. Only a few more paces and he slipped into her room.

The darkness was thick, eerie. Or did it just seem so because of the task ahead of him? How had he gotten himself involved in this? So entangled? How had it come to this? And why had he agreed to it? He did not know how he would muster the courage to do what he had to do.

Just do as I say, her voice whispered in his mind, *and all will be fine. Follow my words, and it will be over quickly and no one will ever know.*

No one but me. His heart sank. There would be no escaping that. He would know what he had done, and he would never be able to blot out that memory.

Karin shifted in her sleep. Images of Pavel and Stepan swirled in her dreams. Her mind tried to work out in her sleep the confused emotions and thoughts surrounding to these two men. In the end, all that came from it was restlessness.

As her mind moved closer and closer to consciousness, she sensed a presence. Was someone in her room? No, only a remnant from her dream. Would she open her eyes to find an apparition of Pavel? Could she bear it? She must.

Karin was slow in opening her eyes to confirm what her mind had envisioned. But, as her lids rose, there he was, no more than a sillhouette standing over her.

Still, it didn't seem like Pavel. The figure was shorter.

A slit in the curtain admitted enough moonlight to gleam against the metal in his hands. The man held a dagger above his head, ready to strike into her heart!

Karin pushed against the bed covers to gain what distance she could, pressing up against the wooden headboard. She screamed.

Everything fell into place—the poison, the carriage accident, the loosened saddle strap, and the stray arrow. All intended for her. They were not coincidences, or the easily explained away happenstances those protecting her pretended they were.

Someone was trying to kill her. And tonight, if the blade over her was telling, he would succeed.

The man followed her movements, pressing his hand over her mouth. Would he now smother her? Why did he not slit her throat and be done with it? Or plunge it into her chest?

He stayed as he was, looming.

She maneuvered against him. Could she free herself enough to scream once more?

His hand slipped, but then clamped down like a vise.

Words filled the space between them. Was he trying to say something?

The moonlight revealed the glint of metal near her head. What could she do? No one was coming to save her. She had to fight for her own life.

Karin reached for the dagger, fighting for a hold on it.

Her attacker pulled at it. There was not much of a struggle; he was too strong.

Whoosh!

Had it happened? Had the blade pierced her?

No, it now protruded from the headboard, just beside her head. How had he missed? Did he do so on purpose?

Seizing the moment, she jerked away. But her hair caught and she fell back on the bed. Whether intentional or accidental, her attacker had driven the dagger into her braid, pinning her to the headboard.

The attacker's hand dropped over her mouth once more and he moved his body closer to hers. His face came down over hers. What was she to endure?

"Karin!" his harsh voice said into her ear.

She could hear little above her muffled screams. But her eyes widened at the sound of her name on his lips. Was he about to—?

The door burst open.

Karin could see nothing but the figure over her.

A scream cut through the night. Had Mary come to her aid?

The figure over Karin pulled up and turned toward the door.

Run, Mary!

Footfalls sounded in the hall. More rescuers?

"Move away!" Stepan's voice! It was forceful and angry.

The weight of the intruder lifted.

Mary was at her side as Karin sat up as much as she could against the headboard. "Milady, are you all right?"

Karin nodded, unsure she believed it herself.

Father was behind Mary.

But Karin's eyes sought out her rescuer.

Stepan was on the other side of the room, pressing the intruder against a wall.

Father reached for Mary's candle. He came behind Stepan, moving the flame toward the attacker's face.

"Luc!" Stepan gasped.

"You will wish you had the sweet release of a dagger when I am through with you," Father ground out.

Karin did not doubt this to be true. Father was mild-mannered enough, but he had a harsh streak and connections in many places. But right now her chest throbbed. It was all surreal.

"Luc," Karin said as hot moisture poured from her eyes. "Why?"

"I could not do it," Luc said through his own tears. "I could not do it...and I did not. I could not."

Stepan kept his arm rigid. His elbow nearly at Luc's throat.

Other servants, who had been roused by Karin's and Mary's screams, started to appear.

Father instructed a couple of manservants to take charge of Luc and rouse the Viscount. He then exchanged a look with Stepan.

As Luc was moved from the room, Stepan stepped to Karin's bedside.

Father exited, doing what he could to manage the growing crowd outside the room.

Karin refocused on Mary. Her hand was on the daggar's hilt, pulling. How long had she been trying to free the weapon?

"Allow me," Stepan said to Mary, but his eyes sought out Karin's.

Mary slid out of the way and shuffled across the room, but lingered.

Stepan removed the knife with little trouble and Karin leaned into his waiting arms, releasing her fear and crying on his strong shoulder.

"I was so scared. I thought he would kill me!" she cried, clinging to Stepan, careful of the bandage on his arm.

He pulled her closer to his chest. "I know. Did he..." Stepan paused. "Did he hurt you?"

She shook her head, burying her face in the warmth he offered. "No."

"I should have been here to protect you."

Karin found a smile for him. She wished, too, that he had been there, but it was not possible. Maneuvering her face so her cheek was against his shoulder, she said, "You cannot be in my bedchambers in the middle of the night."

"I could if we were married."

She pulled back. "What are you saying?"

Stepan took her hands. "This may be the worst possible time, but I cannot hold back my wishes any longer. I love you, Karin. And I want you to be my wife. I want to be with you always—to care for you and protect you."

Karin gasped. What could she say? She could not deny that a part of her had become fond of him. "Stepan, I do care for you a great deal..." Her words trailed. Could her mind work faster?

"But?"

"But my thoughts are spinning. I can't think clearly."

He moved his hands up to her elbows, vying for her attention. "Tell me, dearest Karin, if you want to marry me." His voice was so soft, so gentle.

Karin tried to find some clarity. The fact was that she would be married to Stepan. And she grew tired of fighting the inevitable. She *had* come to care for him...

He drew in a breath and his features calmed. "Take the time you need," he said, caressing her face.

Her eyes closed and she reveled in the feeling of his touch.

Stepan leaned forward and pressed a kiss to the side of her face.

As he pulled away, Karin leaned forward and tilted her face to catch his lips. The kiss was gentle and sweet, not filled with the same kind of passion as when she kissed Pavel. But there was nothing wrong with gentle and sweet.

When they parted, she spoke, "I don't need any more time, Stepan. My answer is yes."

"Yes?" he asked as if he had not heard her.

"Yes. Yes, I will marry you."

Stepan pulled Karin to himself for another kiss. As they broke apart, he enveloped her in his arms once again. She leaned heavily into his embrace.

Soon after, he heard her breathing deepen and felt her body slacken in his arms. He lay her back down on the bed.

It was only then he became aware that Karin's maidservant had remained in the room. He motioned for her to finish settling Karin.

The woman crossed the room and pulled the covers over her mistress's form.

Stepan watched, gazing at the woman he planned to make his wife. Once her handmaiden completed her ministrations, she would beckon him to retire from the bedchambers. As well she should. So he drank in the sight of Karin while the woman worked.

Karin was rather alluring in rest, peaceful. She was free from the worries that had plagued her these last weeks.

This was how he wanted to see her always—at peace. Now that she had agreed to wed, it would be his life's mission that this calm, unfettered rest would find her every day of their lives together.

Karin's handmaiden tucked the blanket around her mistress and stepped toward the candle. Was she preparing to extinguish all lights in the room?

He turned away with reluctance to remove himself from Karin's bedchambers, but with every hope his dreams would be filled with images of his bride-to-be.

CHAPTER II
THE ENGAGEMENT

Hoof steps drew the messenger closer to the residence of the Baron and Baroness Krejik. His journey had been easy and the weather good. It afforded him every opportunity to enjoy the beautiful vistas of the Czech landscape. Though his livelihood gave him many chances to see his country, he never tired of it and never ceased to be awed by the simple beauty.

There were never-ending rounded hills, dotted with the lush greenery of trees and forests, broken up in places by homes. Hills rolled before him, while the distant mountain peaks reached toward the clear blue crystal of the skies. Those same skies in the dark gave way to a million diamonds twinkling overhead.

He longed to one day visit those peaks. Would he be able to touch the stars? The scenery so captivated him that his travels seemed to rush by. Even now, he turned his horse through the entryway leading onto the vast estate of the Krejik home.

The news he carried was neither urgent nor of ill tidings. Of this, he was grateful. He did not relish the idea of being the bearer of bad news—news which may shatter a life or break a heart. It was not that he was often privy to the messages he bore, but he happened to know the nature of this message. Yes, this was an announcement of the happiest kind.

Often, he thought of his station in life, riding though all manner of weather to deliver the greetings, letters, secrets, and announcements of others. His life was different than that of household servants and peasants, but similar in the most essential way—his day-to-day life was not his own. Still, an important difference remained—he could lose himself in the countryside along the way.

On these sometimes lengthy rides, he did wonder after his charges. As the horse crested a hill, he saw in a valley below the residence of the nobleman this message was intended for. So, as he often did, he thought about the man whose name was written on the letter he bore across so many miles. Who was he? What was his life like? What was *he* like, this Pavel Krejik?

The Baron and Baroness were sitting down to eat when they were interrupted by a servant bearing a missive. Marketa watched from her seat as the man pardoned himself, walked to Pavel, relinquished the letter, and stepped back. Did he await further instruction? What word did he bear?

Pavel opened the folds of the papers and read, his features hardened as he did so.

Was the news so concerning? What had disturbed him so?

Pavel nodded to the courier and sent him on his way.

"What is it?" Alexander asked, concern underlying his words.

Pavel glanced toward him. "Stepan sends word. He announces his engagement to the Lady Karin Bornekova. We are invited to a ball honoring their coming wedding."

"This is wonderful news!" his father said.

Marketa beamed as well. This was good news indeed. Yet Pavel did not seem pleased. Stepan was his closest friend. Should he not be thrilled?

"Pavel," she said from the other side of Alex, "Are you not glad for your friend?"

"Of course, Mother."

Alex's eyes met Marketa's. There was a knowing sadness there. Stepan and Pavel were indeed close and had done everything together. Did it bother Pavel to lose their friendship as it had always been?

"Is this the same lady you mentioned? The one staying at the chateau?" Alex attempted to move the conversation along.

Pavel nodded.

"Pray then, tell us more about her. We are eager to hear about the future Viscountess."

Marketa watched the emotions play across her son's face. Why did it seem as if Pavel did not want to talk about this Lady Karin?

"She is pleasant, graceful, intelligent. Karin is a capable horse-woman and an eager conversationalist."

Was this young woman so familiar to Pavel that he would speak her name so informally?

"What a fine match Vlastik has made for his son!" Alex shot Marketa a look. "Such fine qualities for a noble wife."

"Is she pretty?" Marketa tested the subject. She had to know more about the Lady Karin's affect on her son.

"Yes." Pavel's breath caught. "She has fine red hair, sparkling green eyes, fair, smooth skin..." His voice trailed off, and his eyes focused on something in the distance.

Marketa's met her husband's eyes. Did Alex realize?

She looked at Pavel and had nothing more to say. Would that she could pull him into her arms and kiss his hurts away as she had when he was a small boy. But there was no easy cure for his current ailment. Nothing but time would heal this wound.

Clearing his throat, Pavel returned to the present. His fingers rubbed the pages. There was more in the letter from Stepan. But it would have to wait.

"I...I beg your forgiveness. I must excuse myself. I am suddenly unwell." It was the absolute truth—his heart ached. Would it break? This had been the first time since returning home he had allowed himself to conjure an image of Karin and dwell on it. And he found the wound as fresh as the day he left.

Pavel stepped from the great hall and moved through the familiar hallways. He made the necessary turns almost without realizing. His mind was not on where his footsteps fell. As much as he might fight it, his thoughts were miles away, on memories of a certain lady who held his heart. This news of her had devastated his spirit.

Had he not known it was coming? How could he have let it take him by surprise? Had he thought she would resist more? That she would never agree?

He sighed, slowing and leaning against the nearest wall. She had no choice. Her future was in her father's hands, and Petr had made his intentions clear. This announcement was inevitable. Karin would be wed to Stepan.

Pavel turned, his back to the wall. Was the worst yet to come? He would not be able to escape the wedding. Yes, he would have to see her again. Only this time, she would belong to Stepan.

It was too much. How could he have the misfortune to fall in love with the woman who was to become his best friend's wife? There was only one place he could go to seek strength, one place to find some semblance of solace from the turmoil within.

Pavel moved toward his destination again, lengthening his stride and rushing his steps until he arrived at the chapel. The small sanctuary was empty. He closed his eyes and breathed out his relief. Making his way to the altar, he bowed and crossed himself—Father, Son, Holy Spirit. Then he all but collapsed on its sturdy oak frame. And all was silent.

Could he remain in the stillness? Allow himself to feel in the silence? Let his emotions wash over him before he began?

In the end, he had no choice. For it took several moments before Pavel saw through the pain to pray.

Father, I have been so blind. I thought I could be strong on my own, without You. I have struggled with this heartsickness, but nothing could move me toward You because I was so angry.

Yet I am persuaded by the truth of Your love for me. I fall on Your grace. Have mercy on me, O God. It would be my desire that you take this heartache, this pain. Still I know Your will is greater than mine. You have proven that I cannot understand Your will, Your plan. Help me yield.

I confess my bitterness. Help me understand. Help me let her go, because every time I see her face, I feel myself surrender ever more to the love I have for her. I am captured by her beauty and fear I will be a prisoner for life without Your divine intervention.

As Pavel poured out his heart, he fought his mind's shifting focus. Praying over his relationship with Karin caused him to conjure images of her, bringing with it a host of emotions, some of which he was in the midst of confessing. Would he ever be whole again?

Karin slipped onto the corner balcony. It was, perhaps, the smallest of the entire chateau. But it had been the place her father chose for her as she healed. The view of the grounds was not her favorite, but she had come to appreciate it.

Sitting a bit higher than the larger balconies, which boasted the preferred views, this one offered something else. At night, the small platform thrust her into the heavens. Memories of the evening she and Pavel spent stargazing came forth.

Did Pavel think of her? Not a day went by when she did not battle the heartache of being left behind, of watching him go. Her chest felt empty and heavy at the same time.

If he did think of her, may it not be with the sting of regret, but with a fondness. Her heart was steadfast, devoted. That did not mean his had been. Did he still think of her with love in his heart? Or had he found comfort elsewhere?

Karin was haunted by the tender memories of what time they did have and the words they spoke to each other. If he meant those things, if he felt but half as much as she did for him, he still thought on her and their time together.

Perhaps he was resigned to their separate fates. After all, she had accepted Stepan's proposal. Was it the right choice? As much as she had come to care for him, her heart still beat for Pavel.

But what would be the gain in fighting it? Stepan was an honorable man who would care for her. Pavel was gone and would not return. Even if he could, they would remain separated by her father's desires for her to wed the house of Dvorak.

"If you do think of me," she whispered, willing the wind to carry her voice to her beloved, "know that I must try to put you from my mind, as thoughts of you are never far away. You have forever marked my heart. There will never be a day without thoughts of you."

Karin hugged her wrap closer as the wind whipped around her, answering her with a cold rush. With regret, she let the chill of the world turn her back to the chateau and to the warmth it offered.

Stepan, Zdenek, the Viscount, and Radek made a grand show of moving through the village on horseback. The Viscount saw to it that an announcement was posted, telling of negotiations for his son's bride to be held that evening.

Zdenek, whom Stepan had selected in Pavel's absence to be his *kecal*, led the party through the streets. And so the men had taken great care with their appearances that afternoon. Each were garbed in their finest.

They moved beyond the village, with a small contingency of

followers. Were they curious to see the courting negotiations of a noble family? These villagers were led to the doors of the grand chateau.

Karin heard them coming, drawing nearer, pushing her ever closer to her fate. What would the next hours hold? Could she contain the thumping of her heart?

A loud knock echoed through the chateau. They had arrived. The small crowd was soon admitted and led to the Golden Hall.

One table stood at the front of the room. The negotiators would be seated here. Even then, her parents sat, waiting and watching. Zdenek's contingency filled the remainder of the room.

An older woman, Beata, had been selected as Karin's *stara svarby* and she sat at the end of the table. Yes, a stranger would serve as her "old-of-the-marriage".

Karin observed all of this from her place in the corner behind her parents. Why did they put the bride-to-be on such display? She was to be out of the negotiations, but present for the townspeople to stare at.

Once in the room, Zdenek declared, "Good evening. I am coming to you, if it is true you have promised to give your daughter away to us indeed?"

Father nodded.

Zdenek, Stepan, and the Viscount took the other seats at the table. Radek stepped among the people, pressing into the space.

After everyone was settled, Zdenek began the speech he had taken such care to write and memorize, "Most beloved parents! The reason we all come under this roof is the desire of the honorable and high-minded boy, the Lord Stepan Dvorak, son of the Viscount Vlastik Dvorak, to enter the holy state of matrimony with this honorable and innocent lady, the most beloved daughter of yours, Lady Karin Bornekova, who has also clasped him to her heart, having fallen in love with him and chosen him as her accepted spouse in the presence of God."

As he mentioned Karin, a room full of gazes landed on her, but as was her place, she dropped her eyes to the ground, keeping them downcast. She would remain this way the whole of the interchange. Neither she nor Stepan were to speak for most of the meeting. Everything would be done by their parents, Zdenek, and Beata.

With the opening speech concluded, the talks commenced. These were negotiations about Karin's dowry and the property Stepan would bring to the union.

Karin found it difficult to follow the words spoken back and forth. The money and land meant little to her. What mattered was what the conclusion of this ceremony would signify. She would be engaged to Stepan and would marry him. There would be no hope left for a marriage to Pavel.

Once these negotiations were finished, she and Stepan would sign the marriage contract—all but declaring them husband and wife. How could she do this? Her heart cried against it. But did she have a choice? Her father made this arrangement, and she did care for Stepan. Though it was not the same as her longing for Pavel, still there were true feelings for Stepan all the same.

"Karin?" her mother prompted her.

Had the time in the ceremony for her response come? She glanced between her father and mother. All in the room watched her, waiting. Her father must have asked if she agreed to marry Stepan.

She stood and nodded. Her eyes seeking Stepan's.

He offered her a warm smile.

Karin made every effort to return it, yet she found she could not force her lips to obey. So, she averted her gaze.

Soft murmurs from the crowd created a din of sound. What had so fascinated them? Did she care?

Karin sat.

Father pulled out a paper for them to write all which had been agreed. The paper had been filled out prior to these proceedings, it only lacked the final details. It did not take long for those to be penned.

Then it was time for those involved to undersign.

Karin hesitated, seeking a few extra moments by glancing over the papers.

It has been agreed between the Lord Stepan Dvorak, the legitimate son of the Viscount Vlastik Dvorak, belonging with the father's will and consent, as the groom on the one hand, and then the Lady Karin, the legitimate daughter of the Earl Petr Bornekov, with whose consent, on the other hand, the following Wedding Contract had been concluded as the irrevocable conjunction with the exception of the spiritual union...

She continued to read, but the words blurred. No, she would not cry. Not now. Closing her eyes, she gathered hold of her emotions.

"Karin, is something amiss?" Father moved closer and whispered in her ear.

Opening her mouth, she found herself unable to speak. So she shook her head. Her eyes worked their way over the final lines.

This Marriage Contract has been signed true and without pretense by both parties and by three independent witnesses.
In Hradec Kralove on the 22nd of July 1415

Having taken as much time as she possibly could looking over the document, threatening insult to the parties there, Karin took a deep breath and inscribed her name.

Stepan took the quill, his fingers grazing hers. He placed his name alongside hers.

The fathers signed next, followed by Zdenek, Beata, and then Radek.

Now that the marriage contract was complete, the two fathers maneuvered around the table to present Karin and Stepan to the crowd, an engaged couple.

Zdenek put Karin's hand in Stepan's. As far as everyone was concerned, the courting stage was ended and preparations for the wedding would begin.

Applause greeted them.

The doors to the room opened, and servants entered with trays carrying *kolace* and donuts to celebrate, and the men were offered beer.

The Viscount raised his glass. "You are all invited to return this evening for a ball to honor my son and his bride!"

Shouts of gratitude and celebration filled the room. Indeed it seemed everyone was eager to make merry this joyous occasion.

Everyone but the bride.

Luc sat in his cell, wishing the day away. How would it be unlike every other day? Guilt for the lies he continued to tell plagued him, but he must maintain his story for the sake of those who meant more to him than his own well-being: his parents and his sister.

His family had a secret, one that had to be kept at all costs. No one knew that his father's estate was being depleted, and had been, by Father's physicians and care. To no avail. Father's health continued to fail.

They were not independently wealthy, as were many of his friends. No, Luc's family enjoyed wealth because of Father's hard work. But with no money coming in and more and more leaving, it became a dire situation.

Their hopes had been on him rising to a prestigious career, securing an influx of money. Perhaps this would retain their standing and ensure his sister a good marriage.

His sister had found favor in the eyes of a rather wealthy baron. There was but one problem. She had, for a short time, been connected with a man they came to find a philanderer. While he was never with Suzka unchaperoned, her connection, albeit brief, could ruin any chances of an advantageous match. Their secret must be kept.

How *she* found out this dark piece of his family's past, he did not know. But she held it over his head. Still. And so, though he alone was accused of this crime, he dare not speak. As long as he remained silent, there was the chance this secret would remain buried. With Suzka's betrothal so close in the making, he must not betray the one who had controlled him.

No one would understand the burden he bore. Perhaps no one would ever know. What difference would it make should he bring forth what darkness remained at the chateau? A harsh punishment for the crime he had committed marked his future. Regardless. The fact that he had been caroused would not bring a pardon. Luc had commited the deed.

He would spend years of his life in this hole—maybe an even darker hole under the hands of jailers who enjoyed having power over a man of noble standing. Already, he had felt their frustration with the upper class leveled upon him, the only one within their reach.

Even now he heard footfalls nearing his cell. Coming for another round?

Luc was tired, but he turned to face his fate.

A figure wearing a hooded cloak stood beside the jailer.

"You have a visitor," the harsh man's gruff voice echoed off the stark walls.

A visitor? Men guilty of attempted murder were not allowed visitors. They would only break his solitude for a member of a noble family...and a handsome bribe. Was it Stepan come to visit his anger upon Luc?

Luc leaned against the wall, heaving a deep sigh and hanging his head. Where would he find a last measure of strength? He gazed at the man who intruded upon his isolation, the form veiled in darkness.

"How can I help you?" Luc asked, his voice heavy with sarcasm.

"I would have the truth." The man's response was quiet, so much so that Luc could not discern the voice's identity. Now facing away from Luc's position, the figure looked out of the cell's sole window—

a pitiful opening, much too small for even both of Luc's arms to fit through.

"That is a fine request from someone making every effort to conceal his identity."

The figure whirled toward him and threw back the hood, revealing his face in the shadows. Darkness continued to cover much of his features, but Luc did not have to ask him to come into the light. For seconds later, Pavel was face to face with Luc, his nose no more than two inches from Luc's.

"Now there should be nothing preventing you from speaking the truth."

"I have told all there is to tell," Luc lied, a mask going up.

"No!" Pavel's voice was sharp, he shook his head. "Do not lie to me."

" I am not proud of what I've done, but a man must own his actions. I planned to murder Karin."

"That cannot be true," Pavel said, his voice firm. Did he not believe Luc capable?

"Are you so adamant for her sake or for mine?" Luc shot at him.

"Both." Pavel pushed against the wall, thrusting back and creating space between them. "I don't want to see you take the blame for something you were coerced into doing." Pavel took a deep breath. When he spoke again, his voice was calmer. "I know you, Luc. I know you do not have it in you. The fact that you did not hurt her proves it. If you wanted to kill her, you would have. This much I know."

Luc hung his head. What could he say?

"I also know that if the person who pulled you into their scheme is still out there, then he will try again. Can you not see that?"

Yes, he had considered that. But told himself he didn't care.

"Karin is innocent! Can you stand by and let her die while you protect her murderer?"

Pavel didn't know anything. How dare he speak thusly to Luc? He shot to his feet and closed the distance between them. "How can you be so sure it was not me? You may not know me as well as you think!"

The blue eyes that met Luc's were hard. And there was something else? Compassion?

Pavel's steel gaze held Luc's. "This was not the first attempt on her life. There were other times. The carriage..."

Did Pavel truly want to hear all of this? So be it. "I hacked the wheel connections while you were with Karin and the rest were at the pub."

"The horse..."

"It was I who slipped the saddle loose when I checked the straps for her. I slid the burr under the saddle then, too."

"What about the bolt? Was that you? Injuring Stepan?"

Luc nodded. "He got in the way."

"What about Karin's poisoning? That was before we arrived."

Luc became quiet. This was a large hole.

"That could not have been you. We were all in Prague."

What could he say? Pavel spoke truth. Fumbling for his words, Luc was struck with inspiration. "Perhaps it was not a poisoning at all. It could have been an animal just as the doctor said."

"But it was not. We both know that." Pavel's eyes softened. "Think of Karin! Think of how you are allowing an innocent woman to suffer!"

Luc was silent again. As much as he wanted to fight it, Pavel's words penetrated his heart. He protected those close to him with his silence, but what of the cost? Was it one Luc could pay? Even if he did not yield the weapon that finished the deed, would it be as if he did should he not speak up?

"It is not that simple." Luc's whispered, his hard exterior cracked.

"Then tell me." Pavel stepped toward him.

Could Pavel forgive him? Offer him friendship after what he had done?

"I am on your side, Luc."

It was too dangerous. "I cannot."

Pavel shook his head. "Then you truly are a murderer. Whoever hired you will not stop until they succeed. Can you live with that? I couldn't." Moving toward the door, Pavel raised a hand to summon the jailer.

Luc's thoughts jumbled. And his heart raced. Did a part of him want to tell Pavel? He needed someone to know about this war within. Sagging against the wall, he looked at Pavel's back. It was time to tell someone the truth. The whole truth.

"Pavel, wait." His voice was calm, determined. Why so? He feared it would shake as unsteady as his insides had become.

Pavel spun and stepped toward Luc.

Luc took a deep breath, but it came out quite ragged. Then he met Pavel's eyes once more. "Let me tell you a story."

CHAPTER 12
CAUGHT

"My *katka*, you are beautiful this evening," Mother said, pride infused in her voice as she helped Mary affix a headdress to Karin's hair.

"Thank you, Mother." Karin's face lit, from somewhere deep within she found courage. She felt like a princess of a long-ago story, one who graced the fine castles of Prague.

"We must get you to your ball!" Mary said, as she stepped back. Had they finished?

Karin's mother took her hand and led her from the bedchambers and to the top of the grand stairs.

Father and Stepan were there. Waiting.

Stepan paced, moving back and forth across the opening to the stairs. Was he nervous? Having second thoughts?

As Karin and her mother neared, he caught sight of them. It caused him to halt, his gaze fixed on her. His eyes widened and his lips parted.

Karin's face warmed under the intensity of his stare.

Mother released Karin's hand and stepped toward Father.

Stepan's mouth moved, but words were not forthcoming. Was he so struck?

Karin stepped closer.

When Stepan did find his voice, he managed, "Forgive me, I find myself speechless in the presence of such beauty."

"You flatter me," Karin responded.

"No." He shook his head, closing the distance between them. "Karin, you are a vision." Taking her hand with fingers that trembled, he lifted it to his lips.

The warmth of her face deepened as did, certainly, the color.

"Come," Father said, a wide grin on his face. "We must have you announced."

Stepan nodded, offering Karin his arm.

She slid her hand onto it. Was he trembling still?

Father, with Mother on his arm, moved toward the grand stairway. As they closed in upon the stairs, the Viscount and Viscountess joined them. Had they been watching the exchange?

The Viscount delivered compliments to both Karin and her mother, as did Father to the Viscountess. Only then did the Viscount signal a servant to alert the manservant who was to announce them. He then led the Viscountess toward the stairs.

"Your hosts this evening, Viscount Vlastik Dvorak and his wife, the Viscountess Pavla Dvorakova."

As they made their way down the stairs, Karin's parents took their positions. Mother stole a moment to lay a hand to Karin's face and smile.

"The Earl Petr Bornekov and his wife, the Countess Lenka Bornekova."

Both sets of parents remained at the base of the stairs, splitting off each to a side. She and Stepan were to come down and walk between them.

With her parents in place, the caller made his next announcement. "The esteemed Bornekovs and Dvoraks would like to celebrate the engagement of their children, the Lady Karin Bornekova and Lord Stepan Dvorak."

As Karin and Stepan descended, everyone applauded. It was thunderous.

Stepan paused halfway down so everyone had ample view.

Waving to the wonderful people giving them such laud, Karin found it difficult to breathe.

Stepan raised her hand to his lips once again, and the crowd's applause grew louder still.

Everyone was so happy for them. Could she lose herself in the merriment as well?

Stepan tugged on her arm. Was it time for them to continue down the stairs? How long had they stood there? As they set their feet on the floor, the musicians began playing. Another tug and a whirl and she was pulled into a dance.

Karin was truly happy. The people were happy for her. After everything, all was well. The world seemed right.

Karin and Stepan spoke with her parents. Was everything falling into place? She looked at Stepan, so kind, so compassionate. Wasn't he what she needed?

Stepan's eyes wandered toward the entrance to the great hall and they narrowed. Was something amiss? What had distressed him?

Karin glanced in that direction, opening her mouth to ask just that question. And then she saw.

The Constable from Hradec Kralove had entered the great room. Alone. What could be the matter? He scanned the space for some moments and then moved toward the Viscount and Viscountess.

Lowering his head, the Constable spoke to the Viscount, close enough to his ear that no one else could have heard.

"Excuse me. I am sorry to interrupt," Stepan spoke the words to her parents before affording Karin a look as he lay his hand on hers. "But it seems as if the Constable has news. Perhaps about Luc."

As Stepan peeled away from their conversation, Karin's eyes went to her mother's. Turning, she moved off after him.

Stepping out of the great room, Karin saw the Viscount and Viscountess in a tense conversation with the Constable and two armed deputies.

As she moved closer, just a pace or two behind Stepan, she heard the Constable's words. "I must speak with the Viscountess."

"Whatever for?" the Viscount boomed as Stepan and Karin joined them.

There were footsteps slowing behind her. Had her parents followed?

Karin turned. Indeed they had. Were they as concerned as she?

"For the attempted murder of the Lady Karin Bornekova."

The Constable's men came around the Viscountess. Was she being arrested? What insanity was this? Had they not found Luc to be the cause of these attacks? Why would the Viscountess...?

"What? You cannot do this!" Stepan said, his voice rising to a level Karin had never heard. "It is preposterous!"

The Viscountess stood in silence, smirking, and gazing, expressionless into the distance.

"I received information that she was indeed involved. And we have just completed a search of her rooms and found this." He held up a bottle. What was it? What did it prove? "It is the same kind of poison used on the Lady Karin."

"No, it can't be!" the Viscount's voice seemed hollow, shocked, as he stared at his wife.

"What did you expect me to do?" she snapped at him. "Just sit by while you entertained thoughts of this...this girl?"

"What are you saying?" The Viscount's eyes were now quite large on his face.

"I refuse to share my station with anyone, do you hear me? Anyone! Least of all a girl half my age!" She spat in Karin direction.

Stepan pulled Karin into his embrace. This was madness!

The Viscount's eyes cut to the right. What was he thinking? Why would she have to share her station? Had the Viscount previously thought of entertaining a young woman? What had happened to them?

A chill shook Karin's body at this thought. How many?

The Viscount's face fell, his mouth agape. Hands balled into fists at his sides. "What have you done, Pavla?" His voice was not much more than a whisper.

"And you," she said, directing her piercing gaze on Stepan. "Do not be fooled. She is not what she seems. This girl is a manipulative snake. Believe me. You will see—you will all see!"

The Viscountess lunged at Karin, but the Constable's men had her arms.

"You cannot do this to me!" she screamed.

They pulled her toward the large door.

"Let me go! Stepan! Trust me! Don't believe her!" she screamed as she was all but dragged out the door. And then she was gone.

Karin clung to Stepan.

He shifted to look at her and wiped at the moisture on her face. Tears? Was she crying? It had all been so frightful.

Could his mother know she was a Hussite? Was that what she referred to? Or was she simply lashing out in anger? Perhaps the latter.

Karin had no doubt the Viscountess would have exposed her had she known Karin's secret.

She looked into Stepan's face.

His eyes moved between Karin and the door. Was he torn by what had just occurred? What would he do? Believe his raving mother? Or Karin? Dare she hope for his trust? For sure, she was bearing false witness to him.

Drawing her into his embrace once more, it seemed decided. Did he truly love Karin so much? That he would even turn his back on his mother for her sake?

How could she hold back the truth from him? A weight settled in her stomach. She buried her face in his chest and let the tears come.

"It is all right," he soothed.

She pulled back and looked at him. "I should be reassuring you."

"What?" Stepan's brows met as they lowered.

"Your mother...it could not have been easy..."

"No, it was not easy to hear my mother say such things to the woman I love, the woman I am going to marry. But as long as I have you by my side, I can make it through anything."

She dropped her forehead to his chest once more. What was she going to do?

Stepan shifted.

Karin lifted her head to see that his eyes sought his father's. She turned toward the man.

The Viscount still stood in the same spot, head hung. Could he not absorb it? It must be so difficult.

Father stepped to his friend and put a hand to his shoulder.

Stepan gently pulled away and moved toward his father.

Her mother stepped in, wrapping an arm around Karin.

This would be a day forever remembered in the house of Dvorak.

Constable Borivoj breathed in a sigh of relief. His bluff had worked. The doctor's direction on the type of poison had not given him much. Finding the bottle in the Viscountess's room was fortunate. Then she had confessed to the whole thing.

He let his eyes close and pushed out another long breath. They had solved the great mystery of the chateau. Even more, the perpetrators were behind bars. All that remained was for him to fill in some finishing notes in his ledger.

By her own admission, it had been the Viscountess all along. But the only crime they could prove, and thus try her for would be those against the Lady Karin.

Borivoj's heart sank at the realization that she may never be found guilty for her other crimes—the deaths of six young ladies, long since ruled accidents.

If there was a way to find poison in a person, he was certain the poison found in the Viscountess's room would be the same asin those bodies. From the look on the Viscount's face, Borivoj knew he realized it to be true as well.

Borivoj could now close these cases. Solved. Why did that give him so little pleasure? He would do everything in his power to see that she was punished to the full extent of the law.

Even now, the sounds of her shrieking and ranting filled the entire structure.

Jakub had been assigned to record everything she said in case they might catch her in something which could connect her to one of these earlier crimes. Who knew? They may be fortunate again.

Now, he needed to turn his attention to the happenings all over Bohemia. Hradec Kralove would not remain untouched for long. Since the execution of Jan Hus, there had been disturbances and riots breaking out.

Nothing of this nature had happened in his village, to be sure, but he had to maintain an ever-watchful eye. Perhaps it was time to take on another deputy or two.

"That is the last of them," Father said, motioning to the manservant as Mother's large, ornate trunk was loaded onto the carriage.

But Karin cared not. She held her mother's hands. Why did she have to leave?

"I cannot believe Father is being so stubborn." Karin wiped at a stray tear.

"Your father only ever makes the best decisions he can. He has business he must attend to, and you—"

"Yes, yes," Karin looked to the ground. "I know, I have wedding duties here."

"It's only for a week, then you'll be home."

"That does make this easier." Karin sighed. "But I *am* going to miss you, Mother."

They embraced. Heavy foot falls near the entrance to the chateau warned of intruders into their moment. But Karin did not wish to pull from her mother's arms.

Mother leaned back, nodding toward the approaching owner of the steps. She turned and reached for Stepan's hand.

"It has been a real pleasure to know the fine man you have become. Take care of my *katka*."

"Of course," Stepan said, wrapping an arm around Karin's shoulders. "Always."

And though Karin's heart ached, she found comfort in Stepan's eyes. She believed he would keep her safe.

Mother nodded and attempted to smile.

The Viscount stepped toward Father. He extended an arm, which Father grasped.

"I shall miss you, old friend," the Viscount's voice boomed.

"And I you. But the next time we meet, we shall be family!"

The Viscount smiled and glanced at Stepan and Karin. "We did make a fine match, did we not?"

Father nodded, then leaned closer to the Viscount. "Please write if you need anything."

The Viscount bobbed his head. He had not been to the holding facility to see the Viscountess. Perhaps it was for the best.

"I wish you good travels and safe return," the Viscount said, clapping Father's shoulder.

"We will do what we can," Father's smile became crooked.

"And you," the Viscount spoke to Mother, "Keep careful watch on him."

"I always do." She smiled.

The Viscount took her hand and walked her to the carriage, assisting her to a seat.

Father followed in short order, and moments later the carriage was pulling from the portico.

Karin waved until the coach had disappeared from view.

The Viscount turned back to the house, tilting his head to Stepan and Karin as he passed.

But Karin wished to remain and watch after the carriage.

Stepan rubbed her shoulder that his hand rested on. "Are you well?"

Karin nodded, fighting more tears. She had to stop with all the crying. "I have seen my mother so little these last months. It was a breath of fresh air to have her here."

Stepan nodded.

"I am so sorry," she said, turning to look at him. She had no right to complain about being separated from her mother when he would perhaps never see his again.

Stepan shook his head, gazing into her eyes. "It is all right. I understand."

She leaned into him, rising onto her tiptoes and pressing a kiss to his lips.

He accepted it, deepening the contact.

Would she ever not think of Pavel when he kissed her?

Lord Stepan Dvorak,

If you have not been informed of the goings-on in Prague of late, allow me to enlighten you. For our lands have descended into chaos. Since the execution of Jan Hus, the people have become mad. Troubles have broken in many parts of our lands, these heretics driving priests from their parishes and the like. Sigismund has done what he can to stem the Hussite movement, but they grow in numbers every day.

Most recently, there was a procession of Hussites through the streets of Prague. As you can imagine, those who oppose them reacted to their presence—throwing stones from the windows of the town hall. The Hussites then took the matter too far. They threw the burgomaster and several town councilors, whom they thought to have been responsible for instigating the stone throwing, from the windows and into the streets!

Will this madness know no bounds? It is now reported that King Wenceslaus is rather ill from the shock of hearing these dreadful things. I only hope he can recover before these vile things get worse.

Regards,

Professor Evzen

Karin spent her days deep in thought. War had broken out. It still seemed unreal. So much had transpired in her time at the chateau. She still had not quite grasped that Jan Hus was gone. And now this? How could God have let such a thing happen?

Severe fighting between the Hussites and those royal to the crown continued. How she longed for someone to share her pain! But her companions at the chateau were all happiness. And calling for the deaths of all Hussites.

If only Pavel was here! Wiping at a stray tear, she recalled his words of warning: it was more important now than ever that she keep her emotions in check. Her loyalties were on the wrong side of this conflict to be so connected to the Dvorak family.

Did Pavel care of her predicament? Would he come for her? Her heart fell. Such childish notions. Of course he could not. Just as it would be disastrous for her to be found a Hussite, it would be too dangerous for Pavel to travel in these lands.

For certain, he was doing good wherever he was. Her heart ached for assurance that his thoughts were on her. And, as much doubt crept into her soul that they were, she truly knew that he cared and would come if he could.

Karin wanted to feel as if he was near, wanted to know once again that she was not alone, though all around her were those who celebrated each victory against the Hussites. There was still one place she felt Pavel's presence, a place where she continued to go for solitude and reflection—her old tree.

Should she allow herself to dwell on these thoughts of Pavel? Had she not committed her future to Stepan? Yet she could not stop this yearning within.

It was a small matter to slip from the chateau. The walk to her place in the forest near the stream seemed briefer than usual. She paused to take in her surroundings, breathing in the scent of the natural world around her. How long had it been since she had come?

Her days had been filled with dressmaking appointments, Stepan, and wedding plans. Stepan all but consumed Karin's every waking moment. He had thrown himself into the wedding plans since the Viscountess's arrest. She could not begrudge him his need of her. What he was going through was unimaginable, and she would support him in every way she could. If that meant living and breathing wedding, so be it.

But living and breathing wedding was not as easy as she had anticipated. With each day that passed, with each decision made, a little more of Pavel slipped away. It was for the best, wasn't it? She had made her choice.

Karin's hand grazed the weathered wood of the sturdy oak, where she and Pavel had sat when his lips touched hers for the first time. Letting her eyes close, she sighed, a deep breath pushed out.

Her return to these memories must be her last. She would release

Pavel so she might give herself fully to Stepan. That was right, and Pavel would agree. He had agreed, had he not? When he left, his very words spoke that he was removing himself and moving on with his life, so she could get on with hers. With Stepan.

Karin leaned against the tree, gazing down at her feet. Droplets of water bounced off the tips of her shoes. Odd, she had not seen a dark cloud in the sky. As she glanced up, moisture landed on her face. Was it coming from her? She wiped at the tears and returned her gaze to her feet. This would not do! Try as she might, she was unable to contain the emotions threatening to burst forth.

Sinking to the ground, she let it all come. No one was there to bear witness. What did it matter if she fell apart? And so she mourned the loss of what could have been, something she had yet to do, something she needed to do in order to forge ahead and make a life with Stepan.

How long had she sat in her sorrow? It ended as it had begun—in silence, with no one the wiser. She dried her eyes and rose, shaking off her dress and slapping her hands together to shake any dirt loose.

As she turned, her foot struck something solid. She paused. Perhaps it was nothing more than a protruding root. Still, she bent toward the irritant. It was no more than a small bump. Brushing the leaves aside, realization slammed into her—it was the box Pavel had left for her so many weeks ago, a box filled with Jan Hus's writings.

Hungry for the precious words within, Karin dug with her hands. Soon after she had unearthed her prize. She sat, placing the box in her lap. Dare she go one step farther? Would it take her once again father from Stepan and closer to Pavel?

Karin could not contain the desire to hold the papers once more, see her name in Pavel's script. Ripping the box open, she pulled out the papers. There, as she remembered, the words etched which had confused her at one time. They now stabbed at her heart: *For you, Karin.*

Holding the folded papers to her chest, her eyes closed and hot tears brimmed once more. At length, she moved a hand across her face, erasing all evidence they existed. Opening the folds, she poured over the words of Jan Hus as if seeing them for the first time.

Yes, this was truth. This was right.

"Karin," Stepan called for his bride. Where had she walked to? Perhaps these strolls about the grounds were not wise. Turning around a tree, he spotted her red-blonde hair.

He opened his mouth to call to her again, but he paused. She leaned over something, holding it to herself. What was it?

Dare he invade her privacy? Didn't he have every right? Thinking it best not to overreact, he spoke her name.

She jumped, turning her head. Was she attempting to find the source of the sound? Karin scrambled to her feet. Her eyes fell on his as he came around, now face-to-face with her.

"I have looked everywhere for you. The cake maker is here to—" He took in the scene, eyes trailing up and down his beloved. A box set on the ground, her hands and dress dirtied. There was also a hold in the ground. Had she dug the box, buried for some reason, out with her hands? Then he met her gaze. Why were her eyes so wide? Was she so shocked to see him? Why? Was she hiding something?

"Digging for buried treasure?" Would it be best to maintain a calm demeanor?

"No, I..." she fumbled for words, her eyes cutting toward the ground.

He noted the papers in her hands, peeking out, almost hidden within the folds of her skirt. Was she hiding them?

"What do you have there?" He kept a smile on his face, attempting to keep the mood light, but he could not keep the serious edge out of his voice.

Those papers concerned him. Were they love letters? Was she having some secret affair? Was that what his mother tried to tell him?

"N-Nothing," she stammered, burying them further into her skirt, her hands shaking.

The sky rumbled.

She glanced up. "I think it will rain soon. We had better head back to the—"

"Nothing, eh?" He closed the gap between them too quickly for her to react.

Pulling her into his arms, he gained a decided advantage, pinning her. It took little effort, then, for him to extricate the papers from Karin's grasp.

He moved away from her, spreading the papers open. Dare he look? What if they were love letters? If Karin had been untrue to him?

As he tried to read, Karin made a futile attempt to grab for them, reaching around Stepan. He maneuvered his body to keep her to his back, holding the letter at arm's length. Her efforts were futile.

The lines stilled before him and he read. It was something of a scholarly paper. Perhaps even a sermon. Relief washed over him. Could there be anything devious about a sermon?

Then why would she hide them? He read further. As he did so, his anger welled, rising toward the surface.

Stepan turned back to her. "Karin, tell me you do not know anything about these papers."

"What?" Had she not heard him? She backed up until she was under the tree. Did his tone scare her? Cool moisture pelted him. He glanced toward the sky—it had started to rain.

A simple shower would not dissuade him. He leveled his gaze on her once more, stepping toward her. "Tell me you found these and were just curious. They don't belong to you. And you don't know anything about them."

Wouldn't she plead innocent? This could not be happening.

She remained silent for several moments, looking down.

He took another step toward her.

Karin met his eyes. What was there, he could not name. Determination? Sadness? Resolve?

"I cannot tell you any of those things. Because I will not lie to you." Her words were out there, between them.

What did this mean? He was a fool if he ignored the truth. Anger so filled him. Surely his skin would singe the drops of water from the heavens.

"Then you...you are one of...*them*?" He spat the last word at her. Could he not even bring himself to say the word?

Karin squared her shoulders and raised her chin. Defiance?

Then she spoke with a confidence he could not have expected. And it caused his ire to swell again, to dangerous proportions.

"I am a Hussite."

Whatever might happen, Karin had spoken true.

Stepan drew his sword. "Treacherous," he muttered.

Karin took a step back. He could not be serious! Would he truly use his weapon on her? "Stepan, what are you doing?"

"My mother was right. All she was trying to do was protect me. From you! But none of us saw it."

"That's not true, Stepan, you must see that—"

He held up a hand. "Now she is in prison awaiting trial. And the real villain, an enemy of the crown, is free to do as she pleases."

Stepan raised his blade, as if preparing to strike. He wouldn't! Would he? She backed into the tree's trunk. Her faithful oak was no longer friend, but captor.

His eyes narrowed. "How long were you planning on keeping up the act? Until we were married?"

Stepan lunged.

Karin jerked to one side, dodging his sword. He had not been serious with that attack, and she knew it. "Stepan, please let me explain!"

"Your words are venom. Has anything been the truth?" He followed step for step as she attempted to evade him.

"Yes! I am the same Karin, the woman you chose to marry!"

"You are a traitor!" he screamed at her. Stepan swung his sword once more.

Then his movements became measured, more purposeful. Another attack was coming.

"That is a crime punishable by death!" Stepan lept toward her again.

She moved to avoid his thrust, but her foot slipped on the wet grasses and mud. And then she was falling, grasping in futility for a handhold which would prevent her from tumbling down the bank. To no avail.

Her body smacked the rock-clad ground with a thud, knocking the wind from her. When she was able to breathe, she attempted to gain her feet. She had to put some distance between herself and Stepan. But her body would not obey. Pain shot through her torso. Had she wounded her ribs?

Stepan's rough hands twisted her injured body. The rough rocks were at her back, rain stinging her face. She could no longer make out his features. Was she delirious from the pain?

He was only an outline, moving over her. But she saw with clarity that he pulled his sword back and raised it above her chest.

Karin heaved. Breathing only caused her torso to fill with searing pain.

"This is how we deal with traitors," he said, his voice grim.

She closed her eyes. *Lord, let it be quick. I will be with you in a moment.*

CHAPTER 13
HOMECOMING

A rush of movement filled her vision. Followed by the sound of metal on metal. Another man stood over her, deflecting Stepan's strike. She slumped against the rocks beneath her.

The man who had come to her rescue heaved deep breaths, well exerted.

"Why did you stop me?" Stepan yelled. "Do you know what she is?"

"I do," the man replied.

Her heart quickened. *It cannot be!* But it was, undeniably, Pavel.

Stepan's feet crunched. Did he move nearer or farther? Would he and Pavel come to blades again?

"She is a traitor to the crown! Masquerading, enjoying the hospitality...and good opinion...of my family." Stepan's voice was to her right, no longer over her. Had he stepped back?

"I know!" Pavel countered, kneeling beside her. His eyes moved over her form. Was he assuring himself she was well? He scooped an arm under her shoulders, lifting her slightly.

She gasped as pain tore through her.

"You know?" Stepan shouted, the sting of betrayal in his voice. "You knew and did not tell me?"

Pavel's arms offered comfort. He would protect her. All would be well. She sought his eyes, but they were on Stepan.

Shifting his focus, Pavel's eyes caught hers. Bliss.

Pavel looked once again to where Stepan stood. "I could not. I am a Hussite, too."

She did not have to see Stepan's face to distinguish his surprise. Everything began to spin and blurr. Had she the strength to help Pavel? Karin's head lolled against his shoulder. His voice vibrated against the side of her face.

"Believe me, Stepan, I was your friend long before I came to understand and accept the truth of Jan Hus's teachings. I wanted to tell you. But your father's distaste of Hus and his followers made that difficult. I was a coward... I am truly sorry for that. I should have been more trusting, old friend. But I believed you would have to come to understand in your own time."

Stepan twisted away, bringing his hand to his face, and dropping his sword.

Several breaths passed before he turned back to Pavel. There was nothing keeping him from striking them both dead. Did Pavel know this, too? Was he trusting in Stepan's sense of friendship and reason?

Stepan's voice was no longer so loud, but it still had an edge to it. "Why did you come back? To bring such terrible tidings as these?"

Pavel took a deep breath before he answered. " I came back for Karin. I feared for her."

Stepan's volume rose again. "Feared for her? Did you not leave for your own safety?"

"No." Pavel ducked to catch Karin's eyes once more before facing Stepan.

"You were so secretive about it. Now I see you were secretive about many things! Why did you leave if you were so concerned for the safety of your Hussite friend?"

Pavel's voice quieted. "Because I discovered she was intended for you."

Stepan stared, his eyes almost gleaming. They were set on Pavel. Intense. Did he fear what more Pavel had to say?

"Because I could not bear to see the two of you together..." Pavel drew in a breath. "I love her."

Karin's head swam. It became too much for her weakened body, and she lost her hold on consciousness.

"Karin!" Pavel's attention shifted toward her when her body went limp.

Stepan stepped forward. Was that concern on his features? Whereas a few breaths before he was swinging a death blow upon her, now he was worried after her well-being?

Pavel lifted a hand to cup her face. Cold. But he was reassured by her steady breaths.

"I...I cannot." Stepan shook his head. "How can I even...?" His voice trailed.

What could Pavel say to assuage his wounds? He had to let the truth guide him. "You cannot know how much I wish it was not this way. I never meant to bring any pain upon you."

Stepan looked at his sword on the ground, then at Pavel's sword, also laid by the side. "What happens now?"

Pavel's eyes glistened. Was it the rain?

"Please let us leave. Karin needs a doctor, but it is not safe for us to remain here."

It was true. Did Stepan think he should ensure they were penalized for their treachery? Pavel did not think Stepan could bring himself to see harm befall his friends. Not as his head cooled and reason returned. But the Viscount would not hesitate to have them executed.

Stepan spoke, "It is my fault she is injured. Allow me to send you in a carriage."

Pavel nodded. It was the only thing his friend could do for him, and it was more than he dared hope for.

When Karin came to awareness, she was being jostled about. The more aware she became, the more information she took in. She was wrapped in blankets, and Pavel held her body as still as possible. His arms buffered the bumping of the road.

And then the pain returned. Biting back her cries, she maneuvered a hand free of the blankets and reached for one of Pavel's.

His eyes met hers. "How do you feel?"

"Like I was trampled by a horse," she confessed. Her breaths were ragged. A million questions filled her mind, and a few spilled out. "Where are we? What happened?"

"Stepan lent us this carriage. We are bound for your family's home."

There was sadness and pain in Pavel's eyes. The interchange with Stepan had affected him. There would be time later to learn more.

She held Pavel's gaze. Once again, wanting to dive into the pools of his eyes. But this was not the time. There was more to think of. And something she must tell Pavel. "My father will not receive us well when he sees us together, perhaps not at all."

"I know." His attention was drawn elsewhere, but he soon refocused on her. "But you need the attention of a physician, and we are far from safety, from Hussite controlled territory. We have to take the chance."

He was right. Her body was broken. She wouldn't be useful to anyone until her injuries were tended to.

Lord, be with us. Open the way to safety. I pray You will soften the heart of my father to receive us. Prepare the steps before us, Lord. And give us the strength to accept Your will, no matter what it may be. We want Your will to be done.

Karin struggled to maintain her concentration. The darkness warred with her senses, along with an uneasiness in her stomach.

Pavel was speaking. His chest rumbled under her ear.

Karin glanced up at him, but whatever his words, they were muffled. What did he say? She wanted so much to latch onto what he said. But the urge to close her eyes and let go became irresistible.

A loud banging sounded at the door. *Who would come in such a storm?* Lenka moved toward the entryway, preparing to receive the untimely visitor.

Moving through the great hall, she heard a man's desperate plea. The manservant at the door seemed to have difficulty finding words.

"I must see the Lord Bornekov or his wife. Their daughter needs help!" a young man shouted.

All sense of proper decorum flew from her mind. She rushed toward the door. A young man, soaked, stood in the doorway, holding Karin's limp body in his arms.

The manservant's eyes caught Lenka's, still he rushed off. Was he gone to retrieve her husband?

"Please," she said to the young man who bore her daughter, "bring her."

Who was this man? A friend? Or foe? Why did he have Karin? Where was Stepan? Had the hunting chateau been attacked? Was this man charged with her deliverance home?

Lenka led the man farther into the house, turning toward the stairs. Karin would be best suited in her own room.

They were but halfway up the stairs when Petr appeared.

"What is this?" His voice was harsh and his eyes set on the young man. Petr seemed prepared to attack. Did Petr know who the man was?

Lenka spoke, leaning until she was between Petr and the young man. "Karin is injured."

Petr's eyes widened. "There is a war. She is a traitor."

Did Petr speak from concern for them all? Karin as much as himself? Would he stop her? Was he so uncertain how to proceed?

Lenka would not have it.

"*She* is *my* daughter, and she needs our help. And I intend to do everything I can for her." The urge to protect Karin rose within Lenka. No matter who this man was, he had brought Karin home. She would ask questions later, but now was not the time. They must make sure Karin was all right.

Petr's eyes widened ever more. He stepped out of her way just as she pushed by him.

The young man followed, cradling Karin's body. Did he care for her daughter beyond the edict to protect her?

"Send for the doctor," Lenka called out to any servant standing nearby.

As they reached the top of the stairs, Lenka led the young man into the room that used to and, as far as she was concerned, always would belong to Karin. She indicated that he should lay Karin on the bed.

He did so with much care, releasing her weight to the support of the bed. And there was a hesitation in his movements as he stepped aside.

Lenka paid him little mind. She moved to Karin. Leaning over her daughter's body, she heard that her breaths were rattled. Her hands moved over her Karin's face—cold. This was not a good sign.

Karin's clothes and hair were damp.

A servant entered the room, bearing a pitcher of steaming water that she poured into the bedside bowl.

Rolling up her sleeves, Lenka glanced at her daughter's dirtied dress.

Without looking up, she inquired of the young man, "What happened?"

"I do not know the whole of it. I came upon her after the injury had occurred. I believe she fell down some embankment onto rocky ground below, but I cannot be certain."

Lenka nodded. This would mean injuries they could not see. She would have to remove the dress without shifting her too much. But she needed to clean and warm Karin's body in preparation for the doctor's inspection.

When Lenka looked up, it was to catch the eyes of the maidservant who had just finished emptying the pitcher. "I am in need of a knife." The simple request was made without explanation.

The young man stepped forward. "What are you ... ?"

Did he think Lenka would hurt her own child?

"I need to disrobe her." Lenka's eyes met his. The man's true feelings for her daughter were evident in his concerned expression. His eyes told all.

Would hers assure him that Karin would never know harm by her hands? "You should step outside."

He hesitated. Was he so loathed to leave Karin's side? Lingering a few moments more, he stared at Lenka's movements.

Lenka shifted the pillows, and reached for a cloth, dipping it in the warm water. Then she began cleaning Karin's face.

Karin moved under her mother's ministrations but was too slow to consciousness. She did not open her eyes while he remained in the room.

The maidservant soon returned with a cleaned knife from the kitchen. Lenka paused to make eye contact with the young man.

He nodded and took his leave.

Only then could Lenka give her full attention to her work.

Once Pavel was in the hall, a manservant appeared. Where had the man come from? Pavel was only vaguely aware of the happenings around him. He thoughts were on Karin. Would she be well? How badly was she injured?

Pavel stifled a yawn. The physical and emotional exertion had caught him. After questioning Luc, he had remained in Hradec Kralove. He just couldn't leave. Not without making sure she was safe. And then he had found her in their place. How he had wanted to reach out to her.

He almost had. But then Stepan had appeared. Now he thanked God that he had been watching over her, otherwise... Pavel did not want to think what might have happened had he not intervened.

"I have prepared a bath and acquired fresh clothes for you." The manservant indicated that Pavel should follow him.

He wanted to remain. But it would serve Karin better for him to clean up and return. Then the physician may be done.

Pavel nodded, stepping toward the servant. The man led him to a room nearby. Would this be his accommodation? After Karin's warning, he had only dared hope to speak with her parents, convince them to care for her well-being. How could he have thought the Countess would open their home?

His thoughts had only been for Karin. He hadn't even considered when or where he might find respite, a place to lay his head. In his room was a steaming bath. At a glimpse of the warmed water, he became all too aware of his body's aches.

The manservant moved to assist him to disrobe and, though he did not do so often, he allowed himself to be helped.

As much as his body longed to continue soaking in the warm water, he did not permit it. He lingered only long enough to ensure he was clean.

And he stood, rushing the servant along as he dried and helped Pavel into clothes. He found it difficult to force his trepidations down. How was Karin? Had she awakened?

No sooner had the manservant finished, then Pavel was out his door and back at Karin's.

A servant girl came from the room. He caught her attention.

She looked at him, but then lowered her eyes quickly. Had he halted her from her charge?

"Can you tell me how the Lady Karin fares?" Pavel attempted to keep his voice low and calm.

"She is awake, my lord. The doctor has just arrived."

"Thank you." He had hoped the doctor would be almost done with his examination. The weather was to blame. Rain creating mud and puddles, obstacles for horse and carriage alike.

The servant girl returned with clean strips of cloth and entered the room.

Pavel took a step. Would he trespass on Karin's bedchambers while she was examined? Was his concern for her so great? He paused; he must keep her privacy in tact.

As he turned away, Pavel heard the clunk of the door latch. That was odd. Why would they latch the door? He would ensure no other would attempt to intrude.

He stepped to the door, tracing fingers along the rough wood. And he heard Karin's voice. First as guttural moans and groans, but soon it became more clear expressions of pain.

His eyes widened. Must they injure her further? Should he go to her aid?

A scream tore through the hall. His hand landed on the latch. But it was for naught. The door would not budge. He was locked out.

Why would they have done this? Pavel thrust his hand against the door.

Her screams became more intense.

Pavel banged both hands against the door. Was something terrible happening to Karin? What brought her such pain?

"Karin!"

His cries were met with muffled screams. He threw himself against the door. "Let me in! Karin!"

A hand landed on his shoulder. He spun to find himself face to face with the earl.

When Pavel turned and met the earl's eyes, the older man took a step back. Were Pavel's eyes so intense? His movements so aggressive?

"She is all right," Karin's father said, meeting Pavel's eyes again. "We must trust the physician."

Pavel twisted away from the earl's gaze, chest heaving with emotion. He dipped his head. This would not do. Calm. Pushing down the emotions rising, filling his chest, he closed his eyes and breathed deeply.

Karin's father was right. On edge since the meeting with Luc, he had feared the worst. Of course the healer would not hurt Karin. As he had seen, Karin's mother would not let harm come to her daughter. He let out a long breath.

"Pavel," the earl spoke, his voice gentle. Was there some semblance of sympathy in his eyes? "There is nothing we can do for her right now."

Pavel's gaze drifted between the earl and the door. But Karin's father was not correct in his assumption. There *was* something he could do for Karin. Bowing his head and folding his hands, he began to pray. It did not matter that the earl could hear his mumbled whispers. The man stood, quiet and still, while Pavel pled to God for Karin's well-being.

An hour passed before they heard a sound at the door. How long had he waited and prayed out here? Surely he had lived days in the hall. The sound of the bar lifting was unmistakable.

The door swung open.

A portly, balding man with a rounded nose and small glasses made his way out of the room, speaking to the Countess.

Karin's father and Pavel were fairly crowding the doctor.

The physician met the earl's gaze. He halted his conversation with Karin's mother. "My lord, it is always a pleasure. Even if the circumstances are not ideal."

"Agreed, doctor."

The healer opened his mouth to continue, but then set eyes on Pavel.

Pavel hardly noticed. He attempted to peer past the doctor and the countess, and into the room.

"This is Pavel," the earl explained. "A trusted friend. You may speak freely in front of him."

The mention of his name brought Pavel back to awareness of the people in front of him.

He nodded toward the physician, grateful for the earl's words.

"I set the injured bones and wrapped them. The Lady must be immobile for the next two weeks. We may have a better idea at that time as to when she can return to normal activities. Keep her warm, lest she catch cold and further complicate her progress. And see to it she is fed well. She has neglected herself."

The doctor's gaze no longer moved between Karin's parents, but rested on the countess. "When she wakes again, she will be in pain. Encourage her to drink as much of the herbs in a tea as she can. That will ease her discomfort."

Karin's mother nodded.

"Thank you, doctor." the earl's words were more confident than Pavel would have expected. How concerned was he?

"We appreciate you coming with all due haste." The earl's shoulders relaxed. Was he thusly relieved then? To hear that Karin would be well?

Karin's father shifted his attention to the countess and Pavel. Was this an opening to ask any questions of the physician? Pavel had none.

The countess did not respond either.

"Come, doctor, I will show you out."

The doctor nodded. Bowing but slightly to the others, he then moved after Karin's father toward the stairs.

The countess and Pavel were alone.

Pavel's eyes were focused on the bed, straining to see anything he could in the dimness of the bedchambers. Could he go to her? Allow his eyes to confirm what the doctor had said—that she was indeed well?

But this was not his house, and it would be inappropriate for him to rush into her bedchambers unbidden. So, he stood, poised as if he were a caged cat prepared to jump at the first sign of freedom.

The countess moved a step closer to Pavel. Could she sense his turmoil?

"Pavel," she spoke, her voice soft. "I am sure your presence would only strengthen her. Please, sit with her."

He met her gaze, nodding before he stepped into the room.

Karin's mother followed Pavel inside, keeping a step behind as he approached the bed. She touched his arm and pointed to a chair nearby.

A maidservant swept through the room, clearing out Karin's soiled clothing and the cloths used to clean her body and wounds.

"Sharka," the countess spoke to her, "You may leave those. Please station yourself just outside the room, and keep the door open."

Pavel's was intent on Karin's resting figure, or perhaps he would have thanked the Countess for permitting him some privacy while protecting Karin's reputation.

"If you need anything, just ask," the Countess said.

But he was not truly listening. He almost did not take note when she took her leave. Was she, too, bound for a warm bath and the comfort of her bed?

Karin slept. She appeared to be in a deep, peaceful rest. The screams from earlier echoed in his mind. Was it possible those sounds came from this sleeping beauty mere moments ago?

Had she been bathed? Her skin shone bright. It also betrayed the abrasions from the attack she had endured.

Red-blonde hair, still damp, appeared a shade darker. It splayed on the pillow, framing her face and delicate features all the more. After their separation and his fear for her life, the last two days had seemed surreal.

Now that they were together, it all came crashing down on him. Hot tears stung his face, but he did not bother to wipe them away. His hands ached to touch Karin, to confirm that she was not just a vision. But if he reached out to her, would the spell be broken? And so, he sat by her side, caught in indecision as the minutes passed into hours.

Stepan's footfalls crunched on the gravel. His steps bore him closer to the prison. Would he actually go in? He paused. What did he hope to gain?

Glancing at the structure only steps away, he reflected on his decision to come. But he had to know. What was the truth? Everything he thought he knew had been a lie. Karin, Pavel, his mother...

Raising a hand, he knocked on the door. Shuffling within was his answer. Soon after, a man opened the door. Not the Constable. One of his deputies?

His eyes were glazed and he appeared confused. Had Stepan's knock awakened him?

"I need to see one of the prisoners." Stepan's eyes held the man's. How would he be received?

"Do you not know the hour?"

"I do. And I apologize, but I must speak with—"

The man folded his arms across his chest, rising to his full height. He was a rather intimidating picture. "And who are you that I should make such an exception?"

A fire lit in Stepan. This man may be large, but he would not be put off. He could not. "I am the son of the Viscount Vlastik Dvorak. And you, sir, will let me pass." He stepped forward until his features were surely in the candlelight from within.

The deputy glared at him. But could not refuse. After a moment, the man moved aside.

Once within the confines of the jail, the man's eyes narrowed. "And who, praytell, are you to disturb?"

"Luc Reznik."

The deputy gave him a long look before leading Stepan farther in.

To the back of the prison and down a set of stairs, the man went until they reached a lone door in the depths of the building.

Stepan glanced within. A figure lay on the opposite side of the cell, resting. The deputy opened the door and let Stepan pass, a heavy clange sounded behind him as the way was resealed.

As Stepan approached Luc, he stirred, shifting in his sleep. Was he awake?

Luc rubbed his face and then turned toward the intrusion. He had not been treated well. Marks on his face indicated that he had been the brunt of someone's anger.

A thickness filled Stepan's chest and his face heated. But he tried to not let it show. He was here by the deputy's mercy, after all.

"Come back for more?" Luc's voice was ragged, weak. But he spoke with more confidence than one would expect. Could he not see Stepan? The cell was rather dim.

"It's me—Stepan."

"Stepan?" Luc said, unsure. Had his memory been affected? Or was he so surprised to see his one-time friend?

"Yes."

Luc rose and turned toward Stepan. "Why are you here?" His voice caught. Was he fearful? Did he think Stepan had come to hurt him?

Stepan frowned. "I have to know the truth...about my mother."

Luc dropped his head. Would he not tell?

"Please, Luc. I...I have to know."

Luc glanced at him. His eyes darkened. What went through his mind? Was that sadness toward Stepan? Did Luc feel sorry for him?

Stepan would not have it. He continued to hold Luc's eyes. Would that communicate that he was not pitiable?

"What do you want to know?"

Stepan raised his chin. "Everything."

Luc sighed. "I will tell you what I know."

That was all Stepan wanted—answers.

Raising a hand to touch his forehead, Luc winced. Had he opened a cut?

Stepan watched, noting the fresh red on Luc's fingertips.

Luc shrugged. Did he care so little? Then he began, "Your mother wanted Karin dead. I do not know for what reason. Our...relationship was built on demands. She did not readily share information with me."

Stepan searched his memory. As she was taken, his mother screamed that she would not share her position. Had his mother suspected Karin to be his father's mistress? Certainly not.

"She..." Luc paused. Was he deciding if he should continue? At length, he sighed again. As if somehow resigned. "She found out...something...about my family—a secret that must remain hidden. And if I would do as she bid, she would remain silent."

Stepan could not pull his gaze away. Did Luc speak true?

Luc continued, "I did not know what to do. And I chose poorly. It was a choice between my family or a girl who meant nothing to me." His head hung again. "But it was more than that. I bartered with my soul."

Stepan nodded. Would his mother go to such lengths?

"Under her direction, I sawed through the wheel joints of the carriage, which is why it went over the cliff, almost taking Karin and Pavel with it. I loosened Karin's saddle and put the burr underneath to cause a horse accident. And, as you know, I was told to stab her in the night."

The recounting of these events made Stepan's skin crawl. How could his mother be so heartless? How could Luc agree to such actions?

"All of this was planned by the Viscountess. And executed by me... for that, I know I must be punished."

Stepan eyes widened. He had wanted the truth, said he needed to hear it, but had he been ready for it? How could the mother he loved so dearly be so depraved?

"And what will become of you?" Stepan's words were softer than he would have thought.

"I will stand trial in the next couple of days and be sentenced. They will punish me, but I will not be hanged since..." His words trailed off.

"Since they have my mother." Stepan met his eyes once more.

Luc nodded, averting his gaze. Did he feel bad for Stepan?

Stepan's gaze, too, shifted downward. What would become of his mother?

Pavel awoke with a start. He jerked to attention, prepared to fend off the attack he had been resisting mere moments before. Looking around, he found himself in bedchambers. He was safe. It had all been a dream.

His back ached, his shoulders stiff. How long had he been leaning over in an unnatural position? Perhaps hours. The rather uncomfortable chair had been his place of vigil as he watched over Karin. Turning toward the head of the bed, his eyes once again sought her.

Green eyes met his gaze.

"Karin!" He fell to his knees, hands seeking one of hers. How long had she been watching him? How could he have fallen asleep? He had intended to sit with her for some time and then retire to his assigned chambers. But he had been reluctant to do so. It had been impossible to part from her.

"You should be in bed," she croaked.

"I could not leave you." His kept his voice soft. "I was worried."

Karin searched his eyes. There was more in her thoughts. What were they? Would she share? She licked her lips. Was she parched?

"Water," she rasped as she shifted to sit. She cried out.

"Still yourself!" Pavel slipped his arms beneath her shoulders, lowering her down with as much gentleness as he could muster. "You must not try to move."

The servant girl Sharka stepped out of the shadows.

Pavel met her gaze. He had forgotten she remained to chaperone. Guilt filled him. She had been kept from sleep.

Sharka filled a small glass and moved to Karin's other side.

Pavel nodded. "Let's raise her."

With great care, he raised her torso while the maidservant propped pillows behind her back.

Karin bit her lip. Was she trying to keep from crying out? The discomfort was written all over her face.

When Pavel released her weight onto the pillows, they both let out a breath.

She smiled at him before Sharka brought the cup to her lips. Karin pulled in the water in long sips. Then she leaned back, closing her eyes.

"I will wake the Countess," Sharka said, moving toward the door.

"Let her rest," Karin called after the girl.

Sharka halted. "I was instructed to alert her the minute you awoke."

"There is no harm in waiting until morning. See," Karin said, tilting her head in the direction of the window. "It will be dawn in a couple of hours. Give her that much rest. I assure you, I am well enough."

Sharka hesitated.

"Could you prepare the lady some of the tea the doctor left and perhaps some broth?" Pavel spoke with more firmness.

"And some bread from the kitchen." Karin matched her tone to his.

"Of course." Sharka still seemed unsure of her decision. At last, she nodded and stepped toward the door once more, leaving both of the doors to the bedchambers open.

Pavel reached tentative fingers forth to caress Karin's face and moved a stray hair from her forehead. "How are you truly?"

She searched his eyes. What did she seek? "Weary and pained. But thankful...so thankful, Pavel. God has been gracious."

253

"Yes, He has." Pavel's voice broke.

And I ask, Father, that You continue to sustain us through the trials ahead. There may be even greater obstacles to overcome, but Pavel did not wish to worry Karin. For now, she was safe, and that was all that mattered.

"You seem tired." She tried to reach up and graze his chin with the back of her hand but fell short, grimacing from the effort.

He caught her hand and held it to his face.

"Do not worry yourself so, my lady. I am perfectly content as I am."

How long did they remain as they were, gazing at one another? Pavel was unsure. But they were together. A great burden had been lifted.

Footsteps drawing nearer broke the spell. Sharka had returned with the tea and broth. Setting the tray on the stand by the bed, she prepared to feed Karin.

"Allow me," Pavel said, reaching for the bowl.

"Pavel," Karin admonished him. "I would prefer you return to your rest."

"Let me ensure you get something into your stomach, and then I will go. I promise."

Pavel spooned broth into her mouth.

Karin swallowed it, closing her eyes. Was she so calmed by the warm liquid?

He continued to feed her until the broth was gone. Then he helped her sip the tea until it, too, was gone. She leaned back on her pillow. Her green eyes seemed brighter.

Sharka took the empty dishes away.

Pavel stroked the side of Karin's face, allowing his fingers to graze her hair. Her eyes slid closed and she leaned her head in the direction of Pavel's caresses.

He shifted the pillows behind her, maneuvering her back down to a more comfortable sleeping position. Leaning over her, he pressed a light kiss to her lips. "Sweet dreams."

Pavel rose, pulling his torso to a standing position. He could not deny the weary protests of his body. Assured Karin was resting, comfortable, he decided he should go. Resisting the urge to touch her again, he pulled himself from her bedchambers and toward his allotted room for the remainder of the night. As he threw himself into the bed for sleep, he rested in knowing that he would dream of his beloved.

Karin opened her eyes. She was sore all over. As she glanced around, she took in the faces of the small gathering. Pavel, as well as her parents, were nearby. What words were passed between them?

Mother sat on the edge of the bed and Father took a chair nearby.

"*Katka.*" Mother stroked Karin's face. "We were so worried."

A tear escaped Karin's eye at her mother's tenderness. "I am sorry I gave you cause for concern."

"It is all right now. You are safe."

Karin nodded, keeping her movements slight.

"What caused you to become injured?" Father's eyes were difficult to read.

Mother opened her mouth. Would she protest? But she stilled her lips.

Karin's gaze shifted between her mother, father, and Pavel. How much should she tell her parents?

"Will you excuse us, Pavel?" Father said, rising and moving between her and Pavel. Had he misinterpreted her hesitation?

Pavel met Father's eyes, his blue orbs shone with determination. She did not believe he would leave willingly.

"No," Karin said, her voice firm. "He stays."

Silence filled the space between them all as tension thickened between the two men.

"I apologize," Father said, his words seeming forced. "I only thought of your comfort."

Pavel moved closer to Karin.

"I understand. But there is nothing I can say that Pavel cannot hear."

Mother nodded. "We understand that now. Please do tell us what happened." She was ever the peacemaker between Karin and Father.

Karin's eyes met Pavel's. If only she could pull what strength she needed from him. She did not want to revisit those memories, but her parents needed to know what had transpired between she and Stepan.

Pavel slid a hand forward, capturing one of hers.

It was enough for her to gain confidence. She recounted her last hours on the chateau grounds and Stepan's maddening attack on her life. Her parents would have to agree this nullified any arrangement of marriage made.

"It seems Stepan returned to his senses." Father spoke at last.

Karin's eyes widened. She struggled to find a response. It was true, but had her father not heard everything else she said?

"Perhaps," she said, hesitation in her voice. "However, I will not marry him."

"You...what?" Father rose, an edge to his voice. "Karin, this civil unrest will end soon. This Hussite uprising will not last. Then things with the Viscount and Stepan must be made right again."

"Be that as it may, Father, I cannot allow you to barter with my future."

Father's face reddened. "You are a headstrong girl, Karin! You have grand ideas about love. You will need your family, too. Trust me, you do not want to turn your back on us now."

"That is not my desire. But I will do everything in my power to resist if you force me to marry Stepan." She pushed every bit of firmness into her voice.

Mother stood, stepping in front of Father before he could respond. "I think Karin is quite tired, lord husband. Shall we discuss this after we have let all of what she has told us settle in our minds?"

Father's eyes moved to Karin. He opened his mouth, then closed it. Was he preparing to argue further? In the end, he seemed more ready to listen to Mother's words. Perhaps he was more practiced at it. Either way, his anger waned enough for him to turn his back to Karin and storm from the room.

Mother threw a sympathetic glance toward Karin before following Father.

"Stubborn girl!" Petr said, swearing, as his wife escorted him into her cabinet.

"My lord husband, I plead with you not to be so harsh. She has been through much these last few days."

Petr's eyes caught hers. They were darker than she had seen them. "Yet she refuses to see reason. You know as well as I, she will not change her mind once it is set."

"A trait I know all too well," Lenka dared, offering her husband a small smile.

Sharka opened the door. "My lady, did you call?"

"Yes, I would have you bring some refreshment."

Lenka watched her husband as he shifted, turning his back to the servant girl lest she see his anger. She hoped against hope that a break in the strong, emotion-driven words, a chance to take some deep breaths, would calm him. And then he might see reason, and compromise.

However, as Sharka left, Petr's words were no longer as harsh or loud, but they had just as much emotion.

Petr turned back toward his wife after the door closed, and spoke in an even tone. "If she wants to ruin her life on this pursuit of the Hussite life, I cannot stop her. Nor, apparently, can I change her mind. Maybe I should turn her in to the next patrol that knocks on our door. Maybe they can straighten that crooked thinking of hers."

Lenka worked to cover her reaction, but it was difficult to stop her words. "You cannot be serious! Turn in your own daughter?"

"We have sheltered her from the consequences of her actions for far too long."

Lenka saw in her husband's eyes that he meant what he said. Her breath to caught in her throat. Dare she speak against him? Rail against his form of justice? It would be futile. He had spoken, and his word bound her.

She bit at her lip to keep her words of protest in.

Petr crossed the room and out of her cabinet, leaving her to her thoughts and fears.

Pavel sat on the edge of the bed next to Karin and slid an arm around her shoulders.

"You were brave," he said, gazing into her eyes.

Her lip trembled. Was it her father's words that stirred so many emotions? Or his actions? Perhaps both. As he searched her eyes, he saw that, while anger lay at the surface, there was confusion and hurt underneath.

"All will be well." He pulled his arm out to cup her face and shifted his body to face him.

"No. My father is set against my future. Against us."

"He only wants the future he planned for you. A safe future." Pavel softened his voice and touched her hair.

"He refuses to understand. That future can never be. How can I make him see that?" Tears welled in her eyes.

"I do not know." He took her hands in his. "But, I do not know how long it is safe for us to linger. The country is being divided up, and we are not in an area friendly to Hussites."

"What will happen if we are found?" Her eyes displayed the concern within. A concern he shared. But he had to be strong. For her.

"I do not want you to worry. Set your mind on your recovery. As soon as you are well enough, we must make our way into Hussite-controlled territory. It will not be an easy journey, I fear, and I cannot imagine how we will go except as man and wife." He squeezed her hands, his eyes still on hers.

"Are we to pose as a married couple?" She arched a brow.

"No, Karin," he raised a hand to touch her cheek. "I mean to say we are to elope."

"Elope? But I thought..." Her brows furrowed.

He shook his head. "Many things have changed since those things were spoken. This is the only way for us now."

Karin's confusion melted into happiness. Then something else passed across her features. Was she saddened that the union would not be celebrated by family and friends? But this was truly the only way. Would she give all of it up for the to be with him?

She threw her arms around him.

Pavel drew her closer with care, careful of her injured ribs, and kissed her.

Awareness struck him. They were not chaperoned. He pulled back with great reluctance.

"There are preparations I must make," Pavel rose and pressed a kiss to her forehead.

Karin nodded, reaching for his hands one more.

He slid them into hers.

She squeezed them, gazing into his eyes. Much was there in the depths of her green orbs. But he must go.

He tugged and she released his hands. Then he stepped toward the door and out into the hall, leaving her with her thoughts.

The hope of becoming Pavel's wife had been renewed. How long ago was it that she and Pavel had dreamed of marrying—a dream dashed by her father's plans for her to join with the house of Dvorak. Karin had been so devastated, but this, too, seemed a lifetime ago. Now, the dream had new life and new hope. She and Pavel were taking their futures into their own hands. No interference from her father.

Knocks on the door brought Karin back to the present.

"Come," she called. Had Pavel forgotten something? Did he have news already?

The figure that stepped through the door was not Pavel, though. It was her mother. She entered the room with solemn face and downcast eyes. Was something amiss? Her mother never showed so much emotion. Was she troubled?

"Mother?"

She rushed toward Karin, falling on the bed next to her and taking Karin's hands in hers. "Karin... My *katka*."

Were those tears in her eyes?

"Mother?" Karin's voice rose.

"Your father is angry. He says he will not protect you from the patrols."

"Patrols?"

Groups of Royalist guards seeking out Hussites and Hussite sympathizers."

Karin's heart beat faster. Patrols seeking out Hussites? Why? To what end? This was a time of war. And, as Pavel had said, they were not in Hussite-controlled territory.

"If they come, you must renounce that you are a Hussite," Mother pled. "That is your only hope."

How could she respond? She did not want to upset her mother further, but she was determined she would trust God. Taking a deep breath, she caught her mother's eyes. "I will not lie. It isn't that I am not afraid...I am. But I cannot lie about who I am. I will not."

Tears slid down Mother's face. "Then they will take you! And I do not know what will happen to you, my *katka*."

"It will be all right, Mother. Trust me. Trust God. He is on our side. I will pray He will soften Father's heart."

Mother sniffled. "I fear your father is as stubborn as you."

Karin stared out the window at the familiar grounds of her parent's estate. This was her home, wasn't it? It had always been. But the new situation with her father, it would no longer be. Her chest ached. The thought of never returning to this place was...difficult to take in. But she would have a new one. With Pavel. Perhaps not made of stone and wood, but of the heart.

Taps on the door sounded across the space.

"Come." She had given up trying to guess who it may be.

Pavel stuck his head through the narrow opening in the door. His eyes swept the room. Was he seeking someone? Or ensuring they were alone.

His gaze rested on her and he smiled. Then he stepped into the room and crossed to her, seating himself in a chair next to the bed.

Karin continued to gaze past him and out the window.

Pavel remained silent.

She wanted him to. Why wouldn't he speak? Was he letting her dwell in her thoughts for a few moments longer?

"Something has disheartened you, Karin," he said after allowing several moments of silence. "Tell me."

She knew full well what Pavel's response to her news would be, but she was not sure she was ready for what it meant.

Karin met his eyes, determined to share what her mother had disclosed. "Pavel," she started slowly, measuring her words. "There are patrols looking for Hussites. Mother informed me that my father will not protect us if they come. Rather, it is his intention to turn us over."

Pavel's eyes darkened. "Then we must leave before dawn. Are you well enough?"

Karin nodded, tears filling her eyes. Would she ever see her

261

parents again? As much as Father could anger her, she did not wish to part on such terms and live the rest of her life in a damaged relationship. *Father, please find a way to heal our broken fellowship and bring peace between us...somehow...someday.*

"We must travel light," he warned. "Take only what you absolutely need. My parents will help us once we reach Tabor."

Karin nodded. The sadness still thick in her.

Pavel offered her a smile, placing a hand on hers. "At least we will be together."

"And that is all I need."

CHAPTER 14

DANGER

A mist fell over the fields around the Bornekov home. The rolling hills had been a cherished playground for a young girl, all the more so when it came time for her to learn to ride her first horse, practicing a trot, then cantor, and finally gallop, conquering each in turn. And on this dark, damp night, hoofbeats once again fell in these same meadows.

The sound breaking through the field was not the joyful noise generated by the play of a child, but by the clanging of men in dark uniforms—men with a purpose, men with a mission.

They slowed, approaching the large structure looming ahead. This was but the next stop on their list. These men were chosen for this task not because they savored the weightiness of their orders, but because they respected the call of duty. It was not that they were ruthless men by nature, but they would obey their orders or die trying.

As they neared the entry, they pulled their horses to a full stop. The leader among them was the tallest, most intimidating of the brood. He dismounted first and approached the door. His fist landed on the oak of the door in a loud boom three times. It would be a few minutes before a shaken servant answered the door, but one would come. Watching, their leader stepped back and drew his sword partially out of its sheath, just enough so the metal gleamed in the moonlight. They waited.

The servant who answered the door was like all the others—night shift, robe pulled on in haste, half open, and a candle, shaking, betraying the unsteady hand of its bearer. As he opened the door wider to take in the scene, he almost dropped the candle at his first glimpse of the tall, uniformed guard with his weapon at the ready, surrounded by a half-dozen other such men still mounted on their horses. But he dared not slam the door, as he had most certainly seen the royal insignia on the uniform.

Their leader always seemed to enjoy that part of the exchange a little too much. He lowered his voice a few notches below his normal tenor.

"Bid your master come to receive us. We have come on an errand from the king."

The servant tripped over himself backing into the house. Was he so determined not to turn his back on the man with the sword? Though the officer did not use any words indicating immediacy, the servants always took the display of the weapon to mean just that.

The other men dismounted and moved to secure their horses, as it would take a little longer for the master of the house to be roused and made appropriate to receive messengers from the king. But, come he did, with all due haste a man of his station could afford, circumstances permitting. The earl was able to disguise however intimidated he might have been. The nobility was well-practiced in this.

"Gentlemen," the earl said, as he arrived at the door. He, too, was in his night shift and robe, but in much better presentation. "To what do I owe this distinguished honor?"

"We have come to search the premises for Hussites."

Karin had not been able to sleep. The argument with her father was too fresh on her mind. What would he think when the house awoke and found them gone? Would he ever forgive her?

Lord, mend our broken relationship. Soften my father's heart and guide me. It is not my wish that a rift exist between us.

What would the journey hold for she and Pavel? What dangers would they face as they traversed hostile territory? *Oh, Lord, be with us. Keep Your mighty hand on us.*

Her gaze moved about the room. Would she ever see these bedchambers again? Or roam these grounds? This place was as familiar to her as her own reflection. And she would miss it. The people, the servants, the halls and rooms she could maneuver blindfolded, and mother... No, it would be best if she not linger on that thought.

For her sacrifice was not in vain. She made a choice—to leave all of this behind to follow Pavel, to marry him. They had been through much, had overcome...she would not give up what they had for her homesick heart. No, she would have a new home. With him.

After several hours of lying in bed shifting—distracted by her thoughts and uncomfortable with the pain in her limbs—Karin forced herself to sit up. Rising without assistance was difficult. But, inch by inch, she attained greater height. At last, she sat.

From here it would be easier to gain her feet. As much as she wanted to call for a servant, she held her tongue. She would need to accustom herself to moving about on her own. There would not be help for her on their journey, except for Pavel, whose attention would be on many other things. No, she needed to become much more independent.

Karin swung her legs over the side of the bed with great care. Then she tentatively put weight upon them, almost toppling when she did so. Grasping the side of the bed, she maintained her footing. And, little by little, she pressed more weight onto her feet until she was certain her limbs would sustain it.

Once she stood with some confidence, she made her way to the window seat. As she approached the bench-like space, she leaned onto its sturdy structure. Then eased her body onto it. Her eyes sought the sky beyond. How close was dawn?

In the darkness, it was difficult to make out the familiar shapes of the rolling hills. Or was it because something was different? Something moved upon the horizon... Leaning closer to the opening did nothing to increase her visual range, still she did so, narrowing her eyes to focus her vision.

The movement upon the hillside drew near. Approaching. Did it? Or was it her imaginings? She held her breath.

Thud, thud, thud.

The sound was faint but unmistakably at the door below! Who would come to see Father in the dead of night? Should she go for Pavel?

A creak, though faint, sounded and the front door opened, light spilling onto the area around the entrance. The intruders were just visible in the faint candlelight.

Karin scanned the dark figures. What did they want? A flash drew her eyes. Metal? A sword? These men came armed? She honed her vision on the figure at the door. He was tall, dark...looming. This was all the information she could make out from this distance. Were they here for her and Pavel?

Drawing in a ragged breath, she attempted to still her racing heartbeat. She had to get Pavel.

Karin made her way to the back of the bedchambers. The door was just steps away, but her movements were slow, careful. It would not do to injure herself further. As she reached for the latch, it moved under her hand.

She jumped back as the door opened, backing away and opening her mouth to scream.

A hand clamped down on her mouth, and an arm grabbed her, pulling her against the door, closing it.

"Shh, it is all right, Karin," Pavel's familiar voice spoke into her ear.

She relaxed in his arms, nodding against his hand.

He shifted her to hold her more securely and removed his hand. "It is a patrol."

She froze. Her worst fear confirmed. What were she and Pavel going to do? There were so many of them.

Taking a few deep breaths, she attempted to pull the strength she did not have from Pavel.

"We have to go. Now. And we must leave everything behind."

She nodded again.

Pavel released her and then opened the door but slightly. Was he listening? What did he hear?

Karin held her breath.

Turning back toward her, he said, "They are in the house. We cannot use the main stairs. Is there another way down?"

Karin nodded and whispered, "There is an old servant staircase in the library."

Pavel met her eyes. His nod was almost imperceptible. He took her hand and moved through the slim opening.

As they stepped into the hall, Karin listened with every silent step. Her heartbeat quickened when she heard voices. Then there were footsteps on the stairs. The men had mounted the stairway! She and Pavel would have to pass the stairs to get to the library.

We will never make it! Did Pavel know?

Karin glanced at his features.

Pavel frowned and looked up and down the hallway. Then he urged her to quicken her pace.

She did so, as much as she dared while still keeping her footfalls silent.

As they passed the stairs, Karin saw a light approaching and heard the men closing in. Surely they would be spotted if they tried to make it to the library three doors down.

Following Pavel's lead, she pressed her body to the wall farthest from the stairs and chanced making it past another room to slip into her mother's cabinet.

Karin cursed her white nightdress. If not for her light-colored, easily spotted form, they might have been able to chance going farther. She scanned the room for places to hide while Pavel listened at the door. The reality was that they had but one chance: that the men would search the rooms on the other side of the hallway first.

She held her breath and prayed.

"The bedrooms first," a gruff voice said.

A loud knocking sounded through the hall, Three thuds like before. Then the doors were flung open.

Pavel grabbed Karin's hand and pulled her into the hall. The backs of the men were visible at Karin's bedchamber door and another guest room.

It was eerie, but Karin did not have much time to think on it, as Pavel took advantage of the soldiers' focus being on the contents of the rooms to pull Karin into the library.

Once inside, Karin walked to a shelf in the corner and pulled a lever. The bookcase opened to reveal the narrow stairs that were no longer in use, but had been a favorite plaything for her and her childhood playmates.

"Someone was in this room, but has gone. They must have seen us coming," Karin and Pavel heard from the hallway. "Split up. Search the house and send someone to the stables."

Karin caught Pavel's serious look before he moved to descend the stairs. He grabbed for Karin's hand and moved as fast as possible.

Making every effort to keep up, Karin tried to ignore the pain tearing through her torso. As she neared the bottom of the stairs, she moved her hands from holding the skirt of her nightdress to her side. Moving down the stairs with such speed, the nightdress became twisted in her legs, and she lost her balance, pitching to the side. She fell down the last three steps.

Pavel was on his knees in a moment. "Karin!"

She tried to catch her breath. "I'm all right," she managed.

He didn't believe her. One look at her face told a different story. Pavel helped her to her feet, but when she tried to put weight on her right foot, she crumpled.

"You have to go without me," she cried. "Just go!"

How could she even think he could go on with her?

"Your fate will be mine," he said with finality. Leaning over, he reached under her knees and picked her up.

Pavel continued with as much speed as he could bearing her injured body. He rushed to the stables. They arrived before there was any sign of a soldier. But they were on borrowed time. The soldier would be here soon.

Setting Karin in a stall, Pavel began to saddle a horse. His fingers fumbled more than he would have liked, but as the seconds passed, he was nearly done.

"You there!" he heard from behind. "Stop!"

Pavel held up his hands and turned. One of the soldiers stood behind him, sword drawn, moving toward him.

"We should make our way back into the hou—"

There was a thud, and the man sank to the ground.

Karin stood behind the soldier's slumped body, leaning on a shovel. Had she just struck the man?

Pavel closed the gap between them, taking the shovel and kissing the top of her head. Then he lifted her once again.

"Let us make haste." He set her on the horse. They were going to make it!

Just then, men came from all directions. Pavel was wrested from two sides.

Karin's horse shifted nervously, causing the men to give it wide berth.

Go! Pavel's silently pled. This was Karin's chance.

Her eyes met his. *Your fate will be mine.*

Karin stilled the horse and took her hands off the reins.

"I need help dismounting," she said. "I am injured."

"I will assist with that," the earl said as he stepped into view from behind the men. "And I thank you for helping me find my daughter."

The earl walked to where Karin sat on her horse and pulled her down. "My daughter and her betrothed were clearly out for a moonlight horse ride. Unchaperoned. I am most disappointed, and most dishonored that my disgrace will now be made public."

The men appeared confused.

"You thought...oh, be assured not!" Karin's father put on his most jovial laugh. "I have nothing but the utmost respect and complete loyalty to the crown. You would not find me harboring Hussite sympathizers! My daughter and her betrothed are pushing the boundaries of propriety. Though I would not rely on them for good judgment in light of their behavior this night, I assure you they are not Hussite sympathizers. If you doubt me, I invite you to check their rooms."

Karin's father chose his words with care. He was not, in truth, lying about their identities. For they were not sympathizers, but Hussites. But would he be so bold to allow their rooms searched? Did Karin have incriminating materials within?

"We will do so." The leader seemed agitated that his chase had not given way to his imagined prey. "What happened here?" he indicated the soldier on the ground.

"He came after us with a sword," came Pavel's honest reply. "We defended ourselves."

"If I may, I would like to move my daughter and her guest to my solar while you search their rooms and anywhere else you choose," the earl requested. "We have much to discuss."

The leader of the group nodded, a deep frown upon his features. Did he not believe the earl's story? He indicated for two of his men to follow the small group.

Karin's father hoisted her into his arms with ease. And so, he carried her, Pavel following, then tailed by the two guardsmen, back into the house and toward the earl's solar.

Once inside the solar, the earl sought a comfortable chair to set Karin on. The two guards stayed by the door across the room. The earl made a show of examining Karin's leg and ankle, while Pavel came over to offer what assistance he could.

With Pavel's body blocking the guards' view, Karin dared to whisper to her father between grunts of pain from his prodding.

"Father!"

He tilted his head.

"How can you let them search our rooms? There are writings..." She let her voice trail.

"While you two were having your little escapade, I was busy with my own." Tilting his head, he indicated the fire.

Pavel craned his neck, glancing into the fire. But he could not see what the earl might have been referring to. Still, he caught the meaning. The earl had scavenged their rooms and burned every incriminating thing he found.

Karin breathed a sigh of relief and Pavel prayed that Karin's father had, indeed, found everything.

The earl glared at both of them. "If either of you has more on you, now is the time." Just then, Karin's father must have touched a tender spot on her ankle, as Karin let out a yelp before she could contain it, biting her lip to keep from crying out again.

"Can you not see my daughter needs a doctor?" the earl said to the guards, rising and walking to the guards.

Pavel moved a chair closer to Karin so he could sit. He took her hand in his.

"I have done all I can. Now, do you want to be responsible for further pain and injury to my daughter because she was denied the care of a doctor?" the earl continued his rant.

The guards glanced at one another and then at Karin.

Karin chewed on her lip, eyes shut.

Had her father's manipulations of her ankle made things worse?

The guards conversed between themselves, and one left the

room. Did he leave to ask their commander if a doctor could be sent for? Pavel hoped so.

Karin's father caught the other guard in a plea. "My wife may have herbs which can ease my daughter's pain. If I could but bring my wife here..."

It was a ridiculous request. Of course the guard would not leave, nor would he let the earl depart his watchful eye. Perhaps all of this was to distract the guard.

Karin turned to Pavel.

His gaze was fixed on the guard, but he began pulling a small slip of paper from his pocket. Pavel moved his hands over her hair as if to soothe her and leaned in to press a kiss to her forehead.

Then he whispered, "These are the names of safe houses between here and Hussite-controlled territory. I cannot burn it. We need these names if we are to survive." They could not be found with this paper on them, but this paper was too valuable to dispose of.

Karin licked her lips. She accepted the parchment and rolled it, making it quite small. As she watched the exchange between her father and the guard, she let down one side of her hair and re-braided it, concealing the paper within the braid. It was risky, but what choice did they have?

The other guard returned and spoke with the earl. Karin's father seemed somewhat satisfied with what the guard had to say. Turning, he then moved toward Pavel and Karin.

"They have sent a manservant for the doctor," the earl said. "But you two and the solar will have to be searched before the doctor arrives. So, prepare yourselves."

Pavel and Karin exchanged a look. Clasping her hands, Pavel brought his forehead down to rest on Karin's.

"I love you," Pavel said.

"I love you, too," Karin replied.

After a brief moment, he brushed her lips with his.

Karin winced as the doctor moved her ankle this way and that, inspecting her full range of motion. The doctor had arrived and was ushered into the foyer to wait, while the solar was searched along with Karin and Pavel.

Determined to find something amiss in this house, the commander was certain that the trouble centered on Karin and Pavel. But, search as they may, they had been unable to find anything incriminating within the house or on any person. So, they had no choice but to take their leave of the Bornekov residence.

Still, the commander had his own way of letting the master of the house know it was not over and that they would still be watched. Upon exiting the house, he dug a dagger into the door, marking the house with a bold letter "H" scraped across the front. His gut had not led him astray yet.

Now the only fight Karin found herself waging was with the doctor—not so much a fight as a willing surrender followed by a torture session. If only he would ask for information, Karin would certainly give it up.

"It is not broken," the doctor concluded, "but it is sprained."

"What does this mean for me?" Karin asked.

"I will wrap it, but you must not walk on it for one additional week."

Karin did not like this plan. She and Pavel should be leaving the next day, but they must be married first. Never had she imagined a wedding day in which she was carried down the aisle.

"In the meantime...," the doctor began.

"Yes, I know. Drink this tea," she interrupted the doctor as he was reaching in his bag.

He nodded. "As needed for pain."

Karin bobbed her head. Her eyes sought Pavel's. How could she communicate an apology? This recent intrusion had to make him all the more eager to get underway.

Pavel's features were not anxious or frustrated, though. They communicated nothing but his concern and love for her. For that, she was grateful. She would have hated to feel even more like a burden.

The doctor had continued speaking, but Karin was so lost in Pavel's eyes she had failed to catch any of it. Had her mother gathered the important information? Had he even said anything of significance?

When the doctor stood, Karin directed her attention back toward him. "Thank you, doctor."

He took her hand. "Be sure to rest. I will see you in a week."

She nodded. This was perhaps the last time she would ever see this man.

Mother escorted the doctor out of the room.

Pavel came to sit on the edge of the bed, the seat the doctor had recently vacated. He took Karin's hands in one of his and rubbed his other hand over their clasped hands.

"It will be all right," Pavel said, breaking into the silence.

Was he putting on a brave face for her? Didn't he worry about their delayed departure and what it would mean for the safety of their travel?

"Perhaps I will heal faster," she interjected. "We do not have to wait for the doctor's permission."

"I do not want to do anything that may risk injuring you further."

Another silence fell between them.

"The only thing I regret," he said, reaching forward and brushing a stray hair out of her face and behind her ear. "Is that I will have to wait longer before calling you my wife." His hand lingered, cupping her face.

Karin took a deep breath and let it out over several seconds. "Then let's not wait."

His brows rose. "But, you can't walk... How will you...?"

She leaned forward and took his hand in hers. "We will figure it out."

He pulled her hand toward himself and pressed the palm to his lips before clasping that hand to his heart. "I do not want to wait either." Leaning in, he caught her lips with a passion that surprised her. Warmth spread through her entire body, lighting a fire within.

His hands moved to her shoulders, then to her back, one holding her fast, one tangling in her hair.

Her hand, already over his heart, clung to the front of his shirt as if he was her only hold on reality, while her other hand wrapped around his strong shoulder.

They remained, locked in their embrace, lips hungry for more.

Pavel gently broke away, holding her to himself.

When they did draw apart, she still wanted for more. She longed for a second kiss, but it would not come. Pavel was always prudent about their physical interactions, and they both knew this one had reached a limit they dared not cross. A second kiss might invite danger.

CHAPTER 15
PREPARATIONS

Was it possible? Could it be? Lenka's breath caught and she forced herself to exhale. This was a day of celebration. For in a matter of hours her daughter would be married!

Had it only been two evening prior she had found Pavel and Karin, intent on wedding plans, regardless of recent events and Karin's injury. But nothing could give Lenka reason to allow her *katka* to elope. Certainly not! Lenka shuddered at the thought.

Since that time, the house had been a flurry of activity. Even if it were to be a small ceremony, Lenka would have a proper wedding.

Nearing Karin's chambers, Lenka took a deep breath and let it out. How was she ever to contain all of these emotions? How could such excitement and nervousness live inside one person?

She pulled at the latch and stepped into the room already bustling. Karin was only half visible as the seamstress and a maid-servant helped her into the makings of a dress. Would this become her wedding clothes? It was little more than a patchwork of strips of cloth loosely held together.

"I must have you stand, milady. There is no other way to make proper adjustments," the seamstress said as she smoothed hands down the fabric.

"Of course." Karin's eyes were fixed on the mirror.

Lenka opened her mouth to object, but paused. She cocked her head and raised a brow toward Karin. Had not the doctor insisted she stay off the foot?

Karin's eyes caught Lenka's. Had she sensed her mother's stare?

"With assistance, I shall be able to stay upright *and* keep weight off my injured foot." Her tone did not invite debate.

Lenka's word would be final. Should she speak otherwise? What would that accomplish? With a quick nod, Lenka motioned for another maidservant to come alongside Sharka and assist Karin to her feet.

As the seamstress moved about, making minor adjustments here and there, Lenka stepped closer to Karin. What could she make out from the state of the dress? Not much.

A small sound escaped Karin. Lenka's eyes cut to her.

Karin had become slightly more pale and beads of sweat had formed on her forehead.

"Ivana, I think the Lady Karin may need to sit."

"I am almost finished..." the seamstress spoke, focused on her work.

Lenka glared at the woman. Their family seamstress may have become too familiar. Drawing in a breath, Lenka fought to keep calm as she prepared to put Ivana back in her place.

Then the seamstress proclaimed, "There!"

The servants moved Karin toward her chair. She all but collapsed onto its frame.

"Is there adequate time for the dress to be completed?" Lenka asked, an edge to her voice.

Ivana's face became serious. "I will do my best. It will not be as grand as I would wish for you, Lady Karin. But, it will be finished."

"It will be perfect." Karin's breaths came in heaves.

Lenka's attention was on her once again. If she could not manage to stand for this short time, how would she make it through the ceremony? How would she get down the aisle? Through the standing required for the service?

Ivana smiled at Karin. "Thank you, milady. I think it best we leave you to your rest."

Karin did not argue and made no attempt to assist as the maidservants relieved her of the dress.

"The wedding cookies and invitations are being delivered as we speak," Lenka offered as the women worked the dress off.

"I didn't know you were..."

Was Karin surprised? Had it not occurred to her that Lenka would see to every detail? Especially the ones she could not? The cookies, filled with nuts and fruit, were delivered with invitations the day of or the day before the wedding.

Sharka maneuvered Karin's nightdress on and settled her in the bed, propped in a seated position.

"Who have you tasked to do this?" Karin's eyes shone. Were there tears to come? It was, after all, a task normally levied on the bride and groom.

Lenka sat on the edge of the bed and took Karin's hand in hers. "Pavel and your father."

The glistening in Karin's eyes did, after all, produce tears. And Lenka understood. Petr had insisted he take Karin's place. It had touched Lenka too. The thought of her husband, humbling himself to such a menial task. And Pavel, taking on what should be a shared task between them... Karin was blessed with two special men in her life.

Ivana had taken her leave of the room without a sound, and Sharka exchanged a look with Lenka before taking her leave as well.

"That leaves you and I alone for another, most vital charge." Lenka leaned forward.

Karin quirked a brow.

Sharka returned with a tray of rosemary.

Recognition struck Karin's eyes and her mouth parted. Would she speak? Was she too overcome?

"It comes to us to make your bridal wreath." Lenka touched the back of her hand to Karin's cheek.

Karin embraced her mother. "You have thought of everything. Thank you."

And Lenka knew. Karin had consigned herself, imagining that with a quick wedding she would have to give up many of these things. But she had not counted on her mother's determination and craftiness. Lenka was determined to make all her wedding dreams come true.

Pavel walked through the small village, distributing wedding cookies and invitations. It was not quite as arduous as he had first thought. Although much of their assigned task was completed in silence, he and Petr exchanged pleasantries along the way, but no real conversation of any merit. Is this all their relationship would be? What more did he want? And what of Petr and Karin? Would there always be tension between them? Or had they sorted through it?

They turned in the direction the Bornekov's home. Their task now complete. Would their ride back be as their day thus far? Should he make some overture?

"Pavel," Petr's voice shattered the silence and scattered Pavel's thouhts. "I would have you know that I meant no offense upon your person."

Of what did Petr speak? Offense upon his person?

He turned toward his soon to be father-in-law.

Petr's eyes searched his face.

He must have seen the confusion in Pavel's features as he continued. "My refusal to give you my permission for Karin's hand." Petr shifted his attention forward.

"Yes. I knew." And Pavel had known. He had known Petr's refusal was about his agreement with the Viscount. It had little to do with Pavel's merit. Still this knowledge did not alleviate the injury.

"You are a fine young man, and your concern for my daughter has assured me that your intentions are honorable. I know you will do everything in your power to care for Karin. To protect her." Petr's voice caught in his throat.

Pavel glanced at Petr.

Silence fell between them for several seconds.

At last, Petr met Pavel's eyes.

"On my life," Pavel said in a soft but certain voice.

Nothing further was said as they arrived at the stables. They dismounted and handed off their reins to the stable hands before moving toward the entrance. Though naught was spoken between them throughout, the air between them was easier.

As they reached the main structure, a manservant greeted them.

"*Dobry vecer*," the servant spoke a wish of good evening to his master and Pavel.

"*Dobry vecer*," Petr responded in kind.

"There are two men who seek an audience with his lordship Pavel. They await you in the great hall"

Pavel could not stop the look that passed over his features, his surprise plain for all to see. Who would come here to seek him?

His parents would not dare brave the trip. It would be too dangerous. As much as he would wish it possible for them to be with him on his wedding day, they were safely inside Hussite territory and that was where they need remain, awaiting Pavel and Karin's arrival.

Petr dismissed the servant, who bowed and took his leave. He then held an arm up for Pavel to procede him into the grand room.

Though not spoken between them, Pavel was grateful Petr accompanied him. There was always the risk of another patrol come to question him further. After all, the commander had said they were being watched. Was the distribution of wedding cookies suspicious somehow?

As he opened the door, Pavel was tackled by the two men waiting within.

He fought against his attackers, but there were two of them, and they had him in a firm hold before he could do anything about it. Where was Petr? Would he come to Pavel's aid?

Then his capteurs started to sing of what a good fellow he was. He sought out the faces of his subduers—none other than Zdenek and Radek!

Pavel freed his arms enough to clap his friends on their backs and reach to embrace them.

"How? When?" his questions started to come.

His friends released him and started to speak at the same time— a rarity, considering Radek's soft-spoken nature. After a few seconds of garbled talk, they slowed enough to take turns.

"Stepan told us everything," Radek explained.

"Everything?" Could Pavel trust this? What exactly had Stepan told them? The real truth? Or the truth he wanted them to know?

"He felt terrible...he confessed it all," Zdenek said. "Including what happened with Karin."

What else had Stepan told them? That he was a Hussite? A traitor to the crown? What did they think? He had to know. "Did he tell you Karin and I are... ?"

"Getting married?" Radek finished for him.

"Of course! Why do you think we came?" Zdenek took off from there. "You did not think we would let you get married without us, did you?"

Pavel offered them a smile. Should he push further? Was it so important? Yes. "Of course not... But did he tell you we are...Hussites?"

The two became quiet.

"Yes," Radek said, breaking the thick silence that had fallen over the room. "And we respect that you have your reasons, friend. You will not have any problems from us."

Pavel nodded, grateful that at least they were willing to understand.

"So, about the wedding..." Zdenek started.

The next morning, the sun streamed into Karin's window, waking her as it had every morning for as long as she could remember. Though the day started the same as so many before it, the day would close quite differently. For that day, she would become Pavel's wife. It was difficult to imagine, but it was true. Her wedding day was here.

A knock sounded on the door, breaking her solitude. Karin did not speak. But she listened as a maidservant came in regardless of her allowance. Of course they would come. Still, Karin did not look in that direction, resisting the close of her time to welcome this most different and special day.

"Milady?" came the maidservant's tentative question.

Karin's eyes widened. She knew that voice. Yet she had not expected to hear it...perhaps ever. Whipping her head around, her eyes confirmed what her ears had told her. "Mary?"

The maidservant smiled at her lady, folding her hands in front of herself.

"How?" Karin struggled for words as she sat up. "When did you arrive?"

"Late yesterday evening." Mary stepped toward Karin, coming around the bed.

"It is so good to see you." Much to her surprise, Karin truly meant it.

"And you," Mary said before she cleared her throat. "Are you ready for your morning tea?"

"Yes," Karin said, smiling. Was Mary so uncomfortable with the rather familiar interchange?

Mary nodded again before taking leave of her mistress.

Karin sighed. Being reunited with Mary was rather bittersweet. And it would be brief. There would be no servants traveling with she and Pavel.

Now sitting, Karin swung her legs over the side of the bed so she could face the windows. Mother would make her appearance soon enough. And then the day would officially begin. Would there be another chance to just breathe? To take hold of what this day would bring and relish it? Or would it all be the hustling about that she feared?

The door opened once more. Mary entered with her tea. Mother was fast on her heels.

"Ivana will be here any minute. We must get you ready!"

Servants seemed to pour into the room then. Bringing the tub and buckets of hot water. Yes, today would be filled with much activity.

Lenka and Mary were by Karin's side in a moment, urging her to her feet.

Resistance would no longer be allowed. That was apparent in her mother's firm grasp, already drawing her to her feet. Though still a reluctant participant, Karin was up and moving toward the bath with much effort.

Once in the tub, she was scrubbed and cleaned thoroughly, while Mother directed breakfast items be brought.

Karin's knotted stomach did not seem the least bit receptive to the idea of food today.

Commotion in the hall drew Karin's attention away from her stomach. A rather shrill voice yelled, demanded, and shrieked just beyond her door. Who could it be? More servants? What task had been levied upon them?

Mother stepped to the door and opened it but a crack. Was she preparing to silence the breakout of hysteria? Moments later, her voice joined the others, which drew ever nearer until Mother's form appeared again at the door, leading two maidservants in, bearing a cream dress, followed by Ivana.

It was Ivana who screeched at the slightest bounce or droop wrought upon the fine fabric. She directed the maidservants to the far corner of the room where she instructed the dress be laid out.

Karin could not see it as Ivana and Mother, hunched over, blocked her view.

"Milady, I think you must come or else you will wrinkle."

Karin turned toward the maidservant attending her. What had she said? Oh, yes. It was time to exit the comfort of the warm water. Grasping the young woman's arm and Sharka's, she rose. The movement was somewhat unsteady, not at all graceful, but effective. She was on her feet.

The maidservants had her dried and seated in short order. And Sharka brought her tea and her foods to break her fast. Karin offered a smile before turning back toward the wedding dress.

Mother and Ivana were deep in conversation; Mother's hands hovered over the fabric as if she were afraid to touch it.

Ivana made a slight move to the left, and Karin got her first glimpse of the dress.

It was far beyond anything Karin could have imagined when it was but scraps of fabric the day before. The gold-colored dress's structure was simple enough. A scoop neckline and fitted bodice set the stage for sleeves, which had a puff at the shoulder, but were otherwise fitted. And the skirt fell from the fitted waist to sweep the floor, with a modest train flowing behind.

But the uniqueness of the dress was in the details and the fabrics. Lace bordered the scoop neckline, and there were also embroidered flowers and pearls covering the dress in an elegant display.

How Ivana could imagine, much less construct, something of such intricate design was beyond Karin. How was she to wear something so amazing?

Karin found it difficult, but she finished her breakfast in short order. It was not long before she was maneuvered into the gown.

"You have outdone yourself," Lenka said as Mary braided Karin's hair in an elaborate design, sticking pearls in her hair.

"Thank you, milady. It was a labor of love."

Karin caught Ivana's eyes. She knew the woman spoke the truth. Ivana had been making her clothes for many years and was almost like a member of the household.

"All done, milady," Mary said to Lenka.

Lenka brought forth the wreath she and Karin had put together the night before and set it on Karin's head.

Karin stared in the mirror. She was, by all appearances, a bride.

"And now, for a few finishing details," Lenka said, excitement evident in her voice. She walked to a chest at the other end of the room and opened it.

"Finishing details?" Karin asked, confused. Was she not the picture of what every bride should be?

"You need this—your grandmother's veil." Holding it out to Karin, she tenderly placed it in Karin's waiting hands. "And I had this made for your special day." She held out a handkerchief with Karin's new initials embroidered on it. Lenka then clasped a pearl necklace around Karin's neck. "This is mine. I would be honored to have you wear it today."

Karin touched it and tears welled at the thoughtful gifts her mother bestowed upon her.

"There, now," Lenka said, sighing. "You are ready."

Karin was overwhelmed. All of the preparations had been made. Every last one.

But everything was happening so fast. There had been no time to take it all in.

"What is the matter?" Mother asked, touching Karin's hair with light fingertips. Had her thoughts been so evident on her face?

"It is passing me by, Mother. This day. It is happening too fast. I think I need a few minutes."

"Of course." Mother motioned to the servants cleaning up this and that to step out.

"Are you comfortable where you are?" Mother asked, stepping toward the door herself.

Karin sat in a chair across the room from the bed, caddy-corner to a large window. It was a fine place to bask in the sunlight as she sat with her thoughts. She nodded. "Yes, thank you."

It was only a matter of moments before everyone exited. And she was alone. The servants had done fine work cleaning much of the morning's mayhem, but there were still random remnants of breakfast and of getting Karin ready. Her grandmother's veil still lay across the vanity, and the bed had been hastily made.

She removed the rosemary wreath to lean her head back and allowed herself to linger over the things that had happened that morning, letting the anxiety wash over her. Closing her eyes, she took a deep breath and released any remaining uneasiness.

This was a happy day, a day which should be filled with pleasant emotions. So far, her emotions had been uneasy. Was it everything that had occurred this morning? Was it as she said to Mother...that things were happening too fast? Or was it something else?

"Truly you take my breath away," a voice from the doorway said.

She knew that voice. Still, it caused her to jerk her head up, eyes wide all the same.

"Pavel," she admonished him. "You are not to see me yet!"

There he stood, just inside the room, in his wedding clothes, so handsome.

Pavel crossed the room in a few breaths and stood before her. He reached his hands out and she slid hers into them as if that was where they always belonged. Pulling her up with ease, he supported her right side so she could stand. And he took her in top to bottom.

"Forgive me. I could not stay away. I had to see you."

She could not be cross with him. His presence calmed her. It was what she needed.

"You are handsome, Pavel."

"You..." He took a long breath in and out. "You are a vision."

Her face warmed under his scrutiny. She raised a hand to touch his face.

He lowered his head to touch his forehead to hers. "It will only be of a couple of hours. Then we will be husband and wife."

"I can scarce believe it."

"Father God," he began to pray, "We are overwhelmed by Your love for us and Your blessings upon us. You have brought us together and kept us safe. And today we will stand before You, Your priest, and Your people, declaring our intent and making vows, pledging ourselves to one another. We declare that You are our God, and we only ever want to serve You. Be with us today. Guide us."

"Amen," Karin finished.

She maneuvered her face to plant a kiss on his mouth.

"You had better get out of here before my mother returns and finds out you have been here."

He nodded but did not move.

"I am loathe to be parted from you."

She nodded. "I know."

"I love you so much, Karin."

"And I love you."

He caught her lips in another, longer kiss. As they parted, she was left breathless. Easing her back onto the chair, he pressed gentle, swift kisses to her cheeks, her nose, her forehead, and then her lips again before pulling back and standing.

"See you at the church, my love."

She gazed into his eyes. "I will be there."

Not long after, Pavel was in his room, looking at his reflection and pulling at his collar. As a member of the extended royal family, he'd had to dress in formal wear throughout his life for many occasions. But he could never quite get used to it—a fact that always made him feel as if he was a small boy again.

Zdenek and Radek had been groggy company after their night celebrating, and they had begged off after an errand.

Pavel was more than a little concerned what this errand might entail, but there was no sense dwelling on it. He would find out in due time.

There was a bit of activity outside. Was it Zdenek and Radek? Pavel stepped to the window and glanced below. It was only the carriages pulling around to prepare for their passengers.

Pavel continued to gaze out the window, a habit he had picked up from Karin. *Karin...* Since coming to her parents' house, they had not been separated for any stretch of time, save for sleep. On any other day, he would have gone to her as early in the morning as propriety would allow.

And this morning, he had ached to see her. Those few moments with her had quenched that only slightly. What was going through her mind? His emotions were so clouded, for he was both excited and nervous about what the day would bring. He was hopeful about their future, yet overwhelmed at the thought of the responsibility he would take on. But his thoughts were filled with her, how much he loved her, of how much he longed to make her his wife, and of how, after that day, no one could tear them apart.

Pavel was so deep in thought he barely heard the door to his bedchambers open. He did not bother, not even to turn at first, certain it was a servant coming for one reason or another, perhaps to warn him the carriages were preparing to leave soon.

But there was silence. What kind of servant just stands there? Was he waiting on something from Pavel?

After some seconds, the man cleared his throat.

Pavel spun to face him. As he raised his eyes, however, his mouth dropped.

It was not a servant; it was Stepan.

CHAPTER 16
THE BEGINNING OF THE END

Pavel reached the hilt of his sword to assure himself of its protection if Stepan meant him ill will. But he grasped at nothing. In his efforts to dress, he had neglected to place it. Scanning the room, he spotted it leaning against the fireplace several paces away. How long it would take to lunge for it?

The direction of Pavel's gaze did not escape Stepan. His eyes followed.

Pavel watched Stepan, all too aware that Stepan's hand rested comfortably on his own sword.

Stepan looked back at his former friend. His eyes widened. Was Pavel's glare so intense? Only then did he seem to notice his own defensive stance. He held his hands out. "You need not fear me. I did not come to harm you."

Pavel's eyes cut to the sword on Stepan's hip.

Stepan followed his gaze. And with slow, careful movements, he unfastened the sword and tossed it toward the fireplace. Now their swords lay together. Only then did the tension in Pavel's shoulders ease.

"I suppose I cannot blame you, considering the circumstances last we met." There was a depth to Stepan's voice. Sadness? Regret?

Pavel fought a wave of empathy rising within him. There was too much between them. "Why are you here?"

"My best friend will marry today. I had to see him. To wish him well."

"Oh?" Pavel arched a brow. Was that truly the only thing that brought Stepan this distance?

"Whatever has happened, Pavel, you are still like a brother to me. And nothing can change that." Stepan's eyes reflected the sorrow in his voice.

"Though I am a Hussite?"

"Nothing can change that," Stepan said with finality. Were his words meant to convince Pavel? Or himself?

Dare Pavel give in to the emotions pulling at him? Stepan had been so dear to him. Still, it did not sit well with him. Something was amiss.

Stepan took a step toward Pavel.

Pavel jerked back.

Stepan brought his hands back up as if to indicate he meant no harm. "Please, Pavel. Can you not find it in your heart to forgive what I have done? Is there no room for repentance?"

Pavel peered at the floor. The truth was that there was forgiveness aplenty for his friend, for what had happened between them.

Yet what of the beaten servant girl, tossed out, persecuted because she was a Hussite. Would Stepan have spared the sword on her had she been discovered one month later? There was little doubt he would not. What of the next Hussite Stepan would encounter— the others he would abuse, even murder?

Pavel's eyes rose to meet Stepan's again.

"Pavel," Stepan's voice had become firmer, more confident. "Say something."

"I have forgiven you already, my friend." Pavel's hand ached for his sword. But any movement in that direction would only lead to the two of them crossing blades. This was not settled. Yet. " Still I wonder, what of the next Hussite you cross paths with? He is my brother. She is my sister."

Stepan's gaze wandered toward the floor. His features contorted. "I don't know."

At least he was not about to lie.

Silence hung between them.

"Thank you," Pavel spoke into the emptiness. "For sending Zdenek and Radek."

Stepan nodded.

"And thank you...for coming."

"Of course."

Silence fell again. Would they forever remain at odds?

Stepan swallowed hard. "I... have something for you."

Pavel's raised a brow and watched Stepan's movements as he stepped into the hall. He returned with a rolled canvas. A painting? What was this about?

Stepan picked at the corner. Was he having a difficulty finding his words? Would he explain his gift? "I, ah, had a painting commissioned for Karin when we were...betrothed." He met Pavel's eyes. "I want the two of you to have it. But do not tell her it came from me."

Stepan unrolled the canvas.

Pavel took tentative steps toward his former friend. As the painting was revealed, Stepan turned it in Pavel's direction.

It was the chateau. But the vantage point was chosen such that the painting included Karin's favorite view of the grounds as well.

Pavel's eyes shot to Stepan. "I cannot accept this. And I will not let Karin believe that I had this done for her."

"I want her..." Stepan closed his eyes and took a breath. "I want the two of you to have it. To remember where..." His voice caught. "Where it all began." The pain in his voice was evident. "It is so important to me that you take it. I want you to have a piece of the chateau." Stepan held the canvas out between them.

Pavel studied Stepan. After several seconds, he reached forth and took it. "I accept, old friend. But I will not lie to Karin."

"Then tell her you cannot say where it came from."

Pavel rubbed the thickness of the material now in his hands.

They both knew she would know where it came from.

Stepan shook his head. "I delay you. It is time to get to the church." He turned.

"You...could come." Pavel's spoke before the thought had been checked. Why had he said it?

"You know I cannot," Stepan said without turning.

Pavel nodded. He did know.

"Take care of her." Stepan looked back over his shoulder.

"You know I will."

And then Stepan was disappeared into the hall. Only then did Pavel wonder how it came to be that he was in the house unannounced. But it did not matter. Stepan was gone, and it might just be the last time he laid eyes on his oldest friend.

It was time. Everyone surrounded Pavel at the steps into the church. And somewhere nearby, Karin made her way to him. In a few moments, she would be with him. His heartbeat quickened. What would she look like in her bridal accoutrements? Were these thoughts and emotions rushing through her? It became difficult to think, focus.

The small crowd stirred. And the priest craned his neck. Had she come?

Pavel turned, but nothing was visible beyond the movement of the people. Still, he drew in a long, deep breath. Could he calm this racing in his chest? There was now, but one thought: his bride would join him soon.

A shift in the crowd now revealed that which he had long awaited—Karin on the arm of her father. His breath escaped him, and all thoughts vanished. There was only her and this moment.

Karin's progression was slow as she limped, but it mattered not.

Pavel's eyes locked with hers.

Though much effort was required for each step, she managed a smile as she made her way through the people.

If possible, she was even more beautiful in this moment. It seemed like forever, and only seconds, before she stood beside him.

His face flushed with the fullness of her presence. He reached forth his arm and took hers, relieving Petr of his burden.

The priest led everyone in the sign of the cross and continued with a greeting.

But Pavel was listening. His pulse thundered in his ears. And he was all too aware of Karin's breathing, her heartbeat, on the feel of her smaller hand in his. All of his senses were magnified tenfold.

"...Pavel..."

The priest had spoken his name. Pavel looked toward him. But his head was down and his eyes were closed. In prayer? Yes, the priest was in prayer over them. And so, Pavel turned his face toward the ground and attempted to even his breathing.

"Father, You have made the bond of marriage a holy mystery, a symbol of Christ's love for His Church. Hear our prayers for Pavel and Karin. With faith in You and in each other, they pledge their love today. May their lives always bear witness to the reality of that love. We ask You this through our Lord Jesus Christ, Your Son, Who lives and reigns with You and the Holy Spirit, one God, for ever and ever."

While he continued, Pavel entwined his fingers with Karin's.

She squeezed his hand.

Pavel wondered if he would remember anything of this day. Except the way Karin looked. He would never forget that.

The prayer ended and all focus shifted to Pavel and Karin.

Pavel stole a glance at his bride. Her wide eyes watched him as well. What went through her mind? Was her heart threatening to escape its cavity as was his?

"My dear friends," the priest said to them, "You have come together in this church so that the Lord may seal and strengthen your love in the presence of the Church's minister and this community. And so, I ask you to state your intentions. Pavel and Karin, have you come here freely and without reservation to give yourselves to each other in marriage?"

"Yes," they said together.

Pavel's lips curved.

"Will you love and honor each other as man and wife for the rest of your lives?"

"Yes," they said.

As Pavel watched, Karin's eyes began to glisten.

"Will you accept children lovingly from God and bring them up according to the law of Christ and His Church?"

"Yes," they answered again, together.

Was that color upon Karin's face? His bride, so innocent, so pure.

"Since it is your intention to enter into marriage, join your right hands, and declare your consent before God and His Church."

Pavel reached for her other hand. They faced one another.

"I, Pavel, take you, Karin, to be my wife. I promise to love, honor, and respect, to be faithful to you, and not to forsake you until we are parted by death, so help me God. Amen."

Karin shivered as a chill snaked down her spine at Pavel's recitation of those sacred words, his clear blue eyes gazing so intently into hers. How would she remember her part?

She glanced down at their linked hands, bound together in such a way that it would be difficult to separate them. This is what today was about. Linking their persons as intricately as they had linked their hearts. And so, she took a deep breath, licked her lips, and met his eyes again.

"I, Karin, take you, Pavel, to be my husband. I promise to love, honor, and respect, to be faithful to you, and not to forsake you until we are parted by death, so help me God. Amen."

Something fell upon them. Karin sensed it as if the words were spoken. The space between them was thick with the hope of the promises they had just made to one another.

"You have declared your consent before the Church. May the Lord in His goodness strengthen your consent and fill you both with His blessings. What God has joined, men must not divide."

The priest then took a ring in his hand and held it up. "May the Lord bless this ring which you give to as a sign of your love and fidelity."

Pavel took the ring and, clasping Karin's hand, slid it onto her finger, saying, "Karin, take this ring as a sign of my love and fidelity. In the name of the Father, and of the Son, and of the Holy Spirit."

Karin wanted this moment to last, with Pavel clasping her hand, having just placed his ring upon it. This was a moment she wished to live on in her heart.

"You may now exchange a kiss," the priest said.

Pavel leaned forward, wrapped an arm around Karin, and pressed his lips to hers. The contact was simple and pure enough, but it lit something in Karin. Something she was just beginning to understand. Something that both excited and scared her.

The priest stepped forward to pronounce them man and wife. It was done. But from the moment Pavel's lips touched hers; she was lost to goings on around her.

She was only somewhat aware of the people moving around her, congratulating them. All she knew was Pavel's strong arms holding her. Even innocent, his touch caused a response in her body. It soothed her and caused her skin to tingle. One thing was for certain: she hungered for more.

As the crowd moved back toward her parents' home, she turned her thoughts toward heaven.

Father, I pray I would be the wife You have created me to be for Your faithful servant, Pavel. I so desire to bring You glory and honor in all I do.

May my life be a living testament to Your strength and power. Teach me to walk each day in the steps You would have me walk, and grant me strength for the journey ahead. Thank you for the blessing of Pavel. Thank you for the blessing of the love that we share.

As they neared the carriages, a rope decorated with flowers, ribbons, and empty bottles was stretched across their path. The workings of Zdenek and Radek. Had this been their distraction this morning?

Pavel sighed.

Karin turned toward him.

Though he seemed put off, he smiled. Would he rather they forgo this tradition? Still, he produced the money required to pay them to remove the rope so they could pass. And so, Pavel was ransomed from his young sins.

Zdenek and Radek grinned, seeming rather pleased with themselves.

Karin could no longer hide that she had become rather labored. Whether from the excitement, the rush of emotion, or the physical wear on her ankle, she did not know.

One look at Pavel and she knew that he was aware. His brows furrowed and his arm tightened around her waist.

It seemed much time passed before he lifted her into a carriage. How would she make it through the celebration?

Pavel was not quite settled into his seat next to Karin before the carriage jerked into action. As soon as he had his bearings, he faced her, encircling her with one arm and drawing her closer.

"We have done it," he said. His voice held a tenderness she had not known.

She clung to him a bit more tightly.

"And I think," he said, lifting his other hand to touch her face, grazing her features, "That I love you even more now than ever before."

Karin leaned forward and pressed her lips to his. The kiss was everything she would have wanted from their first married kiss, yet propriety would never have allowed in front of the church. His hand cupped her face, tilting her head to deepen the kiss while her hands moved over his chest to his strong shoulders, gripping at his clothing there.

She was eager for more, but Pavel pulled back, a bit breathless. There should no longer be anything barring them. So she moved in for another kiss.

He placed a finger on her lips. "We need only pace ourselves a little longer, my love."

What was he saying? Pace themselves? All she knew was that she wanted to continue kissing him.

"Trust me, Karin. This is not the time or the place to continue this."

Karin did trust him. Though she did not fully understand. Now that the kisses were put on hold, she wanted him to hold her. She wanted to soak in the calmness and strength found only in his arms. Would it carry her through the next couple of hours?

Pavel seemed to sense her need before she spoke it. He pulled her into a firm embrace, holding her fast to himself. She felt his heartbeat, so tight were his arms around her.

Some moments later, the carriage came to a halt just outside her parents' home. Karin started to maneuver her way out of the carriage.

Pavel came around and gathered her into his arms.

Was he to carry her in? She frowned. But would she rather limp into the great hall? Or arrive in her beloved's arms? And so, she conceded.

They led the small crowd into the house and onward toward the great hall, where the meal was being prepared.

Pavel carried Karin to the head of the table where a single bowl of soup and a loaf of bread awaited them. Two servants covered them in a large cloth, under which they would remain while they ate the soup, sharing one spoon. Displaying unity and cooperation.

After they accomplished the task, there was a great feast for all. And the celebration continued with dancing and drinking.

As the wedding feast continued, Karin removed her rosemary wreath, proof of her virginity, and placed it on the plate her mother had prepared with a white scarf.

Zdenek took the plate and, followed by a small parade of guests, brought the plate to Pavel, who accepted the wreath with a smile.

Before she knew it, Radek lifted Karin from her chair and rushed her from the room.

The last thing she saw was Pavel rising, concern upon his face. Did he not remember the traditional kidnapping of the bride? She would be hidden somewhere in the house, symbolizing her separation from her parents, and he would have to find her or pay another ransom to get her back. Find her, he would. Of this, she was certain. And this would be the last time anyone would separate them.

Karin sat while Mary took her hair down. It was not long before waves of red-blonde fell around her shoulders. Her tresses grazed the simple chemise her mother had reserved for this night, this one special night. A wave of apprehension rose within Karin. Her stomach felt a little uneasy at the thought of what this night would bring, but she trusted Pavel. Nothing unpleasant would happen to her as long as she was in his arms. That thought only served to calm the wave of uneasiness a little.

Moments later, Mary gathered the bowl of used water, which Karin had washed her face with, and walked to the window to dump it. It was only a matter of minutes before Mary would set the brushes and pitcher in their proper place and gather the dirtied cloths so she could take her leave.

Try as she might, Karin could not think of any reason to delay her. Did she truly want to? Her anxiety was at war with her growing desire to be comforted by Pavel's arms. Perhaps he could still this disquiet in her.

"Thank you, Mary," Karin said, as she was gathering the last item she would need.

Mary bowed. "Milady. Do you need anything else?"

"Could you help me to the fireplace?"

"Of course, milady."

With Mary's assistance, she hobbled to a chair near the hearth.

"Thank you," she said as Mary laid a blanket over her legs. She need not worry so; the warmth of the fire was more than sufficient to keep away any chill. But Karin accepted it all the same.

Then Karin was alone with her thoughts. Trying to keep her thoughts from running rampant, she focused on the flames, watching them dance and lick at the air. Fire could be so lovely, but also quite dangerous.

It was not long before Karin sensed she was no longer alone, moments before she heard the door close. Was it her beloved come to join her?

Her back was to the doorway, but she did not turn to greet him. Instead she let him come to her. And he did.

Pavel walked through the room almost as silently as he had entered it. He came behind her and laid his hands on her shoulders. She then felt his lips pressing to the side of her face as his hands rubbed down her upper arms. Despite the warmth of the fire, she shivered at his touch, her discomfort getting the best of her. He came around to her left side to crouch between her and the fire, clasping her left hand in his.

"Are you all right, my love?" He used his free hand to push hair from her forehead and behind her ear.

Karin nodded looking down at their clasped hands, avoiding his eyes. "Yes." She brought her right hand around to rub his.

"Truly?"

She glanced up to meet his eyes and shook her head. The movement was so slight it was almost imperceptible.

With a tenderness she only ever knew from him, he touched her face and gently pulled her into his arms. "It is all right," he soothed. "I'm not going to force anything on you."

She nodded against his shoulder.

He pulled back to look into her eyes. "All right now?"

She nodded.

He smiled and continued to smooth back her hair and caress her face. "Let us see to our greater comfortable."

Pavel brought blankets from the bed to create a makeshift bed on the floor in front of the fire.

"There," he said, waving his hands over his work. "The only thing missing is you."

She held out her arms for him to lift her.

He obliged, pressing a soft kiss to her lips before leaning down to lay her on the floor.

Karin found that the knot in the bottom of her stomach was becoming unwound.

Once she was settled, Pavel lay down between her and the fire, half sitting, pulling her to him so she could rest upon his chest. He continued to stroke her hair as they gazed into the fire. His free hand met hers across his body.

She moved her hand to rest over his heart.

Turning his head, he shifted his gaze from the fire to his bride. He pressed a kiss to her forehead and lifted his now freed hand to caress her face.

Karin maneuvered so she could kiss him.

Pavel shifted to deepen the kiss.

Her body flushed with a familiar fire, a fire lit inside her whenever they kissed like this, a fire she had yet to find a way to douse. She clung to him as the kiss continued, the fire threatening to overtake her, spreading through her whole body.

When the kiss broke off, Pavel continued their contact with gentle kisses sprinkled around her lips, her eyes, her cheeks, before he reclaimed her lips in a kiss that was even deeper than the one before.

Karin was lost to the fire burning deep within, which had snuffed any hint of apprehension remaining. All that persisted was this blazing desire.

Their bodies changed position and she was on her back with her husband leaning over her. She moved her hands over his body, tentatively exploring as he continued to stoke the fire within her with his kisses. Karin soon discovered that his hands too could inflame her.

Giving herself completely to her husband, she hoped he could tame the powerful wildfire within her. In his strong arms, at the mercy of his sweet kisses, she found the answer to that question.

Karin was unsure if she was ready for the journey that lay ahead.

Her mother finished repinning her hair with Karin and Pavel's most precious, but incriminating, paper hidden in her braids, a task not to be trusted to a maidservant.

"You are beautiful, my *katka*." Mother placed her hands on Karin's shoulders and gazed with her at their reflection in the mirror.

"Oh, mother!" Karin turned and embraced her mother. "I am sorry for any sadness or disappointment I have brought upon you."

"There is no need," Mother admonished her, pulling back to look Karin in the face. "You have made me so proud, following your convictions, standing for what you believe. And you have made a fine match with an honorable man who loves you and wants to support you. What more could a mother want?"

Karin's face broke into a smile, and she embraced her mother again. "How I am going to miss you!"

"And I you!" Mother tightened her hold. Would this be the last time Karin would embrace her mother? As Mother pulled away, she wiped at tears. "Now, we must get you to your husband, Lady Krejikova."

Another smile lit Karin's face, and she allowed her mother to lead her into the foyer where Pavel and Father waited.

Father stepped forward and enveloped Karin in his arms. He whispered in her ear, "I told Pavel you are not to stop for anything until you reach your destination. If you are stopped, let the coachman do the talking."

She nodded. "Yes, Father."

They pulled away, and she moved to stand next to Pavel.

His arm slid around Karin's waist, supporting her.

"Please take care of each other," Mother said, her voice catching.

"Of course," Pavel assured her, "I would give my life for the care of your daughter, Countess."

Mother smiled at him as if she, too, knew that was true.

Pavel turned to Karin. "It is time."

She nodded. Sharing one more long look with her mother, then her father, she moved to follow as Pavel led her toward the waiting carriage.

Once they were seated within, she peered out the window at her parents, standing just outside, watching and waiting. The carriage jerked as it began to move, and Karin waved at her parents as they grew smaller and became part of the horizon.

"Will I ever see them again?" Karin asked.

"Only God knows."

"I pray He will watch over our journey, Pavel."

Pavel wrapped his arms around his bride and hugged her to himself. "I know He will, my love. We have nothing to fear, as long as we are together."

Karin nestled herself into his chest and found comfort in her husband. She knew he spoke truth. No matter what they faced as they made their way toward Hussite territory, it would not be insurmountable as long as they were together.

This, however, was before they got stopped by a patrol. Before Petr found the true legal obstacles of breaking a marriage contract to

Stepan. This was before Sigismund assumed the throne. Before any of them realized that the Hussite Wars would last fifteen years.

Karin and Pavel's journey was only beginning. But, come what may, they would face it together.

Keep reading for a preview of the next book in The Lady of Bohemia Series!

Thank you, dear reader, for reading along with me! If you enjoyed this story, I would sincerely appreciate if you would submit a review. It would mean so much to me!

To read more about these characters, follow along with The Lady of Bohemia Series. Find it at:
https://saraturnquist.com/lady-bornekova-series/

AUTHOR'S NOTE

Clean Historical Romance...this became a new genre for me in my young adult years. Until then, I was an avid Science Fiction and Mystery reader. But once I was introduced to Clean Historical Romance, I fell in love. Hard. I loved everything about the genre—the historical tidbits, the love stories, the thrill and adventure...and sometimes the mystery and intrigue. I am so honored to be able to write in this space.

Two of the most frequent questions I get as a clean Historical Romance author are "what time period do you write in?" and "why do you write that?" Well, first, I am all over the historical time map with my books as far as eras go. But for my first series, I honed in on this period—Medieval Bohemia. Why?

I spent several summers in the Czech Republic in the early 2000's teaching English in summer camps. I fell in love with the Czech poeple, their culture, the architecture, and the history. Especially the Hussite Wars—religious civil wars that shaped so much about the country. And I began to dig...

It all began, in truth, as is portrayed in this story, with the martyrdom of Jan Hus. He had heretical ideas and challenges to some of the Catholic Church practices of the time, such as the selling of indulgences, the overwhelming wealthiness of the clergy, etc. (some of the same challenges Martin Luther would voice...a man who stated, after reading Hus's work, that he (Luther) himself "was a Hussite all along").

King Wenceslas of Bohemia, who was never given the crown over the Holy Roman Empire, did not stomp out Hus's teachings initially. However, his brother Sigismund is proported to have hated what Hus stood for and sought the man's death. And so, Hus was called to account and would not relent. Following his refusal to submit to the Catholic Church and admit his beliefs (beliefs that Protestants and even, for the most part, Catholics hold today) were heresy, he was burned at the stake.

This martyrdom sparked the unrest that would swell into outright conflict that would become the Hussite Wars.

A SNEAK PEEK
THE LADY AND THE HUSSITES

Karin Krejikova awoke as the rocking came to an abrupt halt, shaking her from a gentle slumber. Eyes now open, she tried to remember where she was. The interior of a fine carriage came into focus and realization cut through the fog of sleepiness. She was traveling to the safety of her now in-laws' home well in Hussite-controlled territory with her new husband. Even then her eyes sought him out—Pavel. Next to her on the narrow bench, his attention was drawn out the small window.

A yawn overcame her and she stretched her arms, relishing the feel of her muscles being re-energized. As she resettled herself and smoothed over her dress, it occurred to her how strange it was they should pause. Had they reached their destination?

The sun sat high in the sky. Hadn't Pavel said it would be nightfall when they arrived?

"Why have we stopped?" Karin placed a hand on Pavel's strong arm. Those arms had brought her protection and comfort each in its own time.

He held a hand up in her direction, but his eyes didn't waver. Something beyond the thin walls of the small, enclosed vehicle had his attention. Her chest tightened. What could it be? Shifting, she maneuvered to glance out her own window, straining to hear what may be outside her visual range.

Men and horses moved about just beyond the reach of the carriage. One of the riders approached. The red of the royal military garb flashed in the sunlight.

Her breath caught and she jerked back into the car, pressing her back against the seat. Closing her eyes, she forced herself to breathe. When she opened her eyes, the blue orbs of her beloved husband were in front of her. He reached for her hand. She slipped it easily into his.

"You can do this," he said, his words measured.

She nodded, drawing in a long breath.

He lifted a hand to touch her red locks, but only lightly. "You are stronger than you know, Karin."

Allowing herself to get lost in his eyes for a moment, she knew he spoke the truth. Karin had been through much in these last months. *They* had been through much. Was there anything they couldn't face together?

She returned his assuring smile.

Moments later, the door to the carriage jerked open. The menacing face of one of the king's men glared in. He eyed them from top to bottom before speaking.

"My lord," the soldier said, all but spitting out the word.

Had the coachman shared that this carriage bore someone of noble title? What else had he shared?

"Would you mind stepping outside?"

"Is this necessary?" Pavel challenged him. His voice remained flat as if he were bored by the irritation of being detained. "My wife is recovering from a foot injury."

The guard shifted his gaze to Karin. She glanced at her fingers, trying to appear nonchalant.

"I apologize, my lord, but I must insist upon it. By order of the king." The man's mouth curled into a slight snarl. Scrapes from above the carriage startled Karin. She gripped Pavel's arm. Were their belongings being unloaded?

"Very well." Pavel moved toward the opening.

The guard took a step back.

Karin froze. How could she follow Pavel? Would these guards find out the truth? That she and Pavel were Hussites? That she bore the names of other prominent Hussites on a paper rolled and braided into her hair?

"But," Pavel continued.

The guard spun, his attention on Pavel.

"I can assure you the king will hear of this."

"Noted," the man said, his brow furrowed and his eyes narrowed.

Once Pavel exited the carriage, he reached in for Karin.

Leaning on his strength, she managed to step out and onto the soggy earth.

Their trunks lay opened and sifted through. The coachman, having been relieved of his seat, stood near the front of the carriage. Another guard questioned him. His gaze landed on Karin. She searched his face. Could they trust him? Or would he give them away to save his own skin?

Prodded forward, Karin lost eye contact with the coachman. She tightened her grip on Pavel's arm. He drew her closer, as if preparing to protect her somehow. But was there anything he could do against these armed men? What could he do should the guards identify them as enemies of the crown?

"I am eager to hear the reason you have relieved my wife of her comfort." Pavel's eyes flashed as he turned to the man who had ushered them out of their seats.

"As you see." The man waved his hand. "This is an inspection. You may be aware that Hussites have infiltrated our peaceful lands. We are only trying to isolate and eliminate their presence and influence. I'm certain you understand. Since you are nothing but loyal to the king."

Pavel did not speak. His eyes hardened and his jaw clenched.

"And so, it is my job to search you . . . and your wife."

What did he mean by that? What was he intending to do?

Pavel pulled her closer.

"You may search me, if you must. But my wife will not be part of your games." Pavel's voice was firm.

"I will determine what will be." A sneer crossed the man's features.

The guard rifling through one of her trunks nearby looked over and stood, walking toward them. Pointing at her, the lead guard spoke to the second. "Let's search her first."

Pavel pulled Karin behind himself, but it was no use. Yet another guard joined the first two and helped extricate Karin from Pavel. Then rough hands pulled her to the first guard, uncaring as she tripped over her injured foot with pained cries.

Then she stood in front of the sneering guard, vulnerable and afraid. Not only for herself but also for Pavel. For them both. For what this guard might find. Her back to Pavel, she could not take comfort or strength from him.

The man made small circles around her, his gaze intense. She closed her eyes against the harshness of his stare, praying it would be over soon. With each round, he moved closer and closer until his breath grazed her neck.

Without warning, his hands were on her shoulders and moving down her arms. She wished Pavel wasn't looking. The hands continued down her back. Jeers sounded from the other men.

Lord, help me!

"What are you doing?" An approaching voice shattered what concentration she had left.

Her eyes shot open to see yet another man in royal garb—the guard who had been questioning the coachman.

"My job," the searching guard replied. His words were edged with a roughness she had come to associate with the man.

The questioning guard's disapproving look gave Karin hope. Was the approaching guard in command?

"Get these trunks loaded and help the lord and lady into the carriage before I decide this merits a letter to the general."

Relief washed over her. The guard in front of her did not seem as pleased. His face twitched, but he did not move. He remained mere inches from Karin.

"Now," the head guard said with more force.

The guard with the sneer took a step back from Karin. Her knees weakened. She gritted her teeth and forced herself to remain upright.

Pavel rushed to her side, steadying her with an arm around her waist. He hurried her back to the carriage. Settling her inside, however, he did not join her. Standing just outside the doorway, he watched through narrowed eyes as the men reloaded the trunks.

The coachman returned to his seat before long and the guards mounted their horses.

"We apologize, my lord, for any inconvenience," the head guard said. "Safe journey."

With that, the men moved away and trotted off into the distance.

Pavel nodded at the coachman before sliding into the seat next to Karin. He gathered her into his arms, holding her securely.

Was it she who was shaking or the carriage?

"I'm sorry," Pavel said over and over. "Karin, I'm sorry. I'm so sorry. I should have been able to protect you."

To read more, find *The Lady and the Hussites* here:

https://saraturnquist.com/the-lady-and-the-hussites/

The Lady Bornekova (Book 1)

The red-headed Karin is strong-willed and determined, she tries to keep her true nature a secret to avoid being deemed a traitor by those loyal to the king.

Karin and her father butt heads over her duty to her family and the Czech Crown. However, her heart soon becomes entangled though her father intends to wed her to another.

The turmoil inside Karin deepens and reflects the turmoil of her homeland, on the brink of the Hussite Wars.

The Lady & the Hussites (Book 2)

Karin and Pavel have found their way safely to his parents home, but things are not as well as they seem. There are secrets between them. A wall goes up. And then Pavel is called into battle.

Radek and Zdenek find themselves pulled into the conflict despite their best efforts to remain neutral, while Stepan finds himself ready for bloodshed.

With tensions mounting within their circle and throughout their country, what will become of Pavel and Karin? Can they find their way back to each other?

The Lady & Her Champion (Book 3)

She needs someone to fight for her. He needs to be rescued.

Karin and Pavel have become separated by war and the destruction of his family's home. When Pavel hears of Karin's predicament, he rushes to his beloved. But what will he find?

Will the pull to remain by her side be stronger than the tug to return to the front lines?

While the Hussites maintain a tenuous hold on their lands, will internal conflict prove their undoing?

The Lady & Her Secret (Book 4)

She seeks the forbidden. He struggles to find peace.

Karin and Pavel are at last reunited. But her desire to take on a task long prohibited has Pavel worried for her safety and that of his new family. She strives to keep her work a secret while he faces his own fight—one of a warrior weary of battle.

While the Hussites wrestle with internal conflict, will the enemy take advantage of their vulnerability...and overtake them?

The Lady & Her Mission (Book 5)

COMING SOON

ACKNOWLEDGMENTS

So many people have influenced and touched my life while pouring into this book. They are just too numerous to count.

To my beta readers—Stacy Schoenwetter, Christina Horton, and Hillary Harvey—I cannot thank you enough for your valuable input and unending support and encouragement. You all have made my work stronger and me more fit for the task.

As well, to the editors who put their mark on the work, I appreciate your hard work and energy into making my work stronger. Your efforts have sharpened my creative process and made me the better for it.

Cora Graphics...wow! You are just amazing. I cannot say enough how much I love this cover.

To VerBull Photography for providing such great author photos. I don't know how you manage to get the best angles every. time. But you do.

To my family for your love, prayers, and support...there are no words to express how much I have gained from being shaped by you.

To Stephanie Taylor and Clean Reads, thank you for taking a chance on me. You have launched me into a career that is exciting and fulfilling in a way I never could have imagined. It is a dream come true!

To God...thank you for every blessing poured on me daily. Especially for touching my life with everyone listed here.

About the Author

Sara is a coffee lovin', word slinging, Historical Romance author whose super power is converting caffeine into novels. She loves those odd little tidbits of history that are stranger than fiction. That's what inspires her. Well, that and a good love story.

But of all the love stories she knows, hers is her favorite. She lives happily with her own Prince Charming and their gaggle of minions. Three to be exact. They sure know how to distract a writer! But, alas, the stories must be written, even if it must happen in the wee hours of the morning.

Sara is an avid reader and enjoys reading and writing clean Historical Romance when she's not traveling.

Please follow along with her journey through her newsletter at: http://saraturnquist.com/list

Happy Reading!

SARA R. TURNQUIST

Author
Editor
Speaker

facebook.com/AuthorSaraRTurnquist

instagram.com/sararturnquist

x.com/sararturnquist

youtube.com/@SaraRTurnquist

pinterest.com/sararturnquist

ALSO BY SARA R. TURNQUIST

CONVENIENT RISK SERIES

A Convenient Risk

An Inconvenient Christmas

A Less Convenient Path

A Convenient Escape

An Inconvenient Acquaintance

These Golden Years

A Less Convenient Arrangement

Ranch Hands Collection (ebook only)

CRIPPLE CREEK SERIES

Hope in Cripple Creek

Christmas in Cripple Creek

Faith in Cripple Creek

Love in Cripple Creek

- Prequels -

Leaving Waverly

Leaving Stoneybrook

RAILWAY ROMANCE SERIES

Laura, The Tycoon's Daughter

ACROSS THE YEARS SERIES

Among the Pages

Between the Lines

STANDALONE NOVELS

The General's Wife

Trail of Fears

Off to War

www.ingramcontent.com/pod-product-compliance
Lightning Source LLC
Chambersburg PA
CBHW061632190726
48289CB00006B/1572